TH3 D4TE
TO⑤AVE

Scholastic Children's Books
An imprint of Scholastic Ltd
Euston House, 24 Eversholt Street, London, NW1 1DB, UK
Registered office: Westfield Road, Southam, Warwickshire, CV47 0RA
SCHOLASTIC and associated logos are trademarks and/or
registered trademarks of Scholastic Inc.

First published in the US by Scholastic Inc, 2017
First published in the UK by Scholastic Ltd, 2017

Text copyright © Stephanie Kate Strohm, 2017

The right of Stephanie Kate Strohm to be identified as
the author of this work has been asserted by her.

ISBN 978 1407 18165 3

A CIP catalogue record for this book
is available from the British Library.

Printed by CPI Group (UK) Ltd, Croydon, CR0 4YY
Papers used by Scholastic Children's Books are made
from wood grown in sustainable forests.

1 3 5 7 9 10 8 6 4 2

www.scholastic.co.uk

TH3 D4TE TO5AVE

STEPHANIE KATE STROHM

▪SCHOLASTIC

For Caitlin, and a friendship that has seen me through the worst of high school and the best of what's come after

THE PROBLEM WITH POST-ITS

ANGELICA MARIE HUTCHERSON, *me*: Colin Von Kohorn has the most annoying Post-it note collection in the entire world.

BECCA HORN, *best friend*: Do I care about Colin Von Kohorn's Post-it notes? No. No, I do not. Do I care about our sad rag of a school newspaper, the *Prepster*? Definitely not. Do I care about the opinion of said sad rag's monomaniacal editor, Colin Von Kohorn? I think you know the answer to that one. I care about his opinion even less than I care about his Post-its.

ANGELICA: They're black. Seriously. Black. The Post-it was designed to *highlight* important information, to call attention to where attention needs to be paid, and Colin specifically chose Post-its that obfuscate information. They're the anti–Post-it, basically. And they tell you pretty much everything you need to know about Colin Von Kohorn.

BECCA: Angelica, however, has still somehow failed to grasp the fact that Colin's marginal position of authority has no real power over anyone, and he is in no way, shape, or form an arbiter of literary merit. Which is exactly why I'm starting my own underground literary magazine, *Riot Prep!* It's coming any day now, and it will blow this school's collective hive mind.

1

ANGELICA: Listen—I get Becca's point about Colin, I do. He's a freckled menace on a power trip. But I still want to be in the *Prepster*, and that makes it sort of impossible to *not* care about what Colin thinks. Avery, my brother's girlfriend, is always going on and on about how validation can only come from within, and emailing me gifs with pictures of unicorns wearing sunglasses with captions like #GIRLBOSS or *No One Can Stop a Self-Actualized Female!* But I obviously know nothing about self-actualization, because I don't understand why a unicorn in sunglasses is a #GIRLBOSS, and it bugs me to no end that Colin won't publish any of my stories. Is it so wrong to want recognition from the establishment? I'm only human!

BECCA: Oh, Colin Von Kohorn is totally the establishment. He's everything *wrong* with the establishment.

ANGELICA: He's part of the West Coast establishment, at least. Because I'm pretty sure that Colin is a direct descendant of nineteenth-century shipping magnate Petyr Von Kohorn, who at one point owned most of Northern California. And if owning part of a state doesn't make you the establishment, I don't know what does.

COLIN VON KOHORN, *editor in chief of the* Prepster, *San Anselmo Prep's only officially recognized publication*: Seriously, Angelica? I finally give you an assignment, and this is what you want to talk about? Post-its? This is not filling me with optimism for your final piece. No, I don't special-order my Post-its. They're right there in the aisle at Target. Why black? Yellow is a frivolous color. I'm putting together a piece of serious journalism, not an Easter egg hunt. Black is clean. Timeless. Precise.

Note: This was almost as bad as the time Colin went on his font rant in English class. Yes, Colin, we all know how you feel about Helvetica.—AMH

ANGELICA: A black Post-it meant doom. That was Colin's signature move, a sticky black note that signifies rejection. There it was, stuck perfectly perpendicular to the top of my meticulously typed page. It was like a pirate flag appearing in a previously calm sea. Next to the Post-it note—which, again, totally defeats the point of using the Post-it note, why use it if you're going to write *on the page?*—he'd scribbled something. After several minutes of squinting at his chicken scratch—seriously, it is *impossible* to read—I deciphered it. "Sorry. Not what we're looking for.—CVK."

COLIN: Angelica isn't a *bad* writer. Not at all. Especially if you're into genre fiction. Personally, it's not my thing, all those spaceship and alien freedom fighters and government drones whizzing about.

Note: The characters in my stories don't "whiz," which Colin would know if he'd read anything I'd written with even the slightest attention to detail.

BECCA: Colin wouldn't know good writing if it jumped out of his Moleskine notebook and bit him on the nose. Angelica is a *great* writer. Which is something that pretty much everyone *but* Colin seems to realize. She's been published, actually published, in a literary magazine! Like one that people subscribe to and *pay* for, unlike the *Prepster,* which they can't even give away. This is exactly why I don't understand *why* Angelica gives a flying fig what Colin thinks about her writing.

Note: I was published in a literary magazine for children when I was eight years old and paid the grand sum of five dollars. Not exactly impressive. But Becca is an extremely loyal best friend, and the kind of person who will defend the literary merits of "The Little Ladybug Poem, by Angelica Marie Hutcherson, Age Eight" until the day she dies.

COLIN: I wasn't trying to give Angelica a hard time. But, as always, I was only accepting material that aligned with my vision for the *Prepster.*

BECCA: Colin's "vision" for the *Prepster* is to induce sleep within fifteen seconds of having struggled through reading the first paragraph.

ANGELICA: Becca will never get it. She laughs in the face of rejection. When she didn't make marching band last year, she tipped her tuba in the trash can and shouted, "I REJECT YOUR MILITARISTIC MUSICAL EMPIRE," and then founded a punk tuba collective that somehow got school funding, even though she was the only member.

BECCA: I decided to retire Blitzkrieg Tuba Factory this year, as it was time for me to pursue other interests. But I'll still do my cover of "I Wanna Be Sedated" by request.

COLIN: Angelica didn't understand the pressure I was under.

CINTHIA ALVAREZ, *associate editor of the* Prepster, *has the great misfortune of being Colin's second-in-command*: All of the "pressure" Colin is under is entirely self-imposed. No one cares what he's doing except for him. I think the primary function of the *Prepster* is to line the hamster cage in the science lab. Does anyone actually read this thing?

COLIN: I have no problem with Angelica writing her little stories. I just don't have room for them in the *Prepster*.
    Note: There are no little stories, only little newspapers.

BECCA: I dread every time I see Angelica head into the computer lab. Each time Colin rejects one of her stories, she spends the rest of the day completely bummed out. Why doesn't she just get *mad*? Sadness accomplishes nothing. Anger is productive. Which Angelica would know if she ever bothered to get mad. In the five years I've known her, I've actually only ever seen her get really mad about one thing—her brother.
    Note: I love my brother. Of course I do. But it sometimes feels like the rest of the world is a little too *in love with him.*

CINTHIA: Colin's created quite a little hobbit hole for himself back here in this corner of the computer lab, aka the newspaper "office." The "office"—note the air quotes, please—consists of a bank of computers he's completely taken over and taped off with PREPSTER STAFF ONLY signs. Colin's desk is demarcated by a brass nameplate that says EDITOR IN CHIEF, which I think is something that should only exist at the *Daily Bugle*.

ANGELICA: I was sitting at the computer next to Colin's editorial "desk" when I saw the black Post-it and deciphered his note. Rejected. Again. My story was good. I knew it was. And I was tired of good stuff getting rejected.

COLIN: I never said it was a matter of quality. It was a matter of *content*.

ANGELICA: I wasn't surprised by the black Post-it note rejecting me—I was used to it at this point, as I'd had a whole year of black Post-it notes rejecting me—but I was *tired* of it. So I decided to try something new.

CINTHIA: Colin hates trying new things. One time I brought in a bag of Cheetos Sweetos—you know, the cinnamon sugar puffs—and all he said was "You have *got* to be kidding me" and pretended he couldn't hear me whenever I offered him any. How are American snack manufacturers supposed to innovate if we don't sample their bold new creations?

COLIN: I'm not opposed to innovation. I just have a healthy respect for tradition, that's all. But I'll listen. So when Angelica asked, "What if I try it your way?" I listened. I was less intrigued by the "and then we'll do things my way" part, but I listened.

ANGELICA: He said, "Go on," and raised an eyebrow before taking a sip of coffee.

MR. DUNCAN, *sophomore English teacher, newspaper faculty adviser*: San Anselmo Prep students aren't allowed to drink coffee. They certainly don't drink it under my supervision. And there are absolutely no liquids allowed in the computer lab.

COLIN: Mr. Duncan is far too busy fussing with his fantasy football team to enforce any sort of policy in the computer lab, let alone one that has anything to do with coffee. Everyone knows a proper newsroom runs on caffeine.

MR. DUNCAN: I swear, I executed one trade during the school day, just one, and that kid somehow knew about it.

COLIN: I am an investigative reporter. Nothing gets by me. Certainly not Mr. Duncan's anemic lineup.

ANGELICA: I told Colin I'd write a news story for the *Prepster*. Plain, straightforward reporting, on any topic he wanted. And if it was good, really good, like knock-his-socks-off good, he'd publish one of my stories. A short one.

COLIN: To be honest, we were understaffed. Right now, it's just me and Cinthia. So I needed someone who could write. And Angelica can write.

CINTHIA: We needed help. The homecoming edition of the *Prepster* is always a big deal. That day in the computer lab, however, we had no idea just how big of a deal it was going to be.

ANGELICA: "Fine," Colin said. "We're short writers for the homecoming edition. You can cover academics. I want two hundred and fifty words on the Academic Battle."

COLIN: "Fine," Angelica agreed. "Two hundred and fifty words on the Academic Battle."

ANGELICA: At the time, I had no idea that those two hundred and fifty words were tickets to a front-row seat at the most epic day in San Anselmo Prep history.

ACADEMIC BATTLE: WHAT IS IT, AND WHY DOES IT EXIST?

BECCA: When Angelica came tearing out of the computer lab, a huge grin on her face, I thought something good had actually happened.

ANGELICA: Something *great* had actually happened!

BECCA: Angelica's great news was that she was forced to write two hundred and fifty words on the Academic Battle? Seriously? That's not great news. That's a cruel and unusual punishment.

ANGELICA: Becca couldn't get away from her Colin-prejudice to recognize this for what it really was: an opportunity. All writers have to start somewhere! Toni Morrison used to be an editor at a textbook publisher in Syracuse. A *textbook publisher.* I can't imagine that was particularly thrilling.

BECCA: You know what's not thrilling? Academic Battle.

CINTHIA ALVAREZ, *Academic Battle team member, associate editor of the* Prepster: Academic Battle is exactly what it sounds like—an academic battle. Eleven events test each team's mental capacity in the toughest possible way. There is a live multiple-choice event called UltraQuiz, followed by an essay, a series of seven multiple-choice tests in different academic subjects, an interview, and an unrehearsed speech, which must be delivered flawlessly even though the competitor doesn't see the prompt until sixty seconds before speaking. Academic Battle is *not* for the faint of heart. Only the toughest cerebral competitors can survive.

BECCA: Okay, fine. There's nothing wrong with Academic Battle. It's certainly more impressive than running a ball from one end of a field to the other end of a field. I just thought it was particularly cruel and unusual for Colin to assign *Angelica*, of all people, to the Academic Battle story.

COLIN VON KOHORN: Of course I purposefully assigned Angelica to the Academic Battle story. I assumed she'd have insider insight.

ANGELICA: Would I have preferred another topic? Obviously. Literally almost anything else would have been better.

BECCA: Angelica's heard enough on the subject of Academic Battle to last for two lifetimes. She doesn't need another two hundred and fifty words about it.

COLIN: Angelica was the perfect person to write this story. Academic Battle was in her blood.

ANGELICA: Academic Battle was *not* in my blood. I just happened to share some DNA with a guy who had lived and breathed it. My brother: James "Hutch" Hutcherson, boy genius, valedictorian, science whiz, perfect son, and the poster child for the Academic Battle. He's not even in the building anymore—he graduated last year—but I probably hear "You're Hutch's sister?!" about as many times a day as I hear my own name. Sometimes I feel like Ralph Ellison's *Invisible Man*. Obviously, my problems are nothing compared to what that guy goes through, but I'd love Ellison's take on being black, female, *and* the younger sibling of San Anselmo's most famous academic overachiever.

BECCA: You have no idea how many afternoons Academic Battle has stolen from Angelica. Her parents made her go to every single one of Hutch's competitions, from Locals to Regionals to Nationals. Can you imagine having to endure four years of sitting around, watching people take multiple-choice tests? On the *weekend*?! I have no idea how Angelica did it. I would have handcuffed myself to the bed or something and refused to go.

Note: Was it boring? Yes. Was I allowed to bring a book? Also yes. So, it could have been worse.

COLIN: I also assigned Angelica to this story because the San Anselmo Prep Academic Battle team stands at a crossroads this year. Angelica knew the team's history and was therefore perfect to cover the potentially dramatic reversal of fortunes the team was facing.

Note: Sorry, Colin, but nothing dramatic has ever happened *at Academic Battle.*

CINTHIA: I think everyone's been expecting an epic fail from the San Anselmo Prep Academic Battle team now that Hutch and Cressida Schrobenhauser-Clonan have graduated. Even my *mom's* expecting us to fail. She's been stockpiling tamales like the apocalypse is coming any day now, and I know they're not for "just in case." They're for in case we *lose*, which we're *not* going to. I don't need those pity tamales! There will be *no* cheer-up tamales in the Alvarez household! I plan to *win*.

BECCA: Hutch has finally graduated, and Angelica is *still* being dragged to Academic Battle. The universe has a cruel sense of humor.

ALLISON WALSH, *Academic Battle team member*: To call this a critical year for us would be the understatement of the century. San Anselmo Prep has been undefeated for the past four years. We couldn't go down in San Anselmo history as the team who'd broken the streak in year five. We had to win.

CINTHIA: You know what would help us win? Getting Angelica on the team. I don't understand why she won't join us. Our team is way too math and science focused, and I know there's always at least one obscure nineteenth-century lit question we miss on the language-and-literature multiple-choice test. I do pretty well with the essay, but Angelica would do better. But she's not interested.

ANGELICA: I'm not interested because of my brother, obviously. Everyone is so obsessed with James, I'm honestly surprised they haven't renamed our Academic Battle team the San Anselmo

Prep Fighting Hutches. If they wore jerseys in Academic Battle, I am one hundred percent confident they would have retired his. The James-worship is off the charts here at school. It's even worse than it is at home. At San Anselmo Prep, I have enough people comparing me to my brother on a daily basis *without* Academic Battle. Can you imagine what people would say if I was actually on the team?! The last thing I needed was another way for people to compare me to James. He was already better than me at almost everything else.

COLIN: I told Angelica I hoped it wasn't a problem that I'd assigned her to Academic Battle. She'd started looking awfully squirrelly when she came back to my office to ask a few clarifying questions.

Note: You know who looks "squirrelly"? Squirrels. That's it.

ANGELICA: I assured Colin that there were no problems at all, and I would handle this assignment, and all future assignments, with the keen professionalism and eye for detail that he would soon come to see were hallmarks of the Angelica Marie Hutcherson writing process.

COLIN: Angelica left my office in quite the hurry. I assume it was because Cinthia had proffered the bag of her abysmal garbage sugar snacks.

CINTHIA: Even Angelica didn't want a Cheetos Sweeto. Maybe I really was the only person eating these things.

ANGELICA: I realized then there was only one thing to do: I had to paint the picture of the Academic Battle's homecoming match so vividly that Colin Von Kohorn would have no choice but to acknowledge my skill as a writer, and finally, finally, *finally* publish my fiction. And I knew there was only one way to vividly paint the picture of an important historical event.

BECCA: Hutch doesn't know we've read Avery's oral history. But it was just *there*, in his room, right on the bookshelf next to the collected works of Isaac Asimov. Normally, I couldn't care less what any of the drones at San Anselmo Prep do, but even I could admit it was interesting. Even if Avery Dennis totally misrepresented me.

ANGELICA: Yes, it was sort of weird to read something that kind of ended up being a love story about my brother. But it was also *fascinating*. And I knew that if I conducted my very own oral history, I could make homecoming just as fascinating as Avery had made prom.

BECCA: Angelica wanted to write an oral history of *Academic Battle*!? Most of Angelica's story ideas are awesome, but this one sounded like it belonged in the trash folder, right along with that fantasy story she'd started, and thankfully abandoned, about the badger coven.

ANGELICA: I could admit that my story about the badger coven had been a mistake. Not every idea is solid gold! But I had a feeling this oral history might be. Yes, I'll admit it, at first, the idea of writing about Academic Battle had made me cringe.

BECCA: Angelica's first response had been right. Writing about Academic Battle was a horrible, terrible punishment that proved my long-held suspicions that Colin Von Kohorn was a sociopath.

ANGELICA: But then I realized that Colin Von Kohorn had actually done me a favor.

COLIN: As a rule, I do not do favors.

ANGELICA: All of my life, I had been trying to run from being the great Hutch's little sister. Here at San Anselmo Prep, it felt like James's shadow loomed so large I could never be my own person. Which is why I never wanted anything to do with science or Academic Battle or tabletop gaming or any of it.

BECCA: Angelica had begged Hutch for years to let her try playing Dungeons & Dragons with him and his friends. Finally, he relented—I think Liam convinced Hutch to let her play; Liam was such a soft touch, so easy to con him out of the snacks he brought over—but then Hutch immediately rescinded his offer when Angelica proudly presented the entire party with copies of the forty-five-page biography she'd written for her character. Because they didn't have time to read it and it would "destroy their rate of play." He told her to get out. Angelica was crushed.

ANGELICA: I wasn't *crushed*. I don't even know why I'd wanted to play his stupid D&D campaign with his grumpy friends anyway. It was a dumb idea, and I'm glad I didn't get stuck with that all summer. It was a valuable lesson learned—I shouldn't try to do the things that James does.

BECCA: Do you know how much time D&D takes? It is *endless*. Hutch had been a complete tool, but I think Angelica had actually dodged a bullet. I sure wasn't going to spend the summer pretending to be a gnome lord, so I was grateful the dungeon hadn't stolen my best friend.

ANGELICA: And this is why I would *never* join the Academic Battle team, but now I was starting to realize that maybe the key to finding out who I really was, as myself, not as "Hutch's little sister," wasn't in avoiding Academic Battle altogether. Maybe I really had to dive in, to enter the belly of the beast. Because maybe the more I understood about James, the more I'd understand about myself. And about how we were different. Or maybe even about how we were the same. Why had Academic Battle been so important to him, anyway? I'd sat in high school auditoriums across the country watching him compete, and I still didn't really get it. To me, it just looked like a way to show off how smart he was, which was already abundantly clear. But maybe there was more to it than that.

BECCA: I don't really believe in self-discovery as a concept. What's to discover? Your self is already, you know, there. But if Angelica felt like doing this Academic Battle thing would help her remove the Hutch-size chip from her shoulder, then I was all for it. Angelica was so much more than just Hutch's little sister. She just needed to see it.

Note: A nice sentiment from Becca, but it's hard not to iden-tify as "Hutch's little sister" when it is literally the only thing anyone ever calls you.

ANGELICA: I just knew that this oral history would be my ticket to a regular feature in the *Prepster*, and the start of my writing career. And hopefully, in the process, I'd learn a little bit more about my brother and myself. And start to figure out what it really meant to be Angelica Hutcherson. Now all I had to do was write this story.

THE TROUBLE WITH TUBAS

ANGELICA: I was writing about Academic Battle in the homecoming edition of the paper. Not just any old edition. The *homecoming* edition. Which meant, of course, that I needed to learn absolutely everything there was to know about homecoming. And at San Anselmo Prep, homecoming means three things: football, marching band, and the Dragon, our beloved mascot.

BECCA: I'm not sure I would call our mascot "beloved." I think I would just call him "there."

ANGELICA: Becca's lack of school spirit extends to our intrinsically adorable mascot. He is the cutest dragon the world has ever seen. Everyone loves him! Well, everyone except Becca. I made her take a picture with me and the Dragon last year, when he was walking around the halls during senior week, and from the way she acted, you would have thought I'd invited her to a polka concert. I have the picture up in my locker because it's hilarious. It's me, hugging the Dragon, and Becca standing about a foot away, refusing to make physical contact with him. Her hands are balled into fists like she's worried she might have to fend him off.

BECCA: Oh, sure, everyone else at this school goes bonkers for some unknown classmate in a furry suit, and *I'm* the weirdo. You don't know who's in there! Who knows what cretin you're hugging? I can easily name at least twenty people that go to this school whom I would never hug, not under any circumstances. Never hug something if you can't see its face, that's my motto.

> *Note: If you ever find yourself at Becca's house, definitely ask her mom if you can see the pictures of Becca's one and only childhood trip to Disneyland. It was not a success. I've never seen Goofy look so rejected.*

CINTHIA ALVAREZ, *associate editor of the* Prepster, *member of the Academic Battle team*: You know what people *don't* usually think of when they think of homecoming at San Anselmo Prep? Academic Battle.

ANGELICA: And that was exactly why I couldn't *just* write about Academic Battle—because it was inextricably bound up with all of homecoming, thanks to when it was scheduled.

CINTHIA: When I saw that the AcaBat Locals were on the same Friday as homecoming, I assumed it was a scheduling mistake. But then I realized that it probably doesn't really matter. I hadn't been planning on going to the game, and I was pretty sure no one else on our team was planning on going, either. Historically, there hasn't been a lot of crossover between the football team and the AcaBat team. So who cares? I actually kind of *liked* that Locals were during homecoming. Most of the school wouldn't care, but Locals were really important to us. This year it would be our own academic homecoming battle, against our detested rivals, San Rafael Academy.

Note: AcaBat is the preferred familiar version of Academic Battle. I usually refuse to refer to it as AcaBat because it implies a cozy familiarity with Academic Battle I certainly do not espouse. It does, however, save a lot of time.

ANGELICA: The story of Academic Battle *was* the story of homecoming. There was no way to separate the two. And that was exactly why I needed to investigate every aspect of homecoming at San Anselmo Prep, even if it didn't appear, on the surface, to relate to Academic Battle. I just didn't expect homecoming to come to *me*.

BECCA: As Angelica and I sat in the cafeteria, enjoying what turned out to be a short-lived lunch, homecoming thundered toward us with the unpleasant velocity of a speeding train. Those feather-hatted miscreants in marching band came for me. I guess I'd always suspected that they might one day. It's not like tuba players grow on trees around here. My days had always been numbered.

ANGELICA: By the time I realized that it was Natalie Wagner who came over to our table, Becca was already on her way out of the lunchroom.

NATALIE WAGNER, *sophomore, San Anselmo Prep Marching Band clarinet:* Of course Becca ran away when I came to talk to her. Well, I knew this was never going to be easy.

ANGELICA: I didn't yet know *why* Natalie Wagner was chasing Becca, but now I had my entrée into what is, perhaps, the most important event of homecoming: the game.

NATALIE: Homecoming is the Super Bowl of marching band. It is our biggest day of the year. I cannot emphasize enough just how important it is.

BROOKS MANDEVILLE, *senior, quarterback of the Dragons, San Anselmo Prep's football team*: Marching band plays during halftime at the homecoming game? You sure about that?
> *Note: How could Brooks not have noticed we have a marching band?! They may be kind of small in numbers, but their half-time shows are legendary. I think more people go to homecoming to see the band than the game. I know I do.*

NATALIE: If the football is like, the, uh . . . football . . . of the Super Bowl, then *we* are the Beyoncé. And we must be *flawless*. Would Beyoncé ever be anything less than flawless? No. No, she would not.

TANNER ERICKSEN, *sophomore, the Dragons' kicker*: Our marching band is *good*. Seriously good. Probably better than our football team. Definitely better than our cheerleaders.

HOLLY CARPENTER, *sophomore, San Anselmo Prep Cheer Squad side base*: We are *terrible*. Hilariously bad. The most epic thing we've ever done was coordinate a mass forward roll, but honestly, who is impressed by eight teenagers somersaulting in unison? Nobody, that's who.

Note: I feel like TV has taught me that cheerleaders are supposed to be mean, but ours appear to just be a group of people who like dancing, fund-raising, and attempting gymnastics, with very mixed results.

TANNER E.: The Dragons almost never win the homecoming game. Our last recorded win was fifteen years ago. Fifteen years! San Anselmo Prep has been playing football since 1920, and I could probably count the number of homecoming game wins on one hand. I had no reason to believe this year was going to be any different.

BROOKS: This year was going to be different. I could feel it. Something in the air. Maybe it was the magic of senior year. Maybe it was the two-a-days. But whatever it was, I woke up every morning sweating Gatorade.

Note: If this was true, I really hope he sought out a medical professional.

TANNER E.: I don't think anybody really even cares about the game. They pretend to, sure, but I think they're all just using it as an excuse to paint their faces and yell stuff.

BECCA: I didn't go to homecoming last year. And I'm not going this year. No matter how many seemingly happy selfies Angelica texts me from the game, I know she doesn't like football that much.

ANGELICA: It's not about the football; it's about the people! Becca doesn't like people watching. In general, actually, I don't think she particularly likes people. And homecoming is full of people. It's emotions running high! The dramatic stakes in the struggle for victory! And of course, our incredible mascot, and whatever amazing medley marching band comes up with. But since marching band is still kind of a touchy subject with Becca, I didn't mention that part.

NATALIE: I care so much about homecoming. More than I care about my GPA. Or where I go to college. Or my dog, sometimes. Oh my God. Don't tell anyone I said that about Buttons. Especially not my sister.

BROOKS: Each night, before I went to bed, I vowed to crush the Knights.
Note: The Knights are the football team at our rival school, San Rafael Academy. They are also not very good at football; we just happen to be even worse.

NATALIE: The Knights don't even have a marching band. Isn't that crazy?! I heard that one time, like, years ago, they tried to bring their jazz band onto the field to play at halftime, but that didn't pan out. So, yes, there was literally no contest—we would be the best marching band on the field, no matter what—but I wanted to blow people's minds. We'd been practicing our Beyoncé medley for *months*. We even came in a couple times over the summer to practice! And we'd been at it every day, twice a day, since the school year started. I was hearing it in my dreams.

BROOKS: I crushed those Knights in my *dreams*. That's the power of visualization.

NATALIE: We were on track to deliver the greatest halftime show San Anselmo Prep had ever seen. But then Martin Shen was sidelined by a serious case of tuba lips and carpal tunnel, and all was lost.

> *Note: For the love of all that is holy, DO NOT google tuba lips!!*

MARTIN SHEN, *sidelined San Anselmo Prep Marching Band tuba player*: I'd forgotten about the heavy toll the constant homecoming practice took on my wrists. And the fact that I'd signed up for a pretty rigorous course load—lots of typing in those honors classes. Basically, I had set myself on a collision course for a carpal flare-up.

BECCA: Martin Shen is a hack. He spent the summer working at Fairfax Scoop. I saw him there when Hutch drove us over to try the lavender-and-honey ice cream. That's when I knew he wasn't serious about tuba. Spending three months scooping ice cream is carpal suicide.

> *Note: Lavender and honey might sound more like a soap than an ice cream flavor, but it was delicious.*

MARTIN: And, well, promise you won't tell anyone in band, but I hadn't worn my wrist brace all summer. I know, I know. I didn't even wear it when I was scooping at Fairfax. I can't even imagine the sounds that would emit from Natalie Wagner if she knew. For a clarinet, she's *very* involved in brass business. Well, she's involved in *everyone's* business.

NATALIE: We'd been playing with fire. What kind of self-respecting marching band only has one tuba? But since Alex Manevitz graduated last year, we were down to only one. And it's hard to cultivate a tuba player, especially at such a small school.

MARTIN: My mom sent out a group text for me letting everyone know that I couldn't play. I couldn't even text! This is how bad it was! The panic flooding into my phone was immediate.

TANNER E., *kicker, definitely not in marching band*: I somehow ended up on the marching band group text. I think they might have meant Tanner P.? But no matter how many times I send out, "Please stop texting me. I don't play any instruments and I don't get any of your jokes about spit valves," nothing works. I should probably just join marching band at this point. As kicker, I've got a lot of downtime.

TANNER PETERSON, *San Anselmo Prep Marching Band trumpet*: Marching band has a group text chain? Are you serious?! I've spent a whole year playing trumpet for these people, and I've never gotten a single text! This explains why I've missed all of marching band's legendary s'mores nights.

NATALIE: I should have texted Martin about his wrist brace this summer. But I just . . . couldn't.

KATE ROWND, *percussion*: Natalie certainly texted *me* plenty of times about Martin's wrist brace. "Kate, do you think Martin's wearing his wrist brace? Kate, have you seen Martin? Was he wearing his wrist brace? Kate, would *you* text Martin about his wrist brace?" No! No, I would not text Martin about his wrist brace; I would not think about Martin's wrist brace. Natalie had texted me the words *wrist brace* so many times they had lost all meaning. It was *summer.* I was busy! I had *better* things to do. I was at percussion camp at Birch Creek in Wisconsin, and it was *awesome,* not that Natalie ever asked. If Natalie was so concerned about Martin's joint health, then she shouldn't have broken up with him in the first place.

MARTIN: There probably haven't been a lot of other relationships that have ended due to a lack of adequate carpal support.

KATE: Yup, it sounds insane, but they broke up because of a wrist brace. Now, that might be the most marching-band sentence that's ever been uttered.

NATALIE: We didn't break up *because* of the wrist brace. We broke up because I wanted Martin to make good decisions, and he wanted to gamble with his health. You can't take care of someone who won't take care of himself. He has a blatant disregard for personal safety, *and* he put the entire marching band in jeopardy, just like I knew he would.

KATE: You would be *disgusted* by how many relationships have blossomed and fizzled in marching band. It's basically *Bachelor* *in Paradise* in uniforms instead of bikinis over here. The drama, the crushes, the tears. We've got all of it.

NATALIE: Martin and I actually got together right after homecoming last year. We had nailed the big finale, which was this incredible remix of Taylor Swift's "Bad Blood," and emotions were running high.

TANNER E., *the kicker, not the one in marching band*: "Bad Blood" was awesome last year. Everyone was going nuts, and thank God, it seems all anyone remembers from homecoming last year is "Bad Blood," and not the fact that we were completely destroyed. It was *brutal*, 48–0. You don't forget a score like that. I'm not sure how marching band will top that at the halftime show this year. "Bad Blood" was insane. But the craziest part was actually what happened *after* they finished.

KATE: Natalie took a running leap toward Martin Shen's face. He caught her, and the rest was history. It was pretty dramatic, even for Natalie.

ANGELICA: This was exactly what I meant about the emotional drama at homecoming! It was *full* of exciting human experiences!

BECCA: Angelica wasn't helping her case. Watching Natalie Wagner make out with Martin Shen isn't exactly high on my list of activities. Why would anyone ever want to see that?

TANNER E.: Martin and Natalie just stood there, kissing, for an uncomfortably long amount of time. The ref had to ask them to leave the field so we could start the second half. The entire stadium booed when they got escorted out of the game. I think everyone would have rather watched Natalie Wagner and Martin Shen make out instead of any football.

NATALIE: I got caught up in the moment, okay? If you had heard Martin's tuba work in "Bad Blood," you would have understood!

Note: I had, in fact, heard Martin's tuba work at homecoming last year, and somehow restrained myself from making out with him.

PRINCIPAL PATEL, *San Anselmo Prep principal*: All displays of public affection at San Anselmo Prep have been, are, and always will be issued consequences.

NATALIE: It was an incredible moment. Like something out of a movie! Totally worth a detention.

KATE: The breakup was inevitable from the moment they first locked lips. I told you. Everyone who gets together in marching band breaks up eventually. If anything, it was only surprising that they dated for seven whole months before it ended. I think that might have been our record for longest relationship. Award for shortest relationship goes to Tanner P. and Damarys Ramos for twelve minutes on the first day of school.

TANNER P., *the one in marching band, not the kicker*: Greatest twelve minutes of the year so far.

MARTIN: Of course Natalie and I had good times. We had some *great* times. Holding hands during breaks at practice. Snuggling on the bus on our way to away games. Getting pizza after practice and ignoring all the "Where are you??" texts from our moms. It was awesome. Until, unfortunately, it wasn't. It started innocently enough. Just a casual suggestion here and there that maybe I should wear my wrist brace more often. And I acquiesced, at first—I could see how it would be helpful to prevent possible torquing while we played Mario Kart—but it snowballed.

NATALIE: Is it a *crime* to care for the person you're in a relationship with? To show concern for their joint health?!

MARTIN: I guess it turned out Natalie was right. I *should* have been wearing that stupid thing the whole time. But I didn't listen, and I'd let the whole band down. I felt terrible. But I couldn't confess to what I'd done—or, more accurately, hadn't done. I know Natalie's small, but she's completely capable of kicking my butt. Or doing something worse.

NATALIE: In the end it didn't matter if Martin had given his wrists the support they so desperately needed. What mattered was that we were out one tuba, and everyone was panicking.

MARTIN: One of our particularly dramatic flautists sent out a text that read "UR KILLING ME SHEN," followed by a bunch of skull emojis. My mom *laughed*. No concern for her only son's safety.

NATALIE: Were we doomed? Sure, it looked that way. But everyone had forgotten that San Anselmo Prep *had* another tuba player—well, everyone had forgotten but me. San Anselmo Prep had the best dang tuba player I'd ever seen.

BECCA: I've told Natalie a thousand times—I had vowed never to audition for marching band again. Never. I don't even know what had possessed me to audition in the first place freshman year.

ANGELICA: I'm not entirely sure why Becca auditioned, either. She wouldn't do French Club with me, although that was kind of a long shot, since she takes Spanish, even though pretty much all we do in French Club is eat stuff and watch movies and sing songs, and who wouldn't like that? And she wouldn't join Art Club back in middle school, even though art is her favorite class, and unlike me, she's actually good. I was just in Art Club to color and relax, not, you know, create anything of value. Becca would have loved Art Club. But as a rule, she doesn't really join things.

NATALIE: I knew Becca would never audition for marching band again. But this was no audition. This was a guaranteed performance spot. Tuba players all over the nation would have killed for this opportunity! I was offering her a featured role in the biggest day in San Anselmo Prep Marching Band history! A

Beyoncé medley comes around only once in a lifetime! Who wouldn't give their last spit valve to be part of those sweet, sweet horns at the beginning of "Crazy in Love"?!

BECCA: It was annoying when Natalie came to talk to me in the cafeteria. It was borderline illegal when she called my home. And I knew it was *bad* when she planted herself in front of my locker and refused to allow me access to my belongings until I spoke with her. I probably should have just left, but I needed my flash cards for Spanish. Avoiding Natalie Wagner wasn't worth tanking a quiz on the subjunctive.

HOLLY: Becca Horn *loves* to argue. Also she loves saying no to things. When I offered her one of my VOTE FOR HOLLY cupcakes, first she said, "Why?" and then when I had no good response, she slowly smushed it with her fist. When it comes to a cupcake, how is "Why?" even a question? Or smushing a viable action? I spent a lot of time frosting those.

Note: Holly is running for sophomore class president—hence the cupcakes. Although one time she handed out cupcakes that said HAPPY TUESDAY, so I think she also just really likes to bake.

MARTIN: And even if we were living in some kind of alternate universe in which Becca Horn would agree to participate in a school activity such as marching band, on homecoming, the single most school-spirited day of the year, how, exactly, did Natalie expect Becca to learn a tuba part that we'd been practicing for months in the span of several days?

BECCA: Can I learn a tuba part in several days? Uh, yeah. Duh. Try several *hours*. Several minutes. I could probably learn a tuba part in ten minutes and walk onstage with the San Francisco Symphony and perform with total confidence.

ANGELICA: One time we were watching TV and Becca pulled out her tuba and played the Meow Mix song perfectly only two seconds after we'd heard it. Now whenever I hear those cats singing, I feel like there's some tuba missing.

BECCA: It wasn't a question of "could." It was a question of "would." As in I absolutely, no way, one hundred and ten percent, would not perform at homecoming. Or anywhere else in the vicinity of San Anselmo Prep.

NATALIE: "Don't worry," I texted the group. "We'll have a tuba. I'm bringing in Horn. Becca Horn. Not another horn. Literally. LOLOLOLOL." Laugh-cry emoji. Laugh-cry emoji. Laugh-cry emoji. Pink bow emoji, because that's my signature.

MARTIN: Natalie's pretty stubborn. Last year she made a senior trombone cry because she insisted we do the bridge in "Seven Nation Army" one last time after three hours of weekend rehearsal. But could Natalie bring in Becca Horn? No way. No one can make Becca Horn do anything. I think even Principal Patel is afraid of her.

PRINCIPAL PATEL: I most certainly am not *afraid* of any of my students. And I have no issues with enforcing compliance from any of them, even the most truculent.

Note: I swear, though, his eye twitched a little when I mentioned Becca's name and the phrase "Blitzkrieg Tuba Factory."

MARTIN: I thought she was crazy, but Natalie promised she would get us a tuba. And if I'd learned anything from dating Natalie, it's that when she wants something, she just doesn't stop. She won't stop. She *can't* stop. So I guess we were all about to see what happens when an unstoppable force meets an immovable object.

BECCA: When it comes to Natalie Wagner, I expect puffy stickers. I expect an ever-changing rotation of cutesy pencil cases. But I never expected blackmail.

HORN VS. WAGNER

NATALIE WAGNER, *clarinet*: Becca Horn and I used to be *best friends*.

BECCA: Best friends? Seriously? She said *best friends*?! Natalie Wagner is deluded. We were barely acquaintances.

ANGELICA: Becca and I have been best friends since I came to San Anselmo Prep. But that was in seventh grade. A lot happened before then.

BECCA: I met Angelica on the first day of seventh grade. Did I see her at the back-to-school pool party? Excuse me? No. I do not attend the elitist institution known as the San Anselmo Prep back-to-school pool party. It's an implicit concession to this classist notion that those of us who don't have pools are somehow less than those who do. Oh, God, I'm complicit in classism just by attending this school. Blame my parents. I'm a minor.

> *Note: Becca talks a big game, but one time I saw her wear a pair of San Anselmo Prep sweatpants. Why get the pants if you didn't have at least a teeny, tiny bit of school pride buried somewhere down deep inside? When I reminded her of this, she shouted, "What was I supposed to do, go to Fairfax Scoop NAKED?!" Naked was obviously not the only option. I know for a fact she owns many pairs of pants. Like at least four pairs*

of ripped black jeans. I find it hard to believe that they all ended up in the laundry at the exact same time.

NATALIE: Becca has never gone to a back-to-school pool party. Not even when my parents hosted it, which, considering the fact that we were best friends, is kind of rude.

BECCA: Natalie Wagner was *not* my best friend. I have only ever had one best friend, and that person is Angelica Marie Hutcherson.

ANGELICA: Being new is the absolute worst. Actually, the exact moment when you enter the cafeteria on your first day of being new is the real absolute worst. There may be dozens of empty chairs, but there is always nowhere to sit. Where are you supposed to go?! It's too stressful. Even in seventh grade, I was self-aware enough to know that I couldn't handle a human social interaction under those circumstances. So I'd brought a book.

BECCA: At that time, I preferred eating alone while reading. At least I'd improve my mind while choking down the assortment of sad salad bar items I'd cobbled together to form a barely passable vegetarian entrée.

ANGELICA: I spotted Becca sitting alone, reading, and figured that was just the area for people to sit alone and read.

BECCA: Angelica sat next to me with this huge doorstopper of a book.

ANGELICA: It was *Jonathan Strange & Mr Norrell*. And then I noticed what Becca was reading.

BECCA: *Stardust*, by Neil Gaiman.

ANGELICA: The look on her face did not suggest that she was enjoying it.

BECCA: Everyone always thinks my face looks like I hate everything! I like *lots* of things. That's just the way my face looks!

ANGELICA: We talked books and swapped books, and pretty soon we weren't reading at lunch at all anymore, just talking. Unless one of us gets really wrapped up in a book, which happens.

BECCA: Thanks to Angelica, lunchtime has actually become an enjoyable experience. Now I think the only person who spends lunch sitting alone and reading is Colin Von Kohorn and his huge stack of newspapers. He even gets *Le Monde*. I'm not sure why. I'm pretty sure he doesn't speak French.

COLIN VON KOHORN, *editor in chief of the* Prepster: Of course I speak French. Angelica, I'm *in* your French class. We were in the same group for the entire "Martinique, C'est Magnifique!" unit. Don't you remember? I did that whole presentation on les bananes.
> Note: Of course I knew Colin was in my French class. How could I forget Colin's presentation on the environmental costs

of the banana trade? I just seriously doubted he had the flu-
ency to read an entire newspaper in French. Unless every
issue of Le Monde *was about the world banana economy,*
he'd be in for a struggle.

ANGELICA: But like I said, I started in seventh grade. Becca
had never, ever said anything about being former besties
with Natalie Wagner, but who knows? There were a lot of
years Becca was at San Anselmo Prep before I got there. She
could have been best friends with Colin Von Kohorn for all
I knew.

NATALIE: Becca's complete denial of the fact that we were
ever friends would be almost insulting if I wasn't well aware
that this is just the way she is. Even back in kindergarten,
when our gym teacher brought out the giant parachute,
which is just, obviously, the greatest thing that can happen in
kindergarten, she would sit under the parachute with this
huge stink face on, looking like she was two minutes away
from slashing holes in the parachute with a shiv fashioned
from a cafeteria spork.

BECCA: I *loved* parachute day. I certainly wasn't about to shiv
anything. Can people just let my resting b-face rest?!

NATALIE: Becca and I became friends in kindergarten the way
most people become friends in kindergarten. A shared snack
here, a game of house there, a playdate or two, a coloring project, and there you are. Best friends.

BECCA: Do five-year-olds even have the intellectual capacity to form friendships? That seems highly unlikely. Natalie Wagner and I were just small humans coexisting in the same space.

NATALIE: Why aren't we friends anymore? Oh, I don't know, really. Nothing dramatic happened to end our friendship; we'd just grown apart by middle school. I got really involved in band, and Becca got really involved in, I don't know, petitioning Principal Patel to allow nose rings to be part of the dress code.
    Note: Becca doesn't even have a nose ring.

BECCA: I'd barely even talked to Natalie in years. Sure, we had the same free period last year, but that didn't mean we *talked*. We just did our homework in the same general vicinity.

NATALIE: Of course I always say hi to Becca in the hallways or in class, even though she just snarls back.

BECCA: She said I snarled? I do not *snarl*!
    Note: Sometimes she kind of does, though.

NATALIE: But this was business. Marching band business. I wasn't going to be deterred by Becca ghosting when I entered the cafeteria, or hanging up even after I'd called her house six times. I waited for Becca by her locker at the end of the day and told her we needed to talk.

BECCA: I waited for her to talk. She stared at me. What was she waiting for? I'm not *in charge* of her. She can talk whenever she wants to.

NATALIE: She just *stared* at me. I knew Becca was going to make this as difficult as humanly possible. Eventually she snarled, "Talk." So I presented Becca with the incredible, once-in-a-lifetime opportunity to be part of the greatest homecoming halftime show San Anselmo Prep had ever seen.

BECCA: I'm sorry, I just—I couldn't. Had Natalie Wagner gone temporarily *insane*?!

NATALIE: She laughed at me. Laughed! In my face!

BECCCA: I didn't *mean* to laugh. Honestly, I didn't. It just slipped out!

NATALIE: I had hoped we could be *civil*. That Becca would help out an old friend, for friendship's sake. That maybe her love of the tuba, or some small part of her that felt school pride deep down somewhere, would compel her to do the right thing. But no. This was Becca Horn we were talking about, and that meant we had to do things the hard way.

BECCA: She looked at me with dead, soulless shark eyes, and said, in this frankly quite terrifying voice, "I had hoped it wouldn't come to this."

NATALIE: I told her I had the picture. And that she had forty-eight hours to learn the tuba part to marching band's Beyoncé medley, or that picture was going *everywhere*. On the Internet, obviously, but that was just a start. I'd already contacted Colin Von Kohorn about buying ad space in the *Prepster*. And he'd told me he could probably also get me a deal on ad space in the *San Francisco Chronicle*, because he interns there in the summer, and he'd gotten their ad guy a *lot* of coffees. I'd made some phone inquiries about billboard space as well, but I wasn't sure I had the budget for it. I was open to creating a Kickstarter page, though.

BECCA: The picture. Dear God. I couldn't believe she still had the picture.

NATALIE: I handed her the sheet music, and told her I'd swing by her house for a uniform fitting tomorrow.

BECCA: It made me respect her, almost, the fact that she'd held on to the picture for all these years, biding her time until the moment was right to exploit my greatest weakness. Maybe Natalie was right. Maybe we *had* been best friends. For the first time, I could kind of see the appeal.

AN EDITORIAL CHECK-IN

ANGELICA: Obviously, I was on fire with curiosity. What could that picture possibly be of??!? I had thought Becca was immune to embarrassment. She farted, just straight-up farted, in the middle of algebra in eighth grade, and as everyone giggled, she said, cool as a cucumber, "I farted. I have a functioning intestinal tract. Deal with it." Couldn't have cared less. If I farted in math class, I'd change my name and move to an uninhabited island in the Swedish archipelago eight hours away from the coast of Stockholm. No one would ever find me.

BECCA: Angelica embarrasses way too easily. She called Ms. Marlow "Mom" by accident once last year, and I thought she was going to die of shame. She spent the next *month* panicking that people were still talking about it. Nobody was talking about it.

ANGELICA: First of all, the Ms. Marlow thing was really embarrassing, and I think anyone with a normal human sense of shame would agree. Also, once Tanner Peterson said, "How's your mom, Angelica?" in this way that was definitely him making fun of me.

BECCA: I'm pretty sure the whole Tanner Peterson "How's your mom?" thing was him actually asking how her mom was, considering that the fateful question was posited the Monday after

Mother's Day, in French class, when they were supposed to be talking about their moms, and Tanner P. clearly just didn't remember any of the vocab.

ANGELICA: I decided to drop the whole Tanner P. thing, since Becca hadn't been there and couldn't know what I knew about his tone. But whatever that picture was of, it must have been *really* bad. So bad I couldn't even think of what it could possibly be.

BECCA: Of course I trust Angelica. I trust her with my life. And I know I could trust her with the picture. Of course I could. I just wasn't ready for *anyone* to see that picture, not even my best friend. I wasn't sure if I'd *ever* be ready. Hopefully, I could get it from Natalie and destroy it. Otherwise, she'd probably hold it over my head and force me to play the tuba for the rest of my high school career. When I think of strapping that marching band hat with the big feathery plume on my head . . . shudder.

ANGELICA: But I didn't bother Becca too much, fiery curiosity or no. I understand that there are some things that need to be kept secret. There are some things I've written that *no one* should ever see. Things that are even worse than the badger coven story.

COLIN VON KOHORN, *editor in chief of the* Prepster: It got back to me, as everything in a school this small eventually does, that Angelica had been asking questions about tubas. *Tubas*, of all things. What, exactly, did that have to do with Academic Battle? Nothing, that's what. I called her into my office to discuss.

ANGELICA: Did Colin understand nothing about the process of journalism? For someone who was allegedly in charge of this newspaper, he seemed to have a very limited view of the art of reportage. I was gathering local color. Setting up the foundation. Painting the picture. And let's not forget that I was writing an article for the homecoming edition of the *Prepster*. Obviously, that meant I had to interview people about every aspect of homecoming! Otherwise, my article would most assuredly be incomplete. Why did Colin have such a bug up his butt about tubas?

COLIN: I informed Angelica that I most certainly did not have "a bug up my butt" about tubas or anything else. Nor were there, in fact, any insects in or about my personage.

ANGELICA: Seriously. Why was he so stressed? I could easily manage writing two hundred and fifty words without the interference of the almighty Colin Von Kohorn. I can write two hundred and fifty words while brushing my teeth. That happened, once, when I forgot about the mini response paper on Grendel in the mead hall, and it turned out totally fine. Mr. Duncan didn't even notice the small blob of toothpaste lurking around the conclusion. Or if he did, he didn't mention it.

COLIN: Stress is for soccer moms and heart surgeons.

CINTHIA ALVAREZ, *associate editor of the* Prepster: Colin's got a whole treasure trove of sayings he trots out on various occasions. He's even worse than my mom, who drops: El que quiera pescado que se moje el culo even if I just ask her to grab my sweatshirt or pass me the hot sauce. So never ask my mom to do you a favor, and never, ever mention that you're stressed around Colin. You'll get a "Stress is for soccer moms and heart surgeons," which, like most of his sayings, makes *no* sense.

COLIN: I'm a sophomore, okay? A *sophomore*. The last time a sophomore was the editor in chief of the *Prepster* was in 1942, when most of the senior and junior class enlisted, many lying about their ages to volunteer to fight in World War II. In their wake, they left behind an editorial staff riddled with vacancies. Bertram "Bugsy" Kopeck led the *Prepster* for three epic years, before going on to edit the *Princetonian* in college and, later, the *Chicago Tribune*. This year, however, the ranks of the *Prepster* have been decimated not by the scourge of war, but by a modern pestilence: apathy. There wasn't a single junior or senior interested in working on the newspaper, which, although it turned out to be to my advantage, is, quite frankly, appalling. Now, I am no Bugsy Kopeck, but on the very first day of school sophomore year, I vowed to do my best to shepherd the *Prepster* into another era of greatness.

Note: Why. Does. He. Know. This. I promise you, there is no "History of the Prepster" class at San Anselmo Prep.

CINTHIA: Is the *Prepster* entering an era of greatness? I'm not sure if I'd say that. Was the *Prepster* ever great? Maybe that time last year we covered the decreasing crispiness of French Fry Friday. That was probably our most popular article ever. Why the decreasing crispiness? Turns out, the cafeteria had switched distributors. You're welcome, world. This is exactly the kind of hard-hitting journalism the *Prepster* is known for.

ANGELICA: It didn't take Sherlock Holmes to deduce that Colin was stressed about being the *Prepster's* editor in chief. But I didn't think it had anything to do with Bugsy Kopeck. I think it had everything to do with August Von Kohorn.

COLIN: No comment.

ANGELICA: "No comment"?! "NO COMMENT"?! I couldn't believe my ears. "No comment" from Colin Von Kohorn, the man who had declared loudly on multiple occasions, "No comment is for cowards"?!

CINTHIA: "No comment is for cowards." Oh, boy, that's a really classic Von Kohorn–ism. Probably the most frequently used Von Kohorn–ism of all time.

ANGELICA: There are three Von Kohorns: Colin, obviously, and his little brother, Sebastian, who's in fifth grade here at San Anselmo Prep, but *always* hanging around the computer lab after school, even though it's just supposed to be for the upper school, and then August, the oldest Von Kohorn. Two years ago, when August was a senior, he won a national prize for high school investigative journalism. I remember it really well, because August Von Kohorn was the only person except for *my* brother who ever made the national news.

CINTHIA: I guess the *Prepster* did have a recent era of greatness—when Colin's brother was editor in chief. But now that I think about it, he actually just submitted that article straight to the contest. It wasn't even published in the *Prepster*. So I'm sticking with my zero-moments-of-greatness thing.

ANGELICA: I'd found the article online. Ironically, for something written by someone who'd spent his whole life in private school, it was an in-depth analysis of the pros and cons of the charter system in the Bay Area. Although I don't usually like nonfiction, I'd enjoyed it. It was interesting, and August was a good writer.

COLIN: I didn't know why Angelica was asking about August. He has absolutely nothing to do with anything. I certainly don't feel like anyone is comparing us.

ANGELICA: I knew that was exactly how he felt, though. I instantly recognized the look of a younger sibling who could never quite measure up. After all, I saw it in the mirror every day.

COLIN: August and I have completely different editorial styles. I certainly wouldn't want to cast aspersions on my own brother, but let's just say he has a more liberal relationship with editorial flair than I'd ever feel comfortable with. And now August is far, far away at Harvard, working on whatever rag they're printing there, and he has absolutely nothing to do with anything.

ANGELICA: It was weird, to think that Colin and I had this in common—the shadow of the perfect older brother. I hadn't thought we had *anything* in common.

COLIN: Shouldn't you be asking questions of someone who counts as a valid source? I'm not the story, Angelica. I'm editing the story. There's a big difference. Interview over.

Note: I had thought we were just having a conversation, but I guess to Colin, there are no conversations, only interviews.

VOTE FOR HOLLY

ANGELICA: I set out to start my Academic Battle interviews, I swear. I really did. But then I walked past Holly Carpenter staple-gunning VOTE FOR HOLLY! posters to the walls with the kind of aggression one doesn't usually expect from the girl our eighth-grade yearbook named "Most Likely to Brighten Someone's Day."

COLIN VON KOHORN, *editor in chief*: Eighth-grade yearbook. Talk about a waste of the perfectly good paper it was printed on. Eighth-grade "graduation" is a non-momentous occasion that deserves none of the recognition that this school so lavishly bestows upon it. This is why our generation won't achieve anything. We're coddled. Weak. Used to being praised for minor "accomplishments" that deserve no praise whatsoever. Do you think Winston Churchill celebrated his eighth-grade graduation? Do you think Angela Merkel celebrated her eighth-grade graduation? I highly doubt it. What? Do I remember my eighth-grade yearbook superlative? I most certainly do not.
Note: I do. It was "Least Likely to Purchase a Yearbook." Shockingly prescient.

HOLLY CARPENTER, *cheerleader, sophomore class presidential candidate*: It was time to depose the tyrant.

ANDREW NITHERCOTT, *tyrant, former freshman class president, sophomore class presidential candidate*: This school lacks one thing: order. No, make that two things: order and discipline. And respect for tradition. Three things. It lacks three things.

COLIN: I don't have an opinion on Andrew Nithercott. Angelica, I told you, you can't edit the story and *be* the story. I'm not a reputable source. Stop asking me questions.

> *Note: I asked him one question. One. Well, I mean, except for all those other questions I'd asked him before. I asked him one question in an official capacity. Just one. Colin is also a tyrant and has a locker next to Andrew Nithercott. If that doesn't spell s-o-u-r-c-e, I don't know what does!*

HOLLY: Freshman year, I was class secretary. I like taking notes. I like keeping things organized. And, I hate admitting this, but I think there was a small, sad, scared part of me that worried I didn't have what it takes to be class president. Or that I would lose. That no one would vote for the dumb cheerleader. But no more.

ANDREW: When I took office last year, my first proposal called for more uniformity in the school uniform. My second for harsher consequences for minor infractions. My third called for an end to the frivolity of locker decorations. The upperclassmen blocked me at every turn.

HOLLY: Andrew Nithercott tried to pass a policy that would have made walking on the left side of the hallway a punishable offense. That was his solution to our totally normal, not even that problematic hallway congestion. What about people who have lockers on the left side? His response: "They'll figure it out." How were they supposed to figure it out? How?!

COLIN: The dress code at San Anselmo Prep has gotten appallingly sloppy, it's true. On that front, I *do* have to agree with Andrew Nithercott. I saw Brooks Mandeville wearing a *striped* Oxford the other day, and I don't believe any consequences were issued. Angelica—stop writing! I'm not a source!

BROOKS MANDEVILLE, *San Anselmo Prep quarterback, last year's junior class president, currently running for senior class president*: Nithercott is stricter than Principal Patel. All of his proposals were nutso. Mandatory shoeshines? How would you enforce that? Who shines their shoes anymore? Where do you even get a shoeshine?

PRINCIPAL PATEL: A mandatory shoeshine would certainly be unenforceable, but perhaps some clearer guidelines about shoe cleanliness would not go amiss. You should see the mud tracked through my hallways during lacrosse season.

HOLLY: "The only thing necessary for the triumph of evil is for good men to do nothing." Or good cheerleaders. Well, a bad cheerleader. But a good person. Hopefully. I try, anyway. And I certainly couldn't let Andrew run unchecked anymore. Sure, he hadn't actually accomplished anything, but he was totally ruining the mood in Student Council. And Principal Patel said he was "seriously considering" the twenty-four-page proposal Andrew had submitted for updates to the dress code. The last thing this school needed was a stricter uniform.

PRINCIPAL PATEL: Has the dress code become too lax? I wouldn't say that. Here at San Anselmo Prep, our students are held to the highest standards in all areas, uniform included. Did Brooks Mandeville wear a striped Oxford last week? What? I have no idea. I mean, no comment.

Note: "No comment is for cowards." Ha!

ANDREW: When I heard my secretary had decided to run against me, I was unimpressed.

HOLLY: I was the secretary to the *class*, not to stupid Andrew Nithercott. And this is his real problem. Forget the uniform thing. Maybe he just really likes knee socks and shiny shoes, and you know what? That's totally fine. To each his own. The problem is the way he treats people. He's a self-important, sexist, condescending oaf. And that's not the kind of person we want representing us. If someone is going to represent the people, they need to respect the people. And Andrew Nithercott respects no one but Andrew Nithercott. And Colin Von Kohorn, maybe. He called him "decent" when the newspaper came up at Student Council once.

COLIN: Andrew Nithercott is *not* my best friend. Do I have any friends?! Yes, of course I have friends! No, I am not going to sit here and list them for you! Can't you see I'm busy? This is what *work* looks like, Angelica!

Note: I'm not actually sure Colin does have friends. Every time I see him in the cafeteria he's sitting alone and reading the New York Times *or something else from his giant stack of newspapers or doing a puzzle from his* Super Sunday Crossword *book. Which is making me feel sort of bad for him—a very unfamiliar feeling. I can't imagine lunch without Becca building strange architectural structures out of green beans almondine.*

ANDREW: This election was going to be a joke. The very idea that Holly had decided to run against me was laughable. I prepared to win by a landslide.

COLIN: Okay, fine. I will answer this one last question. Did I vote for Andrew Nithercott last year? Yes. He outlined a very clear fourteen-point proposal for his term. What can I say? I value structured thought.

HOLLY: I had to beat Andrew Nithercott. I just had to. Because like in *Jaws: The Revenge*, this time, it was personal. What? I like *Jaws*. Is that weird?
   Note: Not weird, necessarily, but if someone had asked me to guess Holly Carpenter's favorite fish movie sequel, it probably would have been Finding Dory.

ANDREW: If it wasn't so sad, running against my ex would be almost funny. Can you imagine if Jane Wyman had run for president against Ronald Reagan?

HOLLY: Yes, I'll admit it. I'm not going to lie to the press. I dated Andrew Nithercott. But it only lasted a week, okay? Just a week! That was it!

ANDREW: What can I say? She flung herself at me.

HOLLY: I wish I had a time machine. I would travel back to the beginning of freshman year and kidnap myself until my moment of madness passed. Maybe I'd take freshman Holly to a nice cabin, somewhere secluded. Give her a great selection of magazines and snacks and keep her far, far away from Andrew Nithercott.

ANDREW: Women are attracted to men in power. It's a fact.

HOLLY: Andrew honestly didn't seem all *that* bad, at first. Sure, he was a little obsessed with the dress code, but he'd had a fourteen-point plan outlined for his term! I *told* you I liked it when things were organized! That fourteen-point plan drew me to him like a moth to a flame. He handed me a copy of his plan on the first day of Student Council, and he'd had it professionally bound, with a laminated cover. My heart skipped a beat. At the fourteen-point plan. Not at Andrew Nithercott.

BROOKS: For Student Council, we all sit around this big, round conference-table-type thing in the AP English Lit room. The seniors are at the head of the table, near the windows, and the freshmen are way down at the other end. I never have any idea what they're doing down there.

ANDREW: Last year, my VP sat on my right side, Holly on my left, so we could confer about the minutes she was taking.

TANNER ERICKSEN, *the Dragons' kicker, last year's freshman class vice president*: It was disgusting. They thought I wouldn't notice, the way Holly kept inching closer to his chair, the way Nithercott's hand would linger on her arm as he asked her to read something back to him after the meeting. I could barely keep my lunch down. It was a real struggle whenever we had Student Council on Meatloaf Day.

ANDREW: I will say this for Holly: Her notes were always exceptional. Her handwriting is so clear it could be a font.

HOLLY: I know I take fantastic notes. I've heard it from every teacher I've had, every study group I've ever been in. I don't need Andrew Nithercott's approval of my notes! But last year, when I was just a young, dumb freshman, and he'd say, "Excellent notes, Holly," at the end of a meeting, my young, dumb self just melted. *Melted.* At Andrew Nithercott! Oh, I'm so repulsed I could just die.

BROOKS: You're telling me Nithercott dated the cute cheerleader last year? The blonde down at the end of the table? *Nithercott?!* No way, man! I have a hard time believing that.
> *Note: Pretty sure Brooks isn't the only one who has a hard time believing it. All the sophomores knew they were dating, because there are no secrets in a school this small, and even though we knew it was happening, we just couldn't believe it was real. I*

think I get along with almost everybody, and I almost accidentally-on-purpose lit Andrew Nithercott on fire with a Bunsen burner in science last year. He is just impossible.

ANDREW: It was obvious that Holly was in love with me. It was cute, really.

HOLLY: I was *not* in love with Andrew. I had a weird crush, for about five minutes, that I have regretted every day since then.

TANNER E.: I could see it coming like a car crash I was powerless to stop. Every time Nithercott handed her a binder, there were practically cartoon hearts shooting out of her eyes. It was the worst. But what was I supposed to do? Yell, "STOP IT!" every time she giggled at him? Construct a barrier out of manila folders to keep the two of them apart? I was on the other side of Nithercott, too far away to have any impact.

HOLLY: One day, though, instead of me showing Andrew my notes, Andrew had something to show me.

ANDREW: I opened my laptop and pulled up the Excel spreadsheet I'd created for our Student Council budget for the rest of the year.

HOLLY: I looked at all the clean lines of the spreadsheet. The columns that balanced perfectly. A fiscal school year all planned out, coming in well under budget for the first time in possibly, well, ever. It was beautiful.

ANDREW: Holly had brought her head so close to mine as we looked at the spreadsheet that we were practically touching. I turned my head to ask her a question, and then all of a sudden, her lips were on mine.

HOLLY: Fine. I admit it, okay?! I *did* fling myself at Andrew Nithercott! I flung, okay?! I flung! I blame Excel!

TANNER E.: If I had actually seen Holly and Andrew Nithercott kiss, I . . . ugh. I don't even want to think about it.

HOLLY: We dated for the next two weeks, although, probably, no one at school even knew we were dating. Andrew's not exactly affectionate.

    Note: We knew. No such thing as a secret at San Anselmo Prep.

ANDREW: Please. How would it look for the person who published the Punishments for Public Displays of Affection proposal to actually engage in a public display of affection? I would never.

TANNER E.: I knew they were dating. And it was excruciating. Holly would do this cute little sigh any time Andrew said something long-winded in class or in Student Council, and I just wanted to murder him. Not literally. Don't print that. I'm not gonna murder him, okay?

HOLLY: I had all these visions of us being a political power couple. Deluded. I was so deluded.

JENNIFER "JENSY" STUDENROTH, *back base on the San Anselmo Prep Cheer Squad*: That week Holly didn't eat lunch with us was the worst! We missed her so much. Well, I guess it wasn't the absolute worst. The worst would have been if Andrew Nithercott had come over and sat with us. Shudder. The other girls on the squad wanted me to have, like, an intervention with her. They thought she'd totally lost it. But I knew she'd snap out of it. Holly is smart. She could figure it out on her own. And who amongst us has not been a fool for love? When I saw Martin Shen play that tuba part at homecoming last year, I was so into him, I would have asked him out right then and there. I was straight-up crying on the field—and not cute crying, like rivers of snot crying—because Natalie Wagner got to him first.

Note: Am I the only person who is immune to the aphrodisiac qualities of Martin Shen's tuba playing?! Maybe being the sole supporter of Blitzkrieg Tuba Factory had tainted the tuba for me. BTF's end-of-the-year concert was two hours and forty-five minutes last year, and Becca's mom and I were the only people who were there. Even good tuba gets a little difficult to endure after two hours and forty-five minutes.

HOLLY: Ironically, the very same spreadsheet that had brought us together was the thing that tore us apart.

ANDREW: Holly had seen the spreadsheet the week before I proposed it in Student Council. She had *already* seen it! It wasn't a surprise. I have no idea why her reaction was so dramatic when I unveiled it in front of the rest of the council.

HOLLY: I hadn't looked at the spreadsheet very carefully, I guess. I'd been swept up in the moment and completely missed just how, exactly, Andrew was proposing to save so much money in the budget.

TANNER E.: Andrew told us at the beginning of the meeting that something big was coming. I ignored this, because the last time he'd said something big was coming, he'd proposed enforcing a uniform shoelace amongst the student body.

ANDREW: I proposed cutting the homecoming dance. I'd wanted to cut all of the dances, but since homecoming is the first dance of the year, it was the one currently on the table. Right now, San Anselmo Prep throws four dances. Four! During one school year! The homecoming dance, the Valentine's Day dance, the Spring Fling, and prom. It's ridiculous. I decided to let them keep prom, because I knew there was no way I could get rid of it. Last year's senior class president was dating the head of the Prom Committee, and I knew enough about politics to know that there was no way I was going to win that one. But homecoming, Valentine's Day, and the Spring Fling had to go. I'd handed every member of the Student Council a binder containing a series of Excel spreadsheets that highlighted just how much money we'd save by cutting these extraneous dances. The savings were significant. No one on Student Council ever had an eye on the budget. All of the treasurers were slacking. I don't even know why most of them had bothered to run for treasurer.

JUSTINE MEUNIER, *last year's freshman class treasurer*: I ran for class treasurer because my mom said it would look good on my college application, and I figured I wouldn't actually have to do anything. I was right.

HOLLY: Maybe it was because my mom had been Homecoming Queen when she was in high school, and I'd hoped one day maybe I could be Homecoming Queen, too. Or maybe it was because I couldn't wait to get all dressed up and put on my makeup with the other girls on the squad. Or maybe it was because I just love dancing, even though I'm terrible at it. It didn't matter what, exactly. I just knew I couldn't let Andrew Nithercott kill the homecoming dance.

> *Note: I had no idea Andrew Nithercott had attempted to kill the dance! That was downright villainous. The guy was clearly allergic to fun. I love our school dances. Even if I still can't convince Becca to go with me.*

TANNER E.: Holly was amazing. Everyone else at the table was still flipping through their binders—there were a *lot* of spreadsheets in there—and she rose to her feet like Ruth Bader Ginsburg or something.

BROOKS: Usually, people don't stand up when they talk at Student Council. It's more of a seated thing.

JUSTINE: I'd been drawing this really elaborate doodle in one of the many, many binders Andrew Nithercott had given us, not paying attention at all, so I wasn't totally sure *why* Holly was standing up until she started talking.

TANNER E.: "No," Holly said in her loud, clear voice that I'd heard cheering "DEFENSE!" from across the field so many times. "No. You cannot do this. San Anselmo Prep will always have a homecoming dance. *Always.* And I will fight you with every last breath in my body to make sure that there is nothing you can do about that." *Every last breath in my body.* I can still hear that ringing in my ears. I really wanted to start a slow clap, but I wasn't sure if it was the right time. Can you slow-clap in Student Council? It seemed like it might not be the right environment.

HOLLY: I'd never spoken up before the whole group in Student Council before. Freshmen usually don't, except for Andrew and all his proposals.

ANDREW: Quiet little Holly had finally decided to say something, and it was about *this*? A *dance*? I'd always known she was silly.

HOLLY: He said, "You don't need to get so *emotional* about it," and boom. The spell was broken. *Emotional?!* Let me tell you, he never would have called Tanner E. or any of the other boys at that table *emotional*. I hate that word. It's sexist. Firstly, it wasn't like I burst into tears at the table or anything. And secondly, what's so wrong with being emotional? It means I care about things. That doesn't make me weak. It makes me a compassionate, dedicated member of the Student Council who is good at what she does, who fights for what she believes in, and who gets things done. Or makes sure things *can't* get done, like if I need to block an Andrew Nithercott proposal.

ANDREW: We broke up immediately after the meeting. I needed to date someone more serious.

Note: Andrew Nithercott is currently single, and has been since those two weeks he dated Holly freshman year. Guess he still hasn't found anyone "serious" enough.

HOLLY: We broke up after the meeting because I could finally see what a complete and total *butthead* Andrew Nithercott is. And now I had to do everything in my power to bring him down.

ANDREW: Holly was clearly taking the breakup very hard. It had been a year, and she was still devastated. How else do you explain her decision to run for an office for which she was completely unqualified? Holly belonged at my side, doing what she did best: taking notes. She doesn't have what it takes to lead.

HOLLY: It wasn't about the breakup! That's the thing I hate the *most* about the fact that I dated Andrew Nithercott. He's using our romantic past to invalidate my candidacy, and that right there is some dirty politics. He thinks I'm running against him just because I'm pissed about our relationship ending, like I'm some kind of crazy ex-girlfriend. And that's not it at all! I'm running against him because he is a bad person, and a bad president. And he needs to be stopped.

TANNER E.: Holly should have been president last year. And she should definitely be president this year.

JUSTINE: Am I running for Student Council again? Are you kidding? Definitely not. No college application is worth that. I folded the flag wrong one time, and Andrew Nithercott unleashed a torrent of verbal abuse that has scarred me for life.

ANDREW: Part of the responsibility of Student Council is raising the flag outside the school every morning and putting it to bed every evening. Part of that responsibility includes folding the flag correctly. It's not rocket science. You just can't, for example, crumple it in a ball and stick it in the trunk of your parents' Volvo.

JUSTINE: I didn't *crumple* anything. I'm just a casual folder, okay?

TANNER E.: Am *I* going to run against Holly this year? No way. I'm running for vice president again. Unopposed, because apparently no one thinks it's sexy to be vice president. But I'll only keep doing Student Council if I can be Holly's vice president. I'm with her.

HOLLY: I think I've got a good chance against Andrew. His increasingly rigid policies haven't exactly made him super popular with the student body. Like, everyone in Student Council complains about him constantly. Tanner E. can't stand him, and I hope that means he'll bring in the football vote. And I know the girls on cheer don't like him, because he tried to pass a measure to make our uniforms fuller coverage.

JENSY: "Fuller coverage." Oooh, that made me so mad I could *spit*. Have you ever seen a cheer supply catalog? Our uniforms are downright *modest*—no exposed navel, long sleeves, bums completely covered, all of it. I would wear my uniform to temple without a second thought, and Rabbi Bearman would probably compliment my cute outfit. She's surprisingly fashion-forward for a rabbi. But no, Andrew Nithercott thinks we should be running around with skirts down past our knees, like we're some kind of rah-rah pom squad from 1925. Do you know how easy it is to trip in those things? Do you know how much we trip *already*? A tea-length skirt would be fatal! Maybe this is actually Andrew Nithercott's secret plan to kill all the cheerleaders. Part of his grand scheme to get revenge on Holly.

HOLLY: But you'd be surprised by how much people tend to stick with what's familiar. They'll vote for Andrew Nithercott because they voted for him last year. Or maybe they'll vote for him because I think his "Holly Carpenter, Crazy Ex-Girlfriend" smear campaign has been unfortunately effective with some of the male demographic here. And we can't underestimate the power of the speeches. Andrew Nithercott is a scary but pretty convincing speaker.

ANDREW: I know everyone thinks Holly is some kind of speech whiz kid because of Academic Battle. Did that make me nervous? Of course not. Academic Battle isn't real life. It's easy to persuade a panel of judges. It's hard to persuade sixty teenagers. There was no way Holly had what it took to cut it in politics. She doesn't understand how things *really* get done.

BROOKS: Andrew Nithercott and Patel are basically BFFs, and *that's* what makes him so scary. He's got Patel in his pocket.

PRINCIPAL PATEL: We have many fine students here at San Anselmo Prep, and Andrew Nithercott is one of our finest.

BROOKS: Patel actually listens to Nithercott. And it seemed inevitable that one of Nithercott's nutso resolutions would pass this year, if he were reelected. Nithercott had no problem going straight over the head of the senior SGA president to talk to Patel. It must be nice to have the principal on your side.

ANDREW: Of course I take my proposals directly to Principal Patel. That was the biggest lesson I'd learned last year. The SGA president never gets anything done. And I had one very special request this year that Principal Patel was more than happy to accommodate.

BROOKS: There isn't a specific date for Student Council elections, or if there is, I don't know what it is. I just knew they'd happened sometime in the fall last year.

ANDREW: When I checked the school calendar online, I noticed that somehow, someone had neglected to schedule the Student

Council elections. Of course, it was my civic duty to point out this oversight to Principal Patel.

PRINCIPAL PATEL: Andrew is an extremely detail-oriented young man, who always has the school's best interests at heart.

ANDREW: I suggested the first Friday in October. We wouldn't want the SGA elections to happen too late in the fall. As always, there was so much to do. And Principal Patel happily agreed, scheduled the elections, and with one click of his computer, assured my victory.

PRINCIPAL PATEL: I don't actually do the scheduling, of course. That's Ms. Hernandez, our registrar. I simply passed along Andrew's suggestion.

MS. HERNANDEZ, *administrative assistant to Principal Patel, registrar*: No, I didn't schedule the Student Council elections this year. Those kinds of big events go through the principal.

ANDREW: So I hadn't been nervous about Holly anyway. But as soon as the speeches were scheduled, I knew the sophomore class presidency was mine. You can't lose to a candidate who doesn't show up.

HOLLY: Homecoming is always the first Friday in October. Game in the afternoon, dance at night. But this year, that Friday happened to be the same Friday of Student Council elections.

I couldn't believe my bad luck. How was it possible that those things had been scheduled at the exact same time?

Note: I didn't know what to do. Should I have told Holly that this scheduling conflict was a direct result of the evil machinations of Andrew Nithercott? What he had done was so beyond unfair. But I could hear Colin telling me not to get involved in the story. And I wanted to prove to him, and to myself, that I was a real reporter, who could be totally objective. But I hated the thought of Andrew Nithercott getting away with what he had done.

TANNER E.: The Student Council elections are at the same time as warm-up for the game? Huh. Good thing I'm running unopposed. Even if people leave their vice president ballots blank I'll still win.

HOLLY: And of course the sophomore class would be at the speeches directly before being dismissed to go to the game . . . except for the cheerleaders and football players, who were being dismissed early to warm up. But how could I cast a ballot for myself if I couldn't give a speech? How would *anyone* cast a ballot for me? Or if I stayed to give a speech . . . how could I let down my part of the pyramid? It would literally crumble without me, and we're not exactly the sturdiest squad on our best days. We've dropped Momo so many times I'm surprised she hasn't sustained any long-term damage.

JENSY: We dropped Momo yesterday and it ripped out one of her earrings. It was super gnarly, but that's why you're supposed to take off all jewelry before practice.

MOMO WAKATSUKI, *freshman, San Anselmo Prep Cheer Squad flyer*: I *couldn't* take my earrings out because I had *just* gotten them for my birthday and they were super nice, so I didn't want to lose them. Obviously, losing an earring would have been preferable to the bleeding stump of an ear I have now, but hey. Hindsight is twenty-twenty. Jensy said she could fix my hair to cover my ear for homecoming.

HOLLY: But no matter how many times we drop Momo, she just gets right back up on top of that pyramid. She's fearless. And we never stop trying *not* to drop her, either. Say what you will about cheerleaders, but there's one thing we've got: commitment.

ANDREW: Commitment. That's the other thing this school was missing. Commitment. My opponent can't even commit herself to be present for the speeches. I think that speaks for itself. Vote Nithercott.

HOLLY CARPENTER, PAGEANT QUEEN

ANGELICA: I realized, of course, while I was talking to Holly Carpenter that she was in fact *on* the Academic Battle team. So I'd actually been doing completely relevant research for my story the whole time! Just like any good journalist, I was being *thorough*.

HOLLY CARPENTER, *cheerleader, sophomore class presidential candidate, San Anselmo Prep Academic Battle team member*: Oh, you want to talk about AcaBat now? Sure, no problem.

ANGELICA: And that was when it hit me. Holly Carpenter had a huge problem. She was on the Academic Battle team. And she was a cheerleader. And she was running for sophomore class president. And now, thanks to horrible Andrew Nithercott, all of our school's most important events were happening on the exact same day, at almost the exact same time. It was impossible!

HOLLY: So, yes, there may have been one teensy-weensy little problem with homecoming weekend. Well, one not-so-teensy problem with everything, really.

CINTHIA ALVAREZ, *Academic Battle team member, associate editor of the* Prepster: I don't really *care* that the Academic Battle

Locals are at the same time as the homecoming game. I don't think any of the AcaBats care. We're not exactly a bunch of sports enthusiasts.

HOLLY: I knew there probably weren't a lot of people interested in going to both the football game *and* the AcaBat Locals. But I was supposed to be at both. And at the Student Council speeches. Basically, I was completely screwed.

ANGELICA: I didn't understand, though, how Cinthia was so nonchalant about the fateful events of that first Friday in October. It was weird. Certainly she'd noticed the conflict awaiting her team's prime speech giver? Cinthia was so geared up about AcaBat I assumed she'd be freaking out.

HOLLY: I think all the AcaBats forget that I'm a cheerleader, and I know that everyone on cheer never thinks about the fact that I'm in AcaBat. And then I almost never see anyone who's on Student Council outside of meetings. I didn't mean to create this, like, secret triple life, but it seemed that was exactly what I'd done. On the plus side, it meant that nobody had noticed the unfortunate situation I'd found myself in, so everyone except for me remained calm while I tried to figure out what I was going to do. But on the not-so-plus side, I had literally no idea what I was going to do. Every single event seemed just as important as the next, and I couldn't bear to miss any of it.

ANGELICA: Poor Holly. I didn't know *what* to say. So I decided to just keep asking her questions about Academic Battle. It seemed like what Colin would have done. Stick to the story. Don't get too involved. But watching the anxiety dance across Holly's face, it was hard *not* to get involved.

HOLLY: Yeah, everybody in AcaBat is completely freaking out.

ALLISON WALSH, *Academic Battle team member*: Now that Hutch and Cressida Schrobenhauser-Clonan have graduated, we're completely screwed. We *needed* them. Did they bring in a lot of points? Yes. We're talking crazy points. All the points. We used to see near-perfect scores on anything even remotely related to math and science. There's no way we can keep those perfect scores without them! I guess we have Mason Baumgartner, and he's not *bad* at science, but he's no Hutch.

CINTHIA: Enough with the AcaBat doom and gloom! Yes, Cressida and Hutch more than pulled their weight. But were they indispensable? No. We're a solid team, even without them.
> *Note: Cinthia's attitude toward my "perfect" brother was incredibly refreshing. I wished more people would listen to her. The world at San Anselmo Prep would continue to turn without James in its orbit.*

ALLISON: Our team is good, I guess, but it could be better. It was definitely better when Hutch and Cressida were here.

CINTHIA: I really want to show everyone that we can hold our own no matter who's graduated. All these doubters need to be shut down. Look at who we've still got! Mason Baumgartner is an economics whiz. Allison Walsh always brings it in the social sciences. And Holly Carpenter gives the best speech and interview I've ever seen.

ALLISON: I'm not sure Holly's ever gotten more than two points off, maximum. So I guess that's something. But it's certainly not enough! There is *way* more to AcaBat than just speech and interview. Those are only two categories! Holly Carpenter can't carry this team on her perma-tanned shoulders.

ANGELICA: I remembered all of Holly's interviews from being forced to watch James compete last year. Honestly, I was reading and not paying a *ton* of attention, but I do remember that the judges were always chuckling and nodding along, like Holly was hosting a party they were all at. Although I can't imagine anything less like a party than AcaBat.

CINTHIA: I don't even know *how* Holly's so good. Even as a freshman last year, she barely needed any training. She just burst forth fully formed, like the Athena of speech and interview.

HOLLY: How am I so good? Well, I like to talk. Just, uh, naturally chatty, I guess?

BECCA: Calling Holly Carpenter "naturally chatty" is the understatement of the century. She was my lab partner in freshman bio and now I can tell you her entire life story, despite the fact that I never asked her a single question.

ANGELICA: Holly *is* naturally chatty. Extremely chatty. Which is why I found it so odd that she barely answered my question when I asked if she'd had any previous experience with speech and interview. Sure, she was probably being modest, but something seemed shifty. She was looking up when she talked, and I felt like I remembered from *Sherlock Holmes* that when people look up, it means they're lying.

MS. MILLER, *academic adviser to the AcaBat team*: Carpenter's had speech training. I don't doubt that for a minute. But it wasn't me. I just helped her polish up a bit, made sure she was hitting all the beats that judges like to see. She came to the San Anselmo Prep AcaBat team with experience. Where from? No idea. That's probably the one thing Carpenter's never talked about.

ANGELICA: Something was going on here. And, okay, maybe the mystery of Holly Carpenter's speech-and-interview training wasn't exactly *Murder on the Orient Express*, but come on! Look at what I was working with! I had been assigned to the Academic Battle, the driest subject of all time. If I wasn't able to punch up this article, there is no way Colin would ever publish my work in the paper. I had to follow any leads I could get.

CINTHIA: I was in the computer lab after school when Angelica stopped by. Colin grunted and toasted her with his coffee. He didn't even bother to look up from his computer.

MR. DUNCAN, *sophomore English teacher, newspaper faculty adviser*: There definitely wasn't anyone drinking coffee in the computer lab. Totally against school policy. No one has ever drunk coffee in the computer lab. I barely even drink coffee.

SEBASTIAN "BASH" VON KOHORN, *age ten*: I was sitting under Colin's desk, trying to make a fort. There are *tons* of old brown stains down there from spilled coffee. Maybe Cinthia's desk would make a better fort, if I could find anywhere to sit in between all her cereal boxes.

> *Note: "Bash" is the preferred moniker of Sebastian Von Kohorn, Colin's little brother. With two such overachieving older brothers, Bash has my deepest sympathies. I'm sure people just call him "the little Von Kohorn." We poor younger siblings need to reclaim our names. Like John Proctor in* The Crucible. *"LEAVE ME MY NAME!"*

CINTHIA: Bash knows the area under my desk is a no-go for forts. I need the storage space, and that kid has crushed way too many Cheetos. You can't eat a crushed Cheeto. It's just dust.

BASH: I like to help Colin with the newspaper. Mom lets me stay after school with Colin, and sometimes she picks us up really late, like even after all the sports practices and play practices are done, because that's how hard Colin works, because he's in charge of the whole newspaper.

CINTHIA: Sure, Bash helps us out. He helps by decorating the computer lab with hand-drawn cat pictures, and by eating—or crushing—all of my snacks.

COLIN: Out of nowhere, Angelica burst into my office, and she said she was "chasing a hot lead off campus" and to "expect big things in the AcaBat story." I naturally expressed thrill at this exciting new development, despite the fact that there was almost no way a field trip could be relevant to her assignment. I also wondered, how, exactly was Angelica planning to get wherever she was going? This was the real problem with having such a young staff. No driver's licenses.

Note: Colin doesn't have a driver's license, either.

ANGELICA: I have a *bicycle*. Why does everyone in San Anselmo seem to have forgotten this mode of transportation? Whenever I visit my dad's office at Berkeley, there are more bicycles than people. I recommended that Colin give a bit more thought to his carbon footprint, and set out.

COLIN: I don't even have a car! I am forced to carpool, by virtue of being a sophomore with no driver's license. My carbon footprint is perfectly respectable.

Note: Told you.

ANGELICA: The student directory really makes an investigative reporter's job easy. I found the address I needed and was there in an easy twenty minutes.

MRS. CARPENTER, *Holly's mom, former Miss Alabama and second runner-up Mrs. World*: The doorbell rang, and there was a girl on my doorstep in a San Anselmo Prep uniform. I was certainly surprised to meet Angelica. I'd met Hutch dozens of times at different AcaBat events—and he'd come over for the big party at our place after the team won Nationals—but I had no idea he had a little sister!

Note: No one ever does.

HOLLY: When I came home from cheer practice and saw Angelica sitting at the kitchen table with my mom, the scrapbook sitting on the table between them, I knew my secret was out.

MRS. CARPENTER: Holly did her first pageant when she was only ten months old. "Bayside Beautiful Babies." She won, of course. Holly was the most gorgeous baby anyone had ever seen. From the moment I carried her across the stage, and her little face lit up like a firework, I knew her destiny was in pageants. Just like mine had been.

HOLLY: I can't believe I'm saying this out loud. I *never* say this out loud. I was a child beauty queen. It's mortifying. I was a toddler with bleached teeth and a spray tan.

MRS. CARPENTER: The last year she competed, not only was Holly crowned Miss Junior Teen California, but she was first runner-up Miss Junior Teen America! First runner-up! And she was only thirteen. Usually it's only the fourteen-year-olds who place. If she really had to "retire," well, she certainly went out on top.

HOLLY: Yes, I'm retired, but being first runner-up Miss Junior Teen America was not the highlight of my life. I refuse to believe that I peaked at thirteen.

MRS. CARPENTER: Pardon my pun, but it was the crowning achievement in an extremely impressive series of achievements.

HOLLY: Look, you're probably thinking it's some kind of creepy thing, like my mom wanted to turn me into her mini me or recapture her lost youth or something, but it's not like that. Mom said that pageants taught her how to be confident when she enters a room, how to stand up straight, how to speak in front of people without being afraid, and how to think on her feet. And she was right—they taught me all those things, too. So I don't regret doing them. Even if they are sort of embarrassing, and I would prefer that nobody at school ever know that I'd done them. No regrets, but I'd rather leave pageant Holly back in the past.

MRS. CARPENTER: I thought it was odd, at first, when Holly mentioned wanting to do AcaBat, but when I first saw her compete, I understood.

HOLLY: So maybe it seems like a weird progression, but pageants led me straight to AcaBat. Do you remember when we had that assembly freshman year, when upperclassmen came and told us about all the clubs and activities we could do now that we were in upper school? The minute I heard about the speech and interview sections in AcaBat, I had a feeling it was destiny. The only part of pageants I ever liked doing was the interview, and now with AcaBat, I can answer much more interesting questions. I mean, I'll probably never do anything as famous as

Hutch's "math is a universal language" speech, but I got a nearly perfect score last year when responding to the prompt "How would you tell someone their fly is down?"

Note: That was really the prompt. I remember because I was sitting in the audience with Mom and Dad, wondering how, exactly, that was an academic question. Although, if anyone was going to tell me my fly was down, I can't imagine anyone doing a nicer, more tactful job than Holly Carpenter. It was a well-deserved near-perfect score.

MRS. CARPENTER: And AcaBat's been surprisingly fun! You should see my baby crush it out there. So many of those other boys and girls just can't carry themselves at all! The posture on them. It's abominable. Holly still lets me do her hair and makeup, too. Even if she says the false lashes are a no-go.

HOLLY: Of course you can't wear fake eyelashes to AcaBat. I'm already usually wearing more makeup than everyone else in the room combined. I can't even imagine what Daphne Leake-Palmer would say if I was wearing fake eyelashes. Well, not that she usually *says* anything, but she always gives me these horrible snotty looks and eye rolls. And once I wore a pink blouse with a pantsuit, and she said, "That was a bold choice." Ugh, it was horrible. For AcaBat, we're supposed to stick to soothing colors, like blue and burgundy, and never something aggressive, like red, and rarely pastels, but it was a very professional pink.

Note: Daphne Leake-Palmer is the new captain of the San Rafael Academy AcaBat team. James used to call her Demon

Sneak-Palmer, which is not even that clever. He should stick to science, not puns.

MRS. CARPENTER: Oh, that Daphne girl is horrible. And she needs more highlighter.

THE FIRST FORAY INTO ENEMY TERRITORY

ANGELICA: I'm not entirely sure what possessed me to call Colin. I think it had something to do with interviewing Holly and her mom. There was this whole other part of Holly that I hadn't even known existed. Sure, maybe it wasn't a total shocker that a cheerleader had once done beauty pageants, but there was a lot more to Holly than just being a cheerleader, or just being on AcaBat, or just running for Student Council . . . Man, Holly made even my brother look like a slacker. The truth is, nobody is just one thing. And I was starting to see how all the AcaBats were smart in different ways, too. Like how Holly was people smart, and Cinthia seemed to love words and graphics equally, and they were all so smart in such a different way from how James is smart. I guess that was something I had missed all those years of watching James compete—that AcaBat celebrates so many different kinds of being smart, with no one way more important than another. It's not like science was more important than music—they were all equal. And, well, I liked that. Maybe all of this thinking about the multidimensionality of humanity was what inspired me to see if there was another side to Colin. There had to be more to him than just an obsession with Times New Roman and a supreme devotion to being antisocial, right? He was passionate about editing the newspaper, after all. I guess that was a quality I admired. Maybe I wanted to see if he had other good qualities, too.

COLIN VON KOHORN, *editor in chief of the* Prepster: The minute the name "Angelica Hutcherson" flashed on the screen of my phone, I knew that giving her my number had been a mistake.

ANGELICA: If Colin didn't want me to call him, he shouldn't have given me his number. Pretty simple.

COLIN: I had given her my phone number for editorial emergencies *only*. Just like I give it to everyone on the *Prepster*. Just like I have everyone on staff in my contacts list, in case I need to contact *them* with an emergency.

CINTHIA ALVAREZ, *associate editor of the* Prepster: One time I almost called Colin to ask him to get me a Red Bull. I felt like my caffeine level was at a state of emergency, but I had a feeling he wouldn't feel the same way. So I just soldiered on and tried taping my eyelids open. Didn't work. I never call Colin, but he texts me all the time. Every time the layout comes in, I'll get a text that says, "DID A CHICKEN DO YOUR FORMATTING?!" or something similar. I always send back a bunch of chicken emojis. He doesn't enjoy it.

COLIN: So far, no one had ever called me with an editorial emergency. Which made me realize that giving my number out had been a mistake. What could possibly have qualified as an editorial emergency, anyway? I take the *Prepster* more seriously than probably anyone ever has in the history of its existence, with the sole exception of Bugsy Kopeck, and even I couldn't come up with an editorial emergency for which I would willingly expose myself to a social call.

ANGELICA: This wasn't a social call. This was straight-up, serious *Prepster* business.

COLIN: I didn't say my phone number was for *Prepster* business. I said it was for *Prepster* emergencies.

ANGELICA: Colin barked, "WHAT'S YOUR EMERGENCY?" Seriously. That's how he answers the phone. He probably says that to his grandma, too.

GRAMMY VON KOHORN, *Colin's grandmother, reigning poker champion at Vivante on the Coast Assisted Living Facility in Costa Mesa:* Young lady, you're assuming Colin actually *answers* my calls. Well, that's not fair. He'll usually pick up on the second try, then shout, "THE PRESS WAITS FOR NO MAN, GRAMMY!" Once he's gotten that out of his system, he'll calm down enough to have a quick chat. That boy needs a vacation. That's the problem with kids today. You spend your summers doing internships. What happened to doing nothing?
    Note: She was very happy to hear that I'd spent my summer doing nothing but eating ice cream with Becca and steadily working through my to-be-read pile, and then suggested I could teach Colin "a thing or twelve."

COLIN: Angelica's call, of course, was in no way, shape, or form an emergency.

ANGELICA: I told Colin I was heading into enemy territory, and invited him along to see some top-notch reporting.

COLIN: Enemy territory. I assumed she was referring to San Rafael Academy, our alleged "rivals." I couldn't care less about our school's athletic organizations, so I have a hard time getting lathered up over some nearby private school we're supposed to arbitrarily hate for no reason whatsoever.

ANGELICA: I don't play any sports, either, but I couldn't understand Colin's blasé attitude. Of course I hate the San Rafael Knights! They are our sworn enemies. And it's not just athletic. They're our enemies in *everything*. Maybe my brother's total detestation of the Knights' Academic Battle team had rubbed off on me. Every narrative needs an antagonist, and every high school experience needs one, too.

COLIN: I have plenty of antagonists. I don't need one the school has manufactured for me.
  Note: I was starting to realize that Colin and Becca were a lot more alike than either of them would ever admit.

ANGELICA: Colin didn't seem to understand that the struggle is what makes life interesting! There's nothing to fight for if there's no one to fight against.

COLIN: And this is why Angelica writes fiction. She's constantly creating narratives, even in cases of straightforward reporting, where absolutely no narrative needs to exist.

ANGELICA: I still didn't understand what, exactly, Colin had against fiction. Why couldn't it be published in his precious *Prepster*, anyway? I was pretty sure they used to publish poems and short fiction pieces. James still had a page of the *Prepster* in his room from a couple years ago that featured a poem called "An Ode to Animal Fries," written by a then-freshman named Avery Dennis. Boy, that crush was a slow burn.

COLIN: The *Prepster* was founded in 1920 as an informational news bulletin for the student body. As they edged into the 1930s, the staff began including satirical fiction pieces, and then, of course, under Bugsy Kopeck's tenure, it entered its heyday as a serious source of journalism. By the 1960s, it had devolved into a literary magazine full of flowery prose and antiwar poetry. The '80s brought a return to hard news, then the *Prepster* of the '90s and early aughts was a mishmash of fiction and fact, marred by a lot of poetry in the unfortunate vein of Jewel. "My hands are small" and all that nonsense. So Angelica wasn't wrong in arguing that there was precedent for including fiction in the *Prepster*. But this was a new *Prepster*, and there was no room for fiction under my stewardship.

ANGELICA: Much to my surprise, Colin agreed to meet me at San Rafael Academy. Maybe he hoped if I did enough straightforward reporting, I'd stop bugging him about publishing fiction. Not very likely, but he didn't need to know that.

COLIN: I'm not entirely sure *why* I said yes. Curiosity, maybe? That week's edition of the *Prepster* was ready to go, so I had no real reason to stay at school. It had also been some time since I'd done any reporting in the field. Last year, I was chasing stories all over the place, but now that I'm editor in chief, it's harder to leave my desk. I just made Angelica promise me I wouldn't have to wear a disguise.

ANGELICA: I have no idea why Colin thought he needed a disguise. I invited him along to do some investigative reporting. I said nothing about going undercover.

COLIN: Angelica seems like the kind of person who would wear a disguise. That's all I'm saying. I was somewhat surprised she hadn't found herself a jaunty hat with a "PRESS" card stuck in the brim, like she was interviewing Shoeless Joe from Hannibal, MO, in *Damn Yankees*.

CINTHIA: The *Prepster* reviews all of San Anselmo Prep's theatrical productions. The fall play, the spring musical, the winter one-act play festival, all of it. Last year, Colin reviewed the middle school's production of *Damn Yankees*. His review was titled "Shoeless OH NO!" and featured such quotes as "This lackluster production certainly wasn't what Lola wanted, but it was what the audience got," "It's not just the ump who's blind, it's the choreographer," and "I'd gladly sell my soul to the devil to erase the last two and half hours from my memory." After several parent complaints, I've taken over doing the reviews this year.

ANGELICA: I told Colin to meet me at San Rafael Academy, and hopped on my bike.

COLIN: There is no greater indignity than being forced to rely on one's mother as a sole form of transportation.

MRS. VON KOHORN, *Colin's mother, chairwoman of the board of the Northern California Society for the Prevention of Cruelty to Animals*: I was very used to picking Colin up at all hours from the computer lab. Luckily, it had been quite some time since the janitorial staff accidentally locked him in. That used to happen fairly frequently. I told him to stop working in the dark. I had to miss book club while I was waiting in the parking lot for someone to come back with keys.

COLIN: I was locked in the school *twice*. That's it. Just twice. And both times, Mr. Ross was at the school within fifteen minutes, and after he unlocked the building, I apologized profusely, and later, I got him a Starbucks gift card. My mother missing her book club hardly qualifies as a national emergency. I know for a fact she'd fallen asleep listening to *The Girl on the Train*, so I doubt she had a lot to contribute to the discussion anyway.

MR. ROSS, *head of the maintenance team at San Anselmo Prep*: Colin Von Kohorn doesn't even hold the record for being locked into the school building the most. Not even close. Twice is nothing. Over the previous four years, this kid named Tripp Gomez-Parker somehow got himself locked in the weight room no fewer than six separate times. What was he doing in there? I don't know, and I don't want to know.

MRS. VON KOHORN: Chauffeuring Colin and Bash around is the least interesting part of the whole mom job description. At least Colin likes to listen to NPR. Bash is going through a really unfortunate techno phase. How, exactly, a ten-year-old was exposed to house music is beyond me, but now we all have to pay the price.

COLIN: I told Bash to pack up his crayons. It was time to get out of the computer lab and see what Angelica was up to. Mom was waiting outside. I tried to brush all the cat hair off the front seat of the car, but it was useless. Mom, for some reason, keeps letting Bash adopt all of these horrible cats no one wants, and then he wants to drive Mrs. Fluff and Li'l Beastie and all his other monsters around with us, so they can "see the city." Those cats couldn't care less about seeing San Anselmo. They spend the entire time they're in the car trying to escape, or attempting to shred my khakis to ribbons.

Note: I tried to picture Colin interacting with a cat, and failed.

MRS. VON KOHORN: I love that Bash has taken such an interest in animal adoption! These cats need homes, and we have more than enough room for them. Colin's always been too fussy about cat hair on his khakis. What's a little cat hair compared to kitty snuggles?

COLIN: I live in a menagerie full of ugly cats. That is my trial. I resigned myself to emerging from the car covered in cat hair, cranked up *Wait Wait . . . Don't Tell Me!*, and we sped off toward San Rafael Academy.

SEBASTIAN "BASH" VON KOHORN, *age ten*: Colin thinks he should always get the front seat, just because he's bigger than me. It's so unfair. And he's so bossy with the radio, too.

MRS. VON KOHORN: Colin wouldn't tell me *why* he needed to go to a different school. His answer, as always, was "official *Prepster* business," with no further elaboration. So I dropped him off, and Bash and I went to pick up the dry cleaning.

COLIN: I barrel-rolled out of the car to avoid having to introduce Angelica to my mother.

ANGELICA: I'd been waiting for Colin in the courtyard, surrounded by a sea of maroon sweater vests.

COLIN: It felt like stepping into a Negaverse, where everything that was usually navy was now maroon. The world had turned upside down.

ANGELICA: We stuck out like sore thumbs in our San Anselmo uniforms. Maybe we *should* have worn disguises after all.

COLIN: I asked Angelica what, exactly, her plan was here.

ANGELICA: I didn't have a plan, but it turned out I didn't need one. Because just at the very moment that Colin asked me what my plan was, Daphne Leake-Palmer walked out of the building.

CINTHIA: Daphne. Leake. Palmer. God, I hate that girl.

ALLISON WALSH, *AcaBat*: Daphne Leake-Palmer is the captain of the San Rafael Academy AcaBat team. She is *scary*. And she knows more about art history than everyone on our team put together. She always crushes us in the art section. She's pretty good at music, too. She's good at all the areas we're bad at, which makes her extra scary.

MASON BAUMGARTNER, *AcaBat*: Daphne Leake-Palmer looks like a Bond villain. Like one of the sexy ones, from Russia, who is hiding a gun somewhere you would *never* expect there to be a gun. If she wasn't our greatest enemy, we'd probably be dating. I'd always felt there'd been a bit of a frisson between us.

ALLISON: Mason is always compulsively fixing his hair and checking his breath whenever Daphne walks by. He packs this kit full of breath mints "just in case" every time we head off to AcaBat Locals. So annoying. Give it up, Mason, it's not happening.

CINTHIA: Allison and Mason kissed once. Maybe they kissed more than once—I only *caught* them once.

ALLISON: Who told you that Mason and I made out? We didn't, okay? This isn't *marching band*. AcaBats are invested in academic performance, not romance. So we just kissed, like, one time. It was nothing. Maybe two times. Okay, fine, six times. It was six times!

CINTHIA: And now Allison seems to think that the worst thing about Daphne Leake-Palmer is that Mason has this unrequited crush on her. Where in fact, the worst thing about Daphne Leake-Palmer is that she's a lizard in human skin.

ALLISON: There's a rumor that Daphne Leake-Palmer once made a judge cry. A *judge*. That girl is ice-cold.
>   *Note: Not a rumor. It happened during James's sophomore year, and I was there.*

DAPHNE LEAKE-PALMER, *senior at San Rafael Academy, captain of the AcaBat team*: Four horrible years of AcaBat shutouts had finally come to a close. Sure, I'd only personally witnessed three of them, but watching Hutch waltz away with a Locals victory year after year was an exercise in excruciating embarrassment. But finally, he had graduated, and the San Anselmo Prep team couldn't rely on him to carry them anymore.

ANGELICA: Daphne was only too happy to talk to us and explain all the ways that San Rafael Academy was going to decimate San Anselmo Prep. Maybe it was a good thing that we'd worn our uniforms after all. She couldn't wait to talk trash.

COLIN: It was shockingly easy. It reminded me of listening to a Bond villain explain all of his evil plans *before* carrying them out, while James Bond nimbly escaped from the giant laser.
>   *Note: Again with the Bond villain thing? Maybe Daphne Leake-Palmer really was one.*

DAPHNE: San Anselmo Prep has always been *so* heavily math and science focused, and now, so sad for them, their two strongest competitors in math and science have graduated. They've underestimated music and art for far too long, and now they're going to pay for it.

MASON: Daphne does this thing in speech and interview, where she takes a dramatic pause, and pushes one inky black lock of raven hair behind one of her perfect shell-like ears. It's *very* effective.

ALLISON: Oh, I hate Daphne Leake-Palmer's stupid hair-behind-the-ear-dramatic-pause trick. As if what she's going to say next is so *profound* we all have to wait for it. I hope the judges this year are smart enough not to fall for it.

ANGELICA: The Daphne Leake-Palmer hair trick was in full effect even in the San Rafael Academy courtyard. It didn't seem to be producing the desired response. Colin kept clearing his throat impatiently every time she did it.

COLIN: Our interviewee kept taking strange pauses to fiddle with her hair. It was very odd.

DAPHNE: Do we have a strategy? We don't *need* a strategy. We have the better team, the stronger team, the more well-rounded team, and we are, quite simply, going to pulverize San Anselmo Prep. I can personally guarantee you that San Anselmo is not going on to Regionals this year. I also wouldn't be surprised if they disbanded the Academic Battle program altogether due to sheer embarrassment.

ANGELICA: Daphne asked me what my name was. I probably should have lied, but I was worried that this might have compromised my journalistic integrity or something. Like maybe you couldn't investigate under false pretenses.

DAPHNE: I couldn't believe it. The little sister of the great James Hutcherson, here at San Rafael Academy, to interview me. It was too much.

ANGELICA: "You tell your brother," she purred, "that his reign has come to an end, and I intend to ensure that there is nothing left of his legacy but smoke and ashes."

COLIN: I rolled my eyes. Smoke and ashes? Seriously?

ANGELICA: Despite myself, I was impressed. It was quite a line. I wondered if she'd written it beforehand, or just come up with it on the spot. I made a mental note to write it down myself, because my goodness, that was really the perfect thing to say to one's enemies before battle. I knew it would make its way into a story eventually. Maybe this would be the line that resurrected the epic tale of the badger coven. Those badgers would destroy their enemies and leave nothing behind but smoke and ashes.

DAPHNE: This was going to be my year. I knew it. Hutch was gone, and a new era of San Rafael Academy victory was dawning.

ANGELICA: I don't know if Daphne Leake-Palmer was right or wrong about the whole new era thing. But she was plain wrong about my brother being gone. James may have graduated . . . but he hadn't really left.

DINNER AT HOME

NINA HOWARD HUTCHERSON, *aka Mom, public defender for the state of California*: James is of course welcome at the dinner table anytime, no advance warnings needed. Your father's not a restaurant, Angelica. James doesn't need to make a reservation.

DARRELL HUTCHERSON, *aka Dad, tenured professor of theoretical math at UC Berkeley*: I always make a couple of extra servings in case James and his girlfriend stop by for dinner. No trouble at all, and if they don't come, then I've got leftovers for lunch the next day.

ANGELICA: James has already come to dinner at home twice, and he's only been at college for a month! See what I mean? That is way too many times to come to dinner! I know they have dining halls at Caltech. I got dragged along on that tour. I've *seen* the dining halls. He can go eat there. He's not even supposed to live here anymore, and he's never left.

JAMES "HUTCH" HUTCHERSON, *older brother, Caltech freshman, former San Anselmo Prep Academic Battle All-Star*: The food at Caltech is fine, but what can I say? My dad's cooking is better, and it's nice not having to pay a machine to do my laundry. I know I don't live at home anymore, but that doesn't mean I can't visit. And even though I moved out, that certainly doesn't give Angelica a right to go in my room and mess with my stuff.

ANGELICA: By his own admission, he doesn't live here anymore. He *moved out*. Ergo, it is no longer his room. Just because Mom and Dad have chosen to leave it all decked out as a James Hutcherson: Perfect Son shrine doesn't mean I have to worship at that altar. And if he was really attached to his stuff, he should have taken it with him to college.

HUTCH: I'd barely moved out and she'd already gone in and messed everything up.

ANGELICA: I hadn't messed anything up! I had borrowed a book, one book, because I'd never read any Isaac Asimov, and I'd thought, "Hey, let's give this a shot." Books are meant to be read and shared and loved, not molder away on a shelf. Sure, I'd *also* found Avery's oral history and read that with Becca, but James didn't know that. I'd been *super* careful about putting that back *exactly* where I'd found it.

HUTCH: She'd completely destroyed my alphabetized shelving system. It was pretty appalling.

AVERY DENNIS, *girlfriend of older brother, Pepperdine freshman*: Even I know not to touch Hutch's books, and we've been dating for less than a year. You've known him for fifteen years. Sorry, Angelica, that one's on you. Just go to the library.

ANGELICA: The first time Avery had come to dinner at our house, of course I'd been surprised. The only girlfriend I ever expected James to have was a robot he'd built himself. How could a human person date him? The mind boggled. But when I showed up for dinner after interviewing Daphne Leake-Palmer at San Rafael Academy, I wasn't surprised to see Avery at all. By this time, she'd become a pretty regular fixture at the dinner table.

AVERY: Mr. Hutcherson makes a veggie burger that will put whatever your sad, sorry idea of a veggie burger is to shame. He always gives me extra avocado to put on top, too. That man is a prince.

ANGELICA: Honestly, I'd rather have dinner with just Avery and no James. Avery doesn't derail the conversation and keep it exclusively focused on string theory. And she's not scared of my mom, which is pretty impressive. Think about it—who could ever have been good enough to date perfect James? No one, that's who. And my mom is a notoriously harsh critic of *everything*. When she met Michelle Obama at this lawyer luncheon, she described her arms as "fine." That's it. She saw Michelle Obama's arms *in person*, and she described them as just "fine."

AVERY: I don't know why Hutch thinks his parents are embarrassing. I think they're awesome. Hutch's mom has all of these pictures with her and Michelle Obama, for Pete's sake! See? Undeniably awesome. My dad, on the other hand, has broken squash rackets over people's heads on three separate occasions. *Three*. And they put pictures of it up at the squash club he was barred from, so that the staff can identify him and remove him at once, if he ever shows up on site again. My dad basically has a squash mug shot. Now *that's* embarrassing.

ANGELICA: I wasn't sure if I should invite Colin to dinner—I didn't want to, obviously, but I could hear my dad in my head telling me it would be rude *not* to invite him just as clearly as if Dad had been standing in the courtyard with us. Fortunately, Colin made a speedy exit before I was forced to sacrifice my enjoyment of dinner for etiquette's sake.

COLIN: The minute my mom's minivan rolled into view I ran, obviously, to once again avoid having to introduce Angelica to my mother. My mother would have undoubtedly invited her over for dinner, and I will subject no one to dinner in the Von Kohorn home. Recently, it's been accompanied by an endless sound track of house music, courtesy of DJ Bash. It's enough to make you lose your appetite.

ANGELICA: Great. So Colin and I had a mutual desire to *not* eat dinner with each other and we went our separate ways. Lucky for me, conversation at the Hutcherson family dinner table turned almost immediately to homecoming and the Academic Battle. Maybe this story had been my destiny after all.

HUTCH: I never, ever, in my wildest dreams imagined that I would come back to San Anselmo Prep for homecoming.

AVERY: Hutch was *always* coming to homecoming. He just didn't know it.

HUTCH: I didn't go to homecoming when I was a student. Football? No. Dances? Well, just that one time. So why would I go back? There was nothing for me there.

AVERY: The whole point of homecoming is for alumni to come back to campus. And I'm the alumni coordinator for our class! That was not a responsibility I took on lightly. It was my *duty* to ensure maximum attendance. Which included Hutch, obviously. I had a *very* persuasive argument prepared. But then it turned out I didn't need it.

MRS. MARTINE HALZBACH, *regional director for the Academic Battle of Marin County*: James Hutcherson is a legend. He's the single most successful Academic Battle competitor I've seen in my fifteen years as regional director.
   Note: All these AcaBat people who know who my brother is totally creep me out. He is not *a celebrity.*

DAPHNE LEAKE-PALMER, *captain of the San Rafael Academy Academic Battle team*: Hutch won *Nationals* for that team. Nationals! The highest honor in American Academic Battle! Can you imagine how humiliating it was, to watch our *rivals* win Nationals? To be separated by mere miles from the champions while we had been brought so low? Never. Again.

ANGELICA: If one more person tells me about the time my brother single-handedly won Nationals with his response to the prompt "Math has been described as the universal language. Discuss," I will scream.

HUTCH: Math *is* the universal language. Actually . . .

Note: The rest of this response has been redacted to preserve the reader's sanity.

MRS. HALZBACH: Including a recent alumnus on the judging panel is a fairly controversial move, especially if said alumnus is evaluating his alma mater. But when I told the board that I wanted to appoint James Hutcherson as a judge, the decision was unanimous.

HUTCH: I had to turn it down, of course. AcaBat judges must have at least a bachelor's degree in the area they're evaluating. Anything less would be unacceptable.

MRS. HALZBACH: In addition to his sterling record of academic excellence, James Hutcherson has exactly the exemplary moral standards we look for in a judge.

Note: Barf.

HUTCH: Once Mrs. Halzbach explained that it was more of a ceremonial judgeship, I was happy to accept. I'm not gonna lie, I was pretty flattered. Even if it was only a ceremonial position, I was still going to be the youngest judge in Marin County AcaBat history. And of course, I couldn't wait to see our team crush the Knights. We've got a pretty young team this year, but I know they'll be way better than whatever flotsam and jetsam Demon Sneak-Palmer has rounded up over at San Rafael.

AVERY: I sent Mrs. Halzbach a very nice note thanking her for appointing Hutch to his judgeship and for so kindly scheduling the Academic Battle Locals during homecoming weekend. It had been an absolute stroke of genius on my part. Of course, I'd been totally happy for Hutch when he told me he'd been appointed a ceremonial judge—dreams coming true and all that—but I was also happy for *me*. The stars had aligned, and I instantly knew what I had to do. Academic Battle Locals hadn't been scheduled yet, and I knew there was one way to guarantee Hutch would attend homecoming—to make sure that homecoming and Academic Battle were at the same time! When I called Mrs. Halzbach, she was only too happy to schedule Locals so Hutch could revisit his beloved alma mater during homecoming weekend. Now Hutch *had* to go to homecoming. I figured I'd still have plenty of time to see the famous Dragon Dougie while Hutch was on a break from judgeship. These things have intermissions, right?

ANGELICA: As Avery went on about the glory of homecoming, and how excited she was for her first Academic Battle experience—little did she know what she was in for—all I could think about was the enormous scheduling mess San Anselmo Prep was heading toward. And part of it was *Avery's* fault?! Well, really, it was James's fault. If he hadn't been so desperate to ceremonially judge something and so *stubborn* about avoiding human social interaction, none of this would have even happened! Why couldn't he just go to homecoming because his girlfriend asked him to, like a normal person? I didn't blame

Avery. This whole homecoming mess was a result of James being difficult. Like always.

HUTCH: I hadn't realized that Academic Battle was the same weekend as homecoming until after Avery had already gotten it confirmed and on the national Academic Battle calendar. Well, it wouldn't be a problem since I had zero plans to attend the homecoming game.

ANGELICA: This was a disaster. Maybe James wasn't going to Academic Battle *and* the game, but I could think of at least one person who was. Holly Carpenter was supposed to be in three places at once. And I had no idea how that was going to be possible. And she couldn't be the only person affected by this scheduling mistake. The story had gotten so much bigger than Academic Battle. And I couldn't wait to see Colin's face when it landed on his desk.

ANOTHER EDITORIAL CHECK-IN

COLIN VON KOHORN, *editor in chief*: Right before the bell rang for fifth-period English, Angelica told me she had something *essential* to discuss. Angelica and I obviously have very different definitions of *essential*, given her liberal views toward using my for-emergencies-only private cell number, but anyway I told her to meet me in my office as soon as school was over.

ANGELICA: How had I forgotten to tell Colin that the Student Council elections were also happening on the first Friday in October? How?! We'd just been standing there at San Rafael Academy last night. I'd had plenty of time to bring it up. Maybe old Demon Sneak-Palmer had unnerved me a little bit more than I'd thought.

BECCA: Something was up with Angelica. She couldn't even focus on the discussion questions, and usually she lives for that stuff. She's always the first one with her hand in the air, and then she'll usually bring up a completely different point two minutes later. Angelica could have a fairly dynamic discussion in English class all by herself. But when I asked what was going on, she said there was "a huge development" in her story for the *Prepster*. I had a hard time imagining anything huge coming out of the *Prepster*, home of the Recipe Roundup, but if anyone could do it, it was Angelica.

COLIN: Recipe Roundup has been discontinued as a feature this year. I do not appreciate the people who keep bringing it up. It is *never* coming back.

> *Note: Recipe Roundup used to be a regular column in the* Prepster, *in which teachers shared favorite recipes. It was the first thing Colin cut when he became editor in chief this year. Ms. Segerson's Snack Mix is still a go-to at my house, though.*

CINTHIA ALVAREZ, *associate editor of the* Prepster: I was eating Cinnamon Toast Crunch out of a coffee mug in the computer lab, trying to convince Colin for the millionth time that listening to music wouldn't "kill productivity," when Angelica burst in.

SEBASTIAN "BASH" VON KOHORN, *age ten*: Cinthia's mug was *full*, and she only put ten little squares of Cinnamon Toast Crunch in my mug! I watched her count them out. So unfair.

ANGELICA: As Bash glowered at Cinthia, I told them everything. That I'd been right, that the story of AcaBat *was* the story of homecoming, because everything was happening *at the exact same time.*

CINTHIA: I'd known AcaBat was at the same time as homecoming, but I guess I hadn't really considered it that big of a deal, since I'd never been to a homecoming game before. But then Angelica pointed out that Holly was supposed to be in both places—which made it, officially, a huge deal, since we needed her to win. And then Angelica said the Student Council elections were also at the same time, which made it, officially, a disaster, because I had to vote to unseat evil dictator Andrew Nithercott, otherwise I'd be spending the next year in a straw boater hat and bow tie or whatever bizarre thing he'd decide needed to be added to the San Anselmo Prep dress code, and how could I do that if I was at AcaBat Locals? And weren't Student Council elections traditionally held in the auditorium, the exact same place we always had AcaBat Locals?! They were happening at the same time *and* in the same place? The panic started to set in. I poured the rest of the Cinnamon Toast Crunch into my mug.

BASH: She poured *the whole box* into her mug. *The whole box!* That's like twenty servings. She could have given me way more cereal.

COLIN: There was no way this could have been right. Either Angelica was confused, which I seriously doubted—I have never seen her confused, not even when we had to memorize "The Wife of Bath's Prologue" from *The Canterbury Tales* in Middle English, and that confused *everyone*—or she may have actually been onto something.

> Note: *"Experience, though noon auctoritee were in this world, is right ynogh for me to speke of wo that is in marriage"*—I *can still do it. This is probably taking up valuable brain space that could be devoted to something else.*

ANGELICA: When Colin started to get excited, I almost couldn't believe it. I'd been a little worried he would dismiss this as me digging for a story when there wasn't one, but I could tell from his response that there was something here.

COLIN: This was a huge oversight. And this kind of incompetence could only have come straight from the top. Maybe this was the exposé that would finally make my career at the *Prepster*.

CINTHIA: I had Cinnamon Toast Crunch to finish, but I wished Colin and Angelica luck as they set off to grill Principal Patel.

BECCA: Angelica was gone when I came to look for her in the computer lab. There was just Cinthia Alvarez, crunching some cereal, and Bash Von Kohorn, spinning around in a computer chair.

CINTHIA: I keep extra boxes of cereal and mugs under my desk, because, obviously, a well-fed writer is a productive writer. Barriga llena, corazón contento. Mr. Duncan would pop a gasket if he knew, and Colin is convinced we're going to get mice, but whatever. I haven't seen any mice yet. And at least I can entertain people when they swing by our dungeon. It's called being a good host. So I opened a fresh box of cereal for Becca.

BASH: The grumpy girl with the blue hair got her own box? Unbelievable. I decided to go exploring. Maybe there would be something stuck in the vending machine I could shake loose.

CINTHIA: About half the time he's in here, Bash'll get bored and wander away while Colin is supposed to be watching him, and we finally get some peace in the computer lab. He always wanders back eventually.

BECCA: I accepted a mug of Cinnamon Toast Crunch, and settled in to tell Cinthia all about my ideas for *Riot Prep!* This school was crying out for an underground literary magazine. It was time to give the people a voice.

MS. HERNANDEZ, *administrative assistant to Principal Patel, school registrar:* Let me just say that at a larger high school, there would be a *team* of people doing my job. A team.

PRINCIPAL PATEL, Angelica Hutcherson and Colin Von Kohorn were not students I saw in my office with great regularity, but of course, I have an open-door policy, and I am happy to meet with any student, at any time.

Note: He winced when he said "open-door policy," though, which made me wonder just exactly how open it was.

MS. HERNANDEZ: Oh, yes, of course Principal Patel has an open-door policy. As long as he's not on the phone. Or writing an email. Or meeting someone. Or busy with anything else.

COLIN: As Angelica and I took our seats across from Principal Patel, and I fixed him with my steeliest glare, I experienced a rush I hadn't felt since Cinthia and I had cracked the decreasingly crispy French fry case. This was what I'd been missing sitting behind my desk. The thrill of chasing the story. The rush of conducting an interview, knowing that I was on the edge of finding something big. I could feel the story thrumming in that room, like a living, breathing thing.

ANGELICA: Colin took an uncomfortably long dramatic pause. Principal Patel was looking at us like we were completely insane.

MS. HERNANDEZ: From my desk outside Principal Patel's office, it appeared as though Colin Von Kohorn was engaging the principal in a staring contest. It also appeared as though Colin Von Kohorn was winning.

ANGELICA: Eventually, after several lifetimes of a dramatic pause, Colin cleared his throat and began questioning Principal Patel.

PRINCIPAL PATEL: Of course I was aware when homecoming was. It was the first Friday in October, just as it was every year. The football game against San Rafael Academy would be in the afternoon, and a dance would follow in the evening.

ANGELICA: Colin teased out his questions gradually, like he was setting Patel up for a fall. I could tell Patel had no idea where Colin was going with this, but I could follow each step of the trap he'd laid.

PRINCIPAL PATEL: Yes, I knew when the Academic Battle Locals were. I didn't have the date right in front of me, but I was sure it was in an email. Mrs. Halzbach, our regional coordinator, had emailed with a proposed date that was mutually convenient for San Rafael Academy, and I'd happily agreed to it.

ANGELICA: I almost felt bad for Principal Patel as he blustered on obliviously.

PRINCIPAL PATEL: Of course I knew when the Student Council elections were. They're at the end of the first quarter, same as they always are.

ANGELICA: I wondered then if Principal Patel was going to say anything about Andrew Nithercott's involvement in picking the date of the Student Council elections. But then he didn't say anything. So I wondered if *I* should say something. But then I didn't, and the moment passed. I felt like I had to tell someone, and it would be the right thing to do, to make sure the truth came out. But I wasn't sure who to tell. Or how that fit into Colin's whole "you can't write the story and be the story" thing. Because if I said something, then I would definitely *be* the story, which I shouldn't be. Except maybe there was a time you *were* supposed to be the story? Like if maybe this was San Anselmo Prep's Watergate?

PRINCIPAL PATEL: Colin Von Kohorn should have asked Ms. Hernandez to check the calendar if he really wanted to know the finalized dates of Academic Battle Locals, or of anything else, for that matter. The calendar is her domain.

MS. HERNANDEZ: The calendar is *not* my domain. Sure, I'll do some day-to-day scheduling, but all big school events are solely the responsibility of Principal Patel. *He* schedules those.

PRINCIPAL PATEL: Ms. Hernandez is the registrar. All scheduling matters should be directed to her. Period.

COLIN: Principal Patel seemed to have no idea why I'd begun this line of questioning, but it seemed as though he'd started to ascertain it was going nowhere good.

ANGELICA: "Were you *aware*," Colin asked, in this incredibly serious sort of voice one expects to hear on a legal drama, "that due to an extreme case of gross negligence, San Anselmo Prep has scheduled all of its major fall events on the exact same day and at the exact same time?"

PRINCIPAL PATEL: All of these events were happening at the same time? No. It was impossible. I told Colin that he must have been mistaken.

COLIN: I never make mistakes. My record on multiple-choice assessments speaks for itself. And I certainly hadn't made a mistake this time. I trusted Angelica's reporting. She had confirmed with multiple sources, in all of these different activities, that the greatest scheduling disaster in the history of San Anselmo Prep had occurred.

Note: The great Colin Von Kohorn trusted my reporting?! This felt like the opposite of a black Post-it note.

ANGELICA: Colin told Principal Patel to check the calendar if he didn't believe him. But I guess Principal Patel doesn't know how to use his calendar, because he started shouting for Ms. Hernandez to come in and open it for him.

PRINICPAL PATEL: Of course I know how to use Google Calendar. It is, quite frankly, offensive to imply otherwise. I simply asked Ms. Hernandez to join us as we perused the calendar, because as I stated previously, the school calendar is firmly in her purview.

MS. HERNANDEZ: Again, scheduling major events on the school calendar? Not my job. But I came into the office when Principal Patel called, because I'm not completely sure he really understands Google Calendar. He once scheduled seventeen dentists' appointments for the exact same time when he tried to merge his personal and work calendars last year, bless his heart.

ANGELICA: As Ms. Hernandez opened Google Calendar on Principal Patel's computer, Colin's face was practically incandescent with glee.

MS. HERNANDEZ: The school calendar is actually a complex web of several different calendars layered on top of each other. There's an academic calendar, a sports calendar, an extracurricular calendar, an arts calendar, even a student government calendar, etc., etc. Each has its own color, and it's possible to hide and show different calendars so you only need to focus on what you're looking for.

ANGELICA: It was immediately obvious what had happened. When Ms. Hernandez clicked on each calendar, at first, it looked like everything was fine. On that fateful Friday in October, there was only one event in the sports calendar (the game), one event in the student government calendar (the elections), one event on the academic calendar (the Academic Battle Locals), and one event in the arts calendar (*Much Ado About Nothing*). *Much Ado About Nothing*? The fall play?! I'd totally forgotten that was *also* happening!. How was it possible that there was *another* event scheduled that day?! At least Holly wasn't also in the drama department. As long as only one calendar at a time was open, it appeared as though there were no scheduling conflicts at all. But with all of the calendars open, it was officially a nightmare. And with the play that day, too—it was even worse now somehow!

COLIN: The mistake was so simple; it was almost brilliant in its stupidity.

ANGELICA: Well, it was immediately obvious to me, anyway. Principal Patel kept saying, "I fail to see the issue here," until Ms. Hernandez had clicked "show" on every calendar, and there stood the biggest snafu in San Anselmo Prep scheduling history, displayed in glorious Technicolor.

MS. HERNANDEZ: I've gotta say, I've been working at this school for six years, and this was the first time I've seen Principal Patel speechless.

ANGELICA: Colin had the kind of fire in his eyes I usually saw when Becca was gearing up to address sexism in our English curriculum.

MR. DUNCAN, *sophomore English teacher*: Listen, there's a certain number of dead white male authors I just have to teach. That's a fact. Don't blame me, blame the Common Core curriculum.

COLIN: I asked Principal Patel how it was possible that such an enormous oversight could have occurred. Who was steering this ship? Was anyone behind the helm here? Or would chaos reign at San Anselmo Prep?

PRINCIPAL PATEL: No comment.

COLIN: No comment is for cowards.

ANGELICA HUTCHERSON, CONSULTING DETECTIVE

COLIN VON KOHORN, *editor in chief of the* Prepster: The first "no comment" is only an opening sally. I knew I'd crack Principal Patel. And Ms. Hernandez seemed disgruntled enough that she'd be more than willing to spill a few San Anselmo Prep secrets. As Angelica and I walked out of the office, I could hear him quite clearly through the doors, shouting that scheduling was *her* job. Academic incompetence at its finest. I decided to let that disgruntlement percolate before we returned to it, and suggested Angelica continue with her assignment in the meantime.

ANGELICA: I swear, I was trying to focus on Academic Battle, I really was. Well, I was also sort of consumed with uncertainty about what to do with what I'd learned about Andrew Nithercott. Although he clearly didn't seem to think that purposefully scheduling the elections so Holly couldn't attend was that bad, since he'd just casually said it to my face. But it *felt* bad. And knowing that Avery had accidentally ensured that AcaBat Locals were at the same time as homecoming just to get my stubborn brother to come certainly wasn't helping! I felt like an accessory to this whole debacle. And now we had the school play that day, too? No wonder I couldn't concentrate on the task at hand. I knew I had to call Avery and get more intel on her role in this scheduling disaster. But before I could call her, the phone rang, with an even juicier mystery on the other end of the line. The stories kept coming to me. In this case, quite literally.

FINN AQUINO, *sophomore*: I had no one to turn to and nowhere to go. Who can you ask for help when the thing you need help with is directly related to a secret so big you had sworn on your life to keep it?

> *Note: I couldn't think of a single way to describe Finn. To the best of my knowledge, at that point, he wasn't involved in a single club, activity, or pastime of any kind at San Anselmo Prep. He was even less of a joiner than Becca, and that was saying something.*

HOLLY CARPENTER, *the biggest joiner at San Anselmo Prep*: Finn Aquino . . . I know he's in our grade . . . but I just don't know much about him, somehow. Gosh, I feel terrible! There are only sixty of us; it shouldn't be that hard!

FINN: Pretty sure the only thing anyone knows about me is that I served lumpia on World Heritage Day last year.

> *Note: Lumpia are Filipino spring rolls, and they are crazy good. Unfortunately, I think World Heritage Day is being discontinued this year due to concern over nut allergies, which stinks, because it was an awesome day of free food.*

BECCA: You've gotta respect a guy like Finn Aquino. Sure, maybe he's not the most charismatic dude, maybe he's not exactly known for doing much, but he doesn't buy into any of the manufactured attempts at school spirit this school is peddling, that's for sure. He goes his own way. He does his own thing. Whatever that thing is. I don't even *know* what that thing is. Pretty impressive.

Note: If she only knew . . .

FINN: My friends and I are the kind of guys who fly under the radar, who prefer to be chilling in the back of the classroom instead of sitting in the front row with our hands in the air like Angelica and the other smart kids. Except for Tanner P. and marching band, we don't really do any clubs, or spend a lot of time at school activities, or seem to do much of anything, really. But I had to fly under the radar. It wasn't a choice. It was a condition of the path I'd chosen. And now that path was in danger of coming to a terrible end.

TIMOTHY "TIMO" WAKATSUKI, *sophomore, confidant*: Finn was in serious trouble. I'd never seen him so stressed about anything. He's usually a pretty relaxed dude.

TANNER PETERSON, *sophomore, the one in marching band, not the kicker*: Timo and I had known Finn's secret since he'd started training last year. That's not the kind of thing you can keep from your best friends. And we'd kept his secret faithfully for him. When he showed up at Timo's house in a cold sweat, I guessed immediately that the Secret of the Dragon was at stake. There's not much else that makes Finn sweat. Except for, like, unprecedented levels of humidity.

MOMO WAKATSUKI, *freshman, flyer for the San Anselmo Prep Cheer Squad*: Older brothers are the dumbest. Lucky for those three idiots, I was grabbing a coconut water out of the fridge when I heard them not-so-subtly whispering about their crisis.

TIMO: I certainly didn't want to bring Momo into this, but she turned out to be the only one of us who had a halfway decent idea.

MOMO: I can't believe they thought I didn't know. I'd known since, like, eighth grade. It was so *easy* to put it together. I think the only reason no one else at school knows is because no one but me, Timo, and Tanner P. has ever seen Finn Aquino dance.

FINN: No one at San Anselmo Prep can ever see me dance. That would be the end of everything. Well, it was all coming to an end now, anyway.

TANNER P.: I told Finn this wasn't the end. No way, man. He had worked so hard for this. After a year of training, it was finally time for him to make his debut, to get the recognition he deserved, and we couldn't let anything stand in his way.

FINN: I needed help. And I didn't want to tell the administration or any of the teachers, because I didn't trust them to help without blowing my cover. Principal Patel isn't exactly known for his subtlety. He probably would have made a school-wide announcement with both my first and last name and sent out an e-blast with a picture of my face. Exactly the opposite of what I needed.

MOMO: I totally got it. This was a matter that needed to be handled with discretion. And I had a feeling I knew just the girl for the job.

TIMO: When Momo suggested going to the *Prepster,* I thought she had lost it.

TANNER P.: The whole point was to keep this quiet! Why would Finn go straight to the school newspaper? That's the opposite of quiet! That sounded as disastrous as telling Principal Patel.

FINN: Go to the *Prepster?* There was no way I could have gone to Colin Von Kohorn. When he was my peer editor at the beginning of the year in English class, he'd written "ABYSMAL" at the top of my paper in red pen. No way that guy would take me seriously. And I guess I could have gone to Cinthia, but last year, she'd written a gossip column for the *Prepster* called "Loose Lips," until Principal Patel had issued an official cease and desist for the column. A gossip columnist? Even though the column wasn't in print anymore, she couldn't be trusted.

CINTHIA ALVAREZ, *associate editor of the* Prepster: I have a lot of regrets about "Loose Lips," okay? It was a mistake from the start. Bizzy Stanhope was always trying to get me to plant negative items about Avery Dennis and trying to bribe me with gift cards and jewelry I would never wear. It was horrible.

Principal Patel will never know how grateful I was for that cease and desist.

MOMO: But I wasn't suggesting Finn go to the *Prepster*. I was suggesting he go to Angelica. I guess she was, like, freelancing for the *Prepster* now, because I'd seen her going in and out of the computer lab. And if she's a reporter now, that's basically what being a detective is, right? They interview people and ask questions and put all the pieces together and solve your mysteries. And since my mom volunteers at the library, I knew for a fact that Angelica had read the collected works of Sir Arthur Conan Doyle many, many times, because I've heard it many, many times, as part of a "Why don't you read more, Momo? That nice girl Angelica who goes to your school reads *all the time*" lecture. So I bet Finn that Angelica could get his dumb head back for him, because she was really smart and obviously knew everything about Sherlock Holmes.

FINN: I objected to Momo calling it "a dumb head," but I didn't actually object to her idea. Angelica *is* really smart. Her brain operates at a level that's much faster and much deeper than mine—I don't even know how she thinks of the things she does in English class. It's always something I never would have thought of, but the minute she says it, I can't believe I didn't think of it, because it makes perfect sense.

> *Note: If he was trying to flatter me to get me to take the case, it was working. It's rare in life to get a compliment on your document-based analysis skills.*

TANNER P.: It seemed too risky. What was to prevent Angelica from exposing Finn in the newspaper? This would have been a pretty serious scoop for the *Prepster*. I mean, a long-hidden secret identity finally coming to light? Come on, that's gold. One of their more recent stories was about how many times Mr. Duncan wore the same tie in September.

MR. DUNCAN, *academic adviser to the* Prepster: Ever since the tie piece ran, I've gone back to proofing the *Prepster* before it goes to print. Clearly, I haven't been giving out enough homework if my staff has time to count how many times I've worn the green tie with the ducks on it.

TIMO: But Angelica didn't have the loyalty to the *Prepster* that Colin or Cinthia had. Momo had said she was just a freelancer. And I'd seen her get pretty antagonistic with Colin in the past. So why should she care how many copies of the *Prepster* people actually read? Besides, I didn't really see what other choice Finn had.

TANNER P.: I hoped Finn wasn't making a mistake. There was more than just a head at stake. Almost fifty years of tradition rested on the slender shoulders of Finn Aquino.

MOMO: You heard it here first, folks: Momo Wakatsuki would go down in San Anselmo Prep history as the Girl Who Saved Homecoming. Well, I guess it would be Angelica who would save homecoming, if she could find the head, but that would be thanks to me. So, yeah, I would totally be the Girl Who Saved Homecoming. Good-bye, life as an anonymous freshman. Hello, destiny.

ANGELICA: When Dad told me Finn Aquino was on the phone for me, I thought he'd heard wrong. Or maybe Becca was making a weird joke.

BECCA: First of all, if I call Angelica, I call her cell. Second of all, impersonating Finn Aquino isn't anyone's idea of a joke, weird or not. What's there to impersonate? No one knows anything about him. He fell asleep, like, twelve times in science last year and Ms. Marlow never noticed. To the best of my knowledge, that is his most significant accomplishment.

FINN: There was no way I could have talked to Angelica at school. That would have been way too risky.

ANGELICA: When Finn asked me to meet him at Marin Coffee Roasters ASAP, I was more than a little surprised. I had assumed he'd called because he'd forgotten the English homework or something. But I could have told him that over the phone. Clearly, there was something much more important at stake than that night's reading and annotations.

FINN: I told her it was urgent, and thank God, she agreed to meet me.

ANGELICA: I was curious. And what did I have to lose, a couple of hours away from the riveting BBC Special, "The Story of Maths, the Language of the Universe"? My dad has the worst taste in television in the history of all time. And he's always hogging the TV, forcing me to watch something "educational," or jumping in with the answers on *Jeopardy!* before I even have a minute to think about it, which totally ruins the fun of watching *Jeopardy!*

DAD: Math *is* the language of the universe. Actually . . .
Note: The rest of this conversation has been redacted to preserve the reader's sanity. I know, it's easy to see where my brother gets it from.

FINN: I sprinted to Marin Coffee Roasters as fast as my legs could carry me.

ANGELICA: Finn was standing in front when I got there. I locked my bike up, and we walked in. He was obviously distressed. He kept fidgeting, anxiously checking the door and tapping his feet.

FINN: We probably should have gone to the Coffee Roasters in Novato, but I didn't feel like asking my mom for a ride. I just hoped my desire for geographic convenience wouldn't cause me to get caught. I kept looking around, and luckily, I didn't see anyone from school. And there was a nice loud buzz of conversation, so we'd be hard to overhear even if someone did stumble in.

ANGELICA: Finn bought me a vanilla frappé and a blueberry muffin, so things were already better than watching "The Story of Maths, the Language of the Universe." We sat down in a corner away from the crowd, and Finn immediately began crumbling his banana bread with nerves.

FINN: Once Angelica promised she'd never tell a soul, and that no part of this interview, or any subsequent interview relating to the topic we were about to discuss, would ever be printed in the *Prepster* in any way, shape, or form, I could finally begin.

HOLLY CARPENTER, *cheerleader*: The San Anselmo Prep mascot is the Dragon, and yes, we have an *actual* dragon! Well, not an actual dragon. You know what I mean. We have someone in a furry dragon suit who performs at the halftime shows and pumps up the crowd at our games. What do I know about the Dragon? Not much. Just that the Dragon is always an amazing dancer. Like, way better than anyone who's on cheer squad. And the crazy thing is, no one knows who the Dragon is! He—she—or it, I guess—is a total mystery.

ANGELICA: It wasn't a mystery anymore. I was sharing a blueberry muffin with the one, the only, *the* San Anselmo Prep Dragon. He'd polished off his banana bread pretty quickly and was now making short work of my muffin.

FINN: It's true. I'm the San Anselmo Prep Dragon. It still sounds weird to say it out loud. I hadn't planned on being a school mascot, that's for sure. A big furry dude who jumps around? No thank you. It's weird, right? But the Dragon chose *me*. And I was powerless to resist.

ANGELICA: I couldn't believe it. Finn Aquino was probably the quietest person in our class. I think the only time I'd ever heard Finn speak was when he taught us a couple words in Tagalog on World Heritage Day. Finn Aquino was the Dragon?! The most charismatic human—er, mythical creature—at San Anselmo Prep? It seemed impossible.

FINN: It all started last year, when I was a freshman. I was new at San Anselmo Prep, and had just met Timo and Tanner P. We'd bonded pretty quickly in the back row of Algebra 2. After school, on a totally random, nondescript Wednesday in September, Timo and I had been goofing around in the hallways, waiting for Tanner P. to finish up marching band practice. They were working on their "Bad Blood" remix for homecoming, and we were dancing in the hall, just messing around, nothing serious.

MOMO: Timo is the worst dancer of all time. It is traumatic. I told him he needs to spend the homecoming dance sticking close to the refreshment table, and hopefully, he'll meet a nice girl who also likes snacks and has no rhythm. But if he does get anywhere near the dance floor, he should preface any moves he makes by shouting "I AM NOT ACTUALLY RELATED TO MOMO WAKATSUKI," even though, unfortunately, he totally is.

TIMO: Finn kept doing crazier and crazier tricks as I egged him on. He was legitimately, expertly, break-dancing in the hallway outside the band room. Holds, freezes, coffee grinders. All of it. It was amazing!

FINN: I was just messing around; it wasn't anything that impressive, I promise.

TIMO: It was beyond impressive. Just as Finn was up in a crazy headstand, this senior named Tripp Gomez-Parker and some redheaded girl tumbled out of a supply closet. I think we all knew what they'd been doing in there.

> *Note: The unidentified redhead remains unidentified, and could not be reached for comment. Tripp didn't even remember her name, which is sort of depressing.*

FINN: Tripp Gomez-Parker was one of those seniors everybody knew. Superstar on the lacrosse team, always dating some hot girl, all the senior parties were at his house, all that stuff. So, yeah, I was pretty surprised when he said he needed to talk to me, a lowly, random freshman. And a new kid.

TIMO: Tripp yelled, "FREEZE, BRA!" which was pretty ironic, considering Finn was, in fact, in a freeze.

FINN: I got out of my freeze and back up to standing. By that time, the redhead was gone, and Tripp said we had "mad urgent business to discuss." I'll admit it—I was intrigued. So I followed him.

TIMO: When a senior asks you to go somewhere, you go. Tripp Gomez-Parker had closets full of redheads! Who knew what untold secrets he was going to bestow upon Finn?

FINN: Unfortunately for Timo, who asked me about the girl Tripp was with many, many times, what Tripp Gomez-Parker told me had nothing to do with redheads.

ANGELICA: I needed another perspective, just to make sure that I had the full picture. Luckily, I had access to all the contact information for last year's senior class, courtesy of Avery Dennis, Alumni Coordinator.

AVERY DENNIS, *alumni coordinator, brother's girlfriend*: When Angelica told me she was writing an oral history, I screamed. Literally screamed! That's how proud I was. Angelica was well on her way to becoming the little sister I had always wanted but never had. And I told her I had something she had *got* to read later.

JAMES "HUTCH" HUTCHERSON, *brother*: Angelica is *never* reading that.
   Note: Too late.

TRIPP GOMEZ-PARKER, *freshman, California State University Los Angeles, graduate of San Anselmo Prep*: I saw an unknown number on my phone, and I'd thought it was the hottie I'd given my digits to on the quad this morning after I'd accidentally slept through econ but thought, Dag, I could still use a breakfast sandwich, so I headed out in my jammy jams. But nope, it was not the hottie. It was some rando girl, no idea if she was hot or not, who started asking me questions about the Dragon. I was *bugging*. Straight bugging. I bugged so hard I hung up, man! But then Avery Dennis texted and told me it was cool. Does Avery Dennis know about the Dragon? Naw, man, only Dragons know about the Dragon. Oh, and random girls of unknown hotness Avery's given my phone number to. But Avery Dennis can keep a secret like it is straight-up her job, so if she said this Angelica girl could be trusted, then aight, I'd trust. When Angelica called back, I didn't hang up.

FINN: I hoped Tripp wouldn't be too pissed I'd told someone not in the Brotherhood about the Brotherhood. But these were desperate times!

TRIPP: The Brotherhood of the Dragon has existed at San Anselmo Prep since they first bought the mascot costume in 1972. The costume isn't the same one from '72, because dag, that would be a seriously smelly piece of fur, but the Brotherhood has been around since then, passing down the ways of the Dragon from Dragon Brother to Dragon Brother.

FINN: That random Wednesday in September, I followed Tripp down into the basement, where the locker rooms and the wrestling gym and all the athletic equipment storage closets are. It's sort of creepy down there. Tripp opened a door in the corner of the weight room, and revealed a small room with mats, a huge mirror like at a dance studio, and, of course, the

San Anselmo Prep Dragon costume hanging in a place of honor. That was the Dragon's Lair, and it became my home away from home.

TRIPP: I named him Li'l Dragon, and I taught him everything I knew. From the Dragon's signature move, the Dragon Dougie, to how to execute a standing backflip that would make every lady on the field lose her head, without losing yours. If a mascot's head falls off mid-performance, it's basically death. Without the head, you're just a weird guy in a fur suit. You need the head, man. There is no Dragon without the head.

FINN: Oh, I was aware there was no Dragon without the head. And that was exactly my problem.

TRIPP: Li'l Dragon and I practiced in secret as much as we could, so that he'd be ready to take my place when I graduated. He was mad chill, and way secretive, as a Dragon should be. My Dragon Brother was always telling me I was, like, "flying too close to the sun" by "showboating" at school dances, and it was only a matter of time before someone figured it out that I was the Dragon. But no one figured it out, ever, so put that in your pipe and smoke it, Keonte.

KEONTE KING, *former San Anselmo Prep Dragon, current senior at Spelman College*: How did you get this number? Who gave it to you? Tripp? Tripp Gomez-Parker? Listen to me. I was not the Dragon. Never was. There is no Brotherhood of the Dragon. But if there were a Brotherhood of the Dragon, which there isn't, Tripp Gomez-Parker would be the person to bring us all down. Of course he would.

*Note: He whispered, "There is no Brotherhood of the Dragon,"
one more time and hung up.*

TRIPP: Still, even though Keonte was mad paranoid, I kind of got his point. I had been a little reckless showing off my sweet skills.

ANGELICA: I was also kind of surprised that no one had figured out that Tripp Gomez-Parker used to be the Dragon. In hindsight, it seemed really obvious. The Dragon was always conspicuously absent during lacrosse season . . .

TRIPP: If the Brotherhood of the Dragon had been busted because of me? I would have felt wrecked fo' sho. I told Li'l Dragon that he might want to keep his sick moves on the DL. Do as I say, not as I do, you feel me?

FINN: I vowed to keep all of my moves on the DL. I would do anything it took to make sure my life as the Dragon was secret and safe. I finally had an identity at San Anselmo Prep. Sure, it was an identity that no one but Timo and Tanner P. would know about, because, hey, I'm not about to keep a secret from my best friends, but it was an identity, and it was mine. It's not like I'd been planning to spend all my time at San Anselmo Prep break-dancing in the cafeteria, anyway. I didn't need to dance as Finn Aquino, because I'd be able to dance as the Dragon, for hundreds of screaming San Anselmo Prep sports fans. I'd get my moment to shine—when I was the Dragon. Only now it looked like that moment might never come.

ANGELICA: I'd gotten so caught up in the lore of the Brotherhood of the Dragon—seriously, I was itching to start brainstorming ideas for a fantasy novel with that title, forget resurrecting the badger coven, *this* was going to be my fantasy story—I'd forgotten that I still had no idea why Finn had wanted to meet for coffee. He'd said it was an emergency. I assumed the emergency wasn't that he really, really wanted to share a muffin with me, considering that we'd had exactly zero previous interactions.

FINN: Homecoming was supposed to be my debut as the Dragon. And now there was no way that could happen, because the head was missing. Someone had stolen it.

ANGELICA: At first, I wasn't sure what Finn meant, because he just kept saying "Someone stole my head!" and panic-eating a second muffin I'd gotten him after the first one disappeared.

FINN: The head of the Dragon mascot costume was missing. And like Tripp had told me, many, many times, you can't be a mascot without a head. Without a head, you're just a weird dude in a furry suit. And worst of all, if I didn't have a head, the identity of the Dragon would be exposed, for the first time in the distinguished history of the Brotherhood of the Dragon. I couldn't be the Dragon who screwed that up! And I also couldn't be the Dragon who pulled a no-show at homecoming. I needed that head. And I had no idea how to get it. Angelica Hutcherson was my only hope.

ANGELICA: A missing mascot head. Zero leads. And *I* was Finn's only hope? I had a newfound sympathy for Obi-Wan Kenobi.

BAND PRACTICE

BECCA: The next day in school, I asked Angelica why she hadn't answered any of my texts. It wasn't an emergency or anything, and Cinthia had done a fantastic job helping me pick fonts for *Riot Prep!*, but it wasn't like Angelica to disappear like that. Usually, as soon as I texted, the three dots that mean "I'm typing" appeared immediately. Followed quickly by a perfectly punctuated text, complete with proper capitalization.

ANGELICA: Without naming any names, because, of course, discretion was of the utmost importance here, I explained to Becca that I'd been hired to track down a missing item of extreme value, one that needed to be recovered as soon as possible.

BECCA: Somehow I couldn't see Angelica going all Jessica Jones, but hey, if Angelica wanted to solve crimes, she could do it. She could find the symbolism in any text, anytime. And she had read *all* of Sherlock Holmes in eighth grade. And then, like, four more times after that. She'd undoubtedly picked up some tips. Tracking down a missing whatever-it-was would be no problem. I briefly considered seeing if she could get the picture back from Natalie Wagner for me, but then I realized that meant that I would have to describe the picture, and that Angelica would probably see the picture, and I just couldn't handle that.

ANGELICA: I told Becca that no matter what the picture was, except if it was of her, like, torturing a small animal, I would never judge her, and would always be her best friend.

BECCA: The only small animal being tortured in that picture is me. Ugh, I'm lying. I *wish* I looked tortured. That would have been way better. Unfortunately, I look blissful. And that's what makes the picture so terrible.

ANGELICA: It was kind of a shock to see Becca carrying her tuba down the hallways of San Anselmo Prep after school again. Brought me right back to the heyday of Blitzkrieg Tuba Factory.

BECCA: I asked Angelica to come with me to . . . shudder . . . oh, God, I can barely say it . . . marching band practice . . . for moral support. There I was. Me. Becca Horn. Participating in an officially sanctioned school activity, seemingly of my own free will. I needed a T-shirt to pull on over my sweater vest that said I'VE BEEN BLACKMAILED. Even just talking about it is making me feel violently ill.

ANGELICA: I knew I had to start tracking down the Dragon's head for Finn, like, yesterday, but I had no idea where to start. Marching band practice would be as good a place as any to brainstorm possible suspects.

MARTIN SHEN, *sidelined tuba player*: When Becca Horn walked through the door, tuba in hand, I couldn't believe it.

NATALIE WAGNER, *clarinet*: There was a teensy part of me that was scared that Becca wouldn't come, that the power of the picture wouldn't be compelling enough. I'd brought it with me, zipped in at the bottom of my pencil case for extra security, but it looked like I didn't need it—not yet anyway. Becca Horn had shown up.

KATE ROWND, *percussion*: The entire band room went completely silent. I couldn't even remember the last time that had happened. Had that *ever* happened?! I honestly didn't think so.

NATALIE: "Take a seat with the other horns," I said super casually, like I wasn't freaking out, but on the inside, I was totally freaking out. Homecoming was saved! And it was all thanks to me. *Me.* I don't know if anyone has ever given out marching band MVPs before, but to me, this seemed like the perfect time to start.

BECCA: Natalie nodded at me as I walked toward the horns like she was the mob boss of marching band. Imagine Don Corleone in a glittery headband. That was what I was looking at.

MARTIN: I went over to get Becca set up, see if she had any questions, that kind of thing, but she just snarled, "I've got this, Shen," so I backed off.

BECCA: Martin Shen got all up in my grill. It was insulting. Did I need help? Of course not. When it comes to tuba, I know what I'm doing. I don't need help from anyone, and certainly not from Martin Shen, of all people. I've forgotten more about the tuba than he'll ever know!

ANGELICA: Becca was *not* being polite. She was being remarkably surly, even for her. I wondered if maybe she'd been more bothered by that rejection from the marching band auditions than she'd ever let on. Even an M&M will melt eventually if you leave it in the sun for long enough.

BECCA: I wasn't thinking about the marching band auditions freshman year. I *never* think of those auditions, except in moments of profound gratitude that I hadn't ended up stuck in that butt-ugly uniform for the next four years. And yet here I was, stuck in said butt-ugly uniform anyway. Curse you, Natalie Wagner. Curse you and your blackmailing, pack-rat ways.

MARTIN: I have to say, though, Becca picked it up remarkably fast. I hadn't brought her up to speed on the piece or anything, and she was already playing perfectly. Was I this replaceable? Apparently, marching band could go on just fine without me. What if Becca Horn decided to stay in marching band *forever*? Would I be out? Who would I sit with at lunch?

NATALIE: Becca was playing perfectly, just as I knew she would. Because I am a certified, grade-A genius.

FINN AQUINO, *secret Dragon*: When I sat down next to Angelica in the band room, she almost stabbed me in the eye with her pen.

ANGELICA: Finn is *silent*! He has the quietest tread I've ever heard. He is seriously taking this "flying under the radar" thing to new levels. If he gets any quieter, he'll be a ninja. Or turn into the Invisible Man—not the Ralph Ellison one, the actually invisible one. All I heard was a "hey" and I jumped out of my seat, whipped around to face him, and ended up accidentally drawing a line of blue pen on his ocular bone.

FINN: Angelica was so distressed. I kept trying to tell her it was fine as she fussed over the pen. That's hardly the worst thing that's ever been drawn on my face. Never fall asleep near Tanner P.

TANNER PETERSON, *the one in marching band, not the kicker*: Oh man, is Finn still mad about that thing I drew on his face? That was *one time*.

ANGELICA: But what, exactly, was Finn doing at marching band practice?

TANNER P.: Timo and Finn come with me to practice every once in a while. I think they're under some delusion that it's going to get them dates.

TIMOTHY "TIMO" WAKATSUKI, *sophomore*: It makes no sense, okay? Tanner P. has had more girlfriends than me and Finn put together. And he's not bad-looking, but he's not, like, an exceptionally handsome dude or anything. So why the end-less parade of girlfriends? How was he making this happen?

I figured it was because of his access to marching band, that hotbed of romantic intrigue.

TANNER P.: I'm single right now, sure, but not for long. Damarys has been giving me some serious heat recently. She has been making some insanely smoldering eye contact during her drum solo. I think she's ready for round two. Maybe this time we'll date for longer than twelve minutes. Crazier things have happened in marching band.

FINN: Timo is convinced that the only reason he doesn't have a girlfriend is that he's not in close enough proximity to enough girls. Our classes are full of girls. I don't think that's the reason.

CLEMENTINE RUTHERFORD, *flautist*: I dated Timo last year—for exactly one date. He took me out for fro-yo. Didn't bother to verify whether or not I can digest dairy, which I most certainly cannot. There was no date two.

TIMO: Clementine and the fro-yo were a bust, but maybe one of these other girls would start to think I was cute, if I hung around long enough. Like how the first time you hear a pop song, maybe you don't like it that much, but before you know it, you're singing along to every word?

TANNER P.: I didn't have the heart to break it to Timo, but I was pretty sure Clementine had told all the other girls not to date him. There was a full-on Timo Wakatsuki dating ban. So all the hours he'd put in in the band room were probably worthless.

CLEMENTINE: Oh, sure, no flautist, or anyone else in that room, was ever going to date Timo Wakatsuki. They wouldn't even touch him with a ten-foot pole. Harsh, maybe? We've all dated a lot of the same people *within* marching band, but it felt different with an outsider. I wasn't dating Timo anymore, due to his lack of respect for lactose intolerance, but I didn't really want anyone else dating him, either.

FINN: Timo was looking for a homecoming-date-slash-future-Mrs. Wakatsuki, but I was looking for a missing head. I figured marching band practice would be as good a place as any to brainstorm for suspects. No one can hear anything in there unless you get right up close to them.

ANGELICA: I wondered if there was anyone at our school who had maybe wanted to be the Dragon but didn't get to. That seemed like a pretty good motive for sabotage.

FINN: I didn't know if anyone else had wanted to be the Dragon. Tripp had asked me to do it so out of the blue *and* in complete secret. It's not like there had been formal auditions or anything like that where I could have scoped out the competition.

ANGELICA: I asked Finn to help me think if there were any other fantastic dancers in our class. That was a prerequisite, right?

FINN: Ideally, you want a Dragon who can dance. In years that there weren't great dancers, the Dragon has been just a charismatic guy who can pump up the crowd, but usually, you're looking for a dancer.

ANGELICA: A guy? I wondered if the Dragon had to be male. If so, that seemed needlessly sexist. Women can be anything. Including mythological creatures.

FINN: The Brotherhood of the Dragon might sound like it's all-male, but it's not. I think there have been more dudes, statistically, but girls can definitely do it. Amy Nuttelman was the last female Dragon, and that was only three Dragons ago. Not that long.

ANGELICA: So who were some possible would-be dragons? Jensy Studenroth, on the cheer squad. She's the only one of them who can dance.

FINN: Harrison Baxter, who does all the musicals. Traditionally, the Dragon doesn't really tap, but hey, the Dragon didn't used to crump, either.

ANGELICA: I was having trouble thinking of anyone else. We are not a school with a lot of rhythm.

BECCA: Angelica was providing very little moral support, scribbling in her notebook with Finn Aquino.

ANGELICA: I was not scribbling. Well, I was scribbling, but I was also conducting a serious investigation.

BECCA: Good thing I didn't need any moral support, because I was slaying it.

ANGELICA: I added Momo Wakatsuki to the list, too, because she wasn't a terrible dancer. And she *did* know that Finn was the Dragon. Although then why would she ask me to help him find the head if she'd stolen it? I crossed her off the list again. Maybe I wasn't cut out for this investigative stuff. If I was having this much trouble even making a list of suspects, how would I ever find the head?

FINN: Somehow, though, I couldn't see any of these people stealing the head. You'd have to be pretty seriously disgruntled to ruin homecoming over not getting to be the mascot. And why would a cheerleader, of all people, want to ruin homecoming? That was their big day, too.

ANGELICA: I agreed with Finn. I'd do my due diligence at school, but I had a feeling our culprit lay somewhere else.

FINN: San Rafael Academy. Of course. Our rivals must have decided they'd do whatever it took to break us.

ANGELICA: I'd always known the Knights were evil. And I bet that the trail to find the missing mascot head would lead right to their door.

"A RETURN TO TRADITION"

ANDREW NITHERCOTT, *sophomore class presidential candidate*: A heinous crime had been committed.

ANGELICA: It seemed we were having a bit of a crime wave here at San Anselmo Prep. Of course, when I mentioned this at dinner, Mom said, "Some high schools have *actual* crime, Angelica," and handed me an article to read on socioeconomic disparity in California. I expected nothing less from the woman who had a "Check Your Privilege" magnet holding up the China Villa menu on the fridge. Still, for San Anselmo Prep, this was an unusual string of "illegal" activity.

BECCA: The last major disciplinary action at San Anselmo Prep had happened last spring. For last year's senior prank, someone stuffed a bunch of lobsters in the toilets. Which I suppose could have been hilarious, if it hadn't been the most elitist, entitled crime of all time, and extremely unfair to the maintenance team.

ANGELICA: The entire school reeked of shellfish for a whole week. It was the worst.

TRIPP GOMEZ-PARKER, *obviously the mastermind behind the lobster prank, I have no idea how Principal Patel didn't catch him*:

Dude, the lobsters were hilarious!!! And yeah, it was mad stanky, but sometimes life is stanky, you know? It was a commentary on, like, life and graduation and stuff.

MR. ROSS, *head of maintenance at San Anselmo Prep*: When you start a career in maintenance, you certainly don't expect to be pulling lobsters out of toilets. That definitely wasn't in the job description. Some of those lobsters were still alive, too. And they were *feisty*. But Gomez-Parker's not a bad kid. He stayed after school to get all the lobsters out, after asking the maintenance team not to report him to Patel. There wasn't much he could do about the stink, though.

ANDREW: I had been *vandalized*. What had been done to me was nothing compared to a toilet full of lobster.

HOLLY CARPENTER, *sophomore class presidential candidate*: In order to understand the beautiful genius of what happened to Andrew Nithercott, you first need to understand what his campaign posters looked like.

TANNER ERICKSEN, *the kicker on the football team, last year's freshman class vice president, not the one in marching band*: Nithercott has wallpapered the school with his face. Everywhere I go, he's staring at me. It's scary. And the last thing I need is *more* Andrew Nithercott.

BECCA: Those campaign posters are downright terrifying. Imagine a dystopian future in which the world is ruled by a fair-skinned boy-king in a madras bow tie. That's the reality I envision every time I see one of Andrew Nithercott's campaign posters.

HOLLY: The top of the poster has A RETURN TO TRADITION, Andrew's campaign slogan, printed in big block letters. Then there's a portrait of Andrew, shooting a deranged glare off into the distance.

BECCA: The American flags waving in the background and the bald eagles flying past his head really add that certain patriotic je ne sais quoi to the whole shebang.

ANDREW: Classic. Timeless. Inspiring. That's how I would describe my campaign posters. Or how I would have, before they were vandalized.

HOLLY: When I walked into school, I felt like a kid on Christmas morning.

TANNER E.: Someone had drawn a mustache on every single one of Andrew Nithercott's billion campaign posters. Every. Single. One.

ANDREW: This miscreant had turned me into a laughingstock. Everywhere I went, my constituents were pointing and laughing at my face. At my *face*! How could I expect to be taken seriously when my likeness had been transformed into a poorly drawn caricature of Salvador Dalí?

HOLLY: And these weren't just any plain old hastily drawn, boring, generic mustaches, either. Each mustache was a work of art. And they were all different, like snowflakes!

TANNER E.: There were handlebar mustaches. Muttonchops. Goatees. A Fu Manchu.

HOLLY: There were more kinds of mustaches than I ever even knew existed.

ANGELICA: My favorite one featured a handlebar mustache *and* a monocle. Very classy.

HOLLY: It was like walking into an art gallery. I was so sad when Principal Patel had the maintenance team take them all down. They were creative!

PRINCIPAL PATEL, *principal at San Anselmo Prep*: Vandalism is a serious offense here at San Anselmo Prep. Whoever drew the mustaches on Andrew Nithercott's campaign posters would be found, and would be issued severe consequences.

ANDREW: I had no faith in the administration. Patel was as incompetent, if not more so, than the Neanderthals in student government who blocked me at every turn. As much as it pained me to go outside the law, I knew if justice were to be served, I would be the only one who could dish it up. It was time to go rogue.

HOLLY: Did *I* do it? Gosh, no! I guess I seem like the obvious suspect, since I'm running against Andrew, but I would never interfere with the democratic process like that. I want to beat Andrew Nithercott because I'm the better candidate, not because of some funny mustaches.

BECCA: I don't know who did it. But whoever did deserves a medal.

TANNER E.: No idea. It could have been anyone. Nobody likes that guy.

BROOKS MANDEVILLE, *quarterback, last year's junior class president*: Whoever 'stached Nithercott is my *hero*. I hope this means he doesn't get elected. I'm hoping to be senior class president this year, and I would prefer a chill office, one with no Nithercott in sight. I have this great idea for SGA Nacho Wednesdays, and I know Nithercott won't get on board with the nachos. He said we were already allocating too much money toward the snack budget, which is insane. We had pretzels, like, once last year, and that was it. And they were the little pretzels. Not even jumbo.

> Note: Brooks Mandeville had also hung up campaign posters. His featured a cheesy platter of nachos, below which was written, YOU KNOW YOU WANT IT. #NACHOTYPICALPRESIDENT. Nowhere on it did it say anything about voting for Brooks Mandeville, but from what I'd heard in the halls, he seemed to have clinched the senior vote.

TANNER E.: Listen, I'm all for making Andrew Nithercott look dumb. That's always a plus. I just hoped that the whole mustache situation would help give Holly the win. She deserved it.

HOLLY: Tanner E. has been so helpful with my campaign. He photocopied so many posters for me, and made these cool buttons, because he apparently has a button maker, which is so awesome.

TANNER E.: Um, yeah, I have a button maker. And I had it before Holly decided to run. I didn't, you know, buy it *for* Holly, or anything.

> Note: If Tanner E. owned a button maker before this election, I'll eat a button.

HOLLY: He even called while I was frosting my VOTE FOR HOLLY cupcakes just so I'd have someone to talk to, because he knows my mom teaches Zumba at night. He has been such a rock star.

TANNER E.: I didn't do anything for Holly that I wouldn't have done for any qualified candidate. I just think we need to have the best person for the job. And if Holly doesn't win, I'm resigning. The sophomore class doesn't really need a vice president. You know what they say: "The vice presidency isn't worth a bucket of warm spit."

COLIN VON KOHORN, *amateur presidential scholar*: Ah, the old bucket of warm spit. That quote is actually impossible to verify. John "Cactus Jack" Nance Garner, FDR's vice president, may have told Roosevelt that the vice presidency "was not worth a quart of warm spit," and he may have told Lyndon Johnson, "the vice presidency isn't worth a pitcher of warm spit," so whether it was a bucket, a quart, or a pitcher, it has unfortunately been lost to time. Garner's low opinion of the office, however, is without question. He definitely did once say that being elected vice president was the worst thing that ever happened to him.

Note: Things Colin likes: Newspapers. Presidential trivia. Crossword puzzles. World War II. Colin Von Kohorn is basically my grandpa. I wonder if Colin also listens to Smokey Robinson when he's in a good mood.

TANNER E.: Being elected vice president was the best thing that ever happened to me. Sure, I had to deal with Andrew Nithercott, but hopefully, he was on his way out. And maybe, once he was gone, Holly Carpenter would finally notice me.

INTERROGATION ONE:
THE CHEERLEADER

ANGELICA: I had my suspicions that San Rafael Academy was behind the missing head. But I didn't want my detestation of the Knights to blind me to any suspects who might be lurking behind the cozy doors of San Anselmo Prep. I may have been a new detective, but I wanted to be a good one. And that meant I had to do due diligence, no matter what my personal prejudices were.

FINN AQUINO, *dismayed Dragon*: I was worried it would be too suspicious if I went with Angelica as she interviewed people, but she told me to just wear a hat and keep my head down.

PRINCIPAL PATEL, *principal*: Hats are expressly forbidden by the San Anselmo Prep dress code.

ANGELICA: If anyone asked, I'd say he was my intern.

BECCA: All of a sudden, Angelica was spending a lot of time with Finn Aquino, which, sorry to be blunt, was bizarre. He was probably the most boring person in our grade. No one knows anything about him. He doesn't do anything, he doesn't say anything, he's just *there*. And yes, I have lots of respect for those who opt out of the propaganda machine that is San Anselmo Prep, but you can still have a personality and refuse to participate in school activities. Or have other things you're interested in outside of school. And Finn appeared to be interested in nothing, which made him officially boring, whereas Angelica is probably the least boring person I know. She can turn a trip to Walgreens into an adventure. It was perplexing.

ANGELICA: Finn isn't boring. He's quiet. There's a difference. But I wasn't surprised that Becca didn't get it. "Quiet" is not a mode that Becca Horn operates in. Ever.

BECCA: I'm just saying. Angelica had time to hang out with Finn Aquino, but she didn't have time to return my texts? What were these priorities?!

Note: I certainly hadn't intended to ignore Becca, but I was starting to feel a little guilty. It was hard not to get wrapped up in all the homecoming drama! Once I (hopefully successfully) concluded my investigation, I vowed to make more best friend time.

COLIN VON KOHORN, *editor in chief of the* Prepster: Angelica had hired an intern? She had no jurisdiction to do that. First of all, the *Prepster* doesn't have interns. We're all already unpaid. We don't need a second tier of unpaid labor. And even if we did have interns, for some unknown reason, it would be up to the editor in chief to select them. Not a freelance reporter who keeps forgetting that she should be reporting on the Academic Battle Locals and only the Academic Battle Locals.

ANGELICA: Colin just can't comprehend the idea that not everything is about the *Prepster*. I told Colin that Finn wasn't my newspaper intern, he was the intern for my work as a consulting detective.

COLIN: So apparently, Angelica was now running a detective agency. Sure. Of course she was. By next week, she'd be an astronaut and a gourmet chef.

JENNIFER "JENSY" STUDENROTH, *San Anselmo Prep Cheer Squad back base*: Homecoming is my most favorite, favorite day of the year.

ANGELICA: Jensy certainly didn't look like she had recently committed a crime as she sat in the cafeteria beaming at me and Finn. I mean, she does have extremely long arms, which I suppose could be useful for pilfering a mascot head. But if she was suffering from any guilt, she was psychopathically good at hiding it.

JENSY: We all know we're not a very good cheer squad. The only thing we've ever won at competition was a participation medal, and it was made out of plastic. Nobody at school ever seems particularly jazzed to see us perform, either. Becca Horn ended up in the front row of the school spirit assembly we danced at during the first week of school, and it looked like she was trying to stab her eyes out with a pen.

Note: She was. Well, she was mime-stabbing her eyes out, obviously, but still, that was the intended effect. I quietly confiscated the pen, because, yes, our cheerleaders may be pretty terrible, but they at least deserve a polite audience.

BECCA: School assemblies are the seventh circle of hell. Check Dante's *Inferno.* It's in there.

TANNER ERICKSEN, *the kicker, not the one in marching band*: Hey, the football team appreciates the cheerleaders. Sometimes the only people at our games are the cheerleaders and our parents. And the cheerleaders are louder. And they're not on their phones. Well, they're usually not on their phones. I'm pretty sure Momo Wakatsuki was playing Fruit Ninja during most of our first game this season.

MOMO WAKATSUKI, *San Anselmo Prep Cheer Squad flyer*: I'm sorry, do you know how *long* a football game is? I was not adequately warned. I'll bring a book or something next time if being on my phone is such a problem. I can't watch *hours* of bad football. There are limits to what humans can endure!

JENSY: So for most of the year, literally no one cares we exist. I think most of the school forgets San Anselmo Prep even has a cheer squad. But for those fifteen minutes of halftime at homecoming, the eyes of the whole school are upon us. It's the only football game that everyone in the school actually attends. And yes, we have to share those fifteen minutes with the Dragon, and with the marching band, and it's sort of embarrassing because they're actually good and we suck at everything, but for those fifteen minutes, I don't feel like we suck. I feel like everyone is behind us, cheering for us, for once, instead of us cheering for them. And it feels like we're all part of something big. Call it school spirit or whatever, but I like that feeling of being part of something, of feeling like the whole school is on my side. And those might be my favorite fifteen minutes of the whole year.

ANGELICA: Jensy definitely had the requisite school spirit to be the Dragon. And despite all her protestations about cheer squad's suckage, she was actually a pretty good dancer. Not to mention I'd seen her do a split on multiple occasions, and once she almost successfully completed a roundoff. These were all qualities a Dragon usually had.

JENSY: I love the Dragon! He's so cute. I always take, like, a million pictures with him whenever he's at a game. My Dragon collage was my most liked Instagram of last year.

FINN: Jensy thought the Dragon was a he? Did this mean she knew *I* was the Dragon? How much did she know?!

ANGELICA: Finn was nervously sweating for no apparent reason. It was pretty obvious that Jensy didn't know the Dragon was Finn; she just assumed it was a guy, like everyone else does.

JENSY: Is the Dragon a guy? Oh, I don't know. I just assumed, I guess? Because, like, aren't all Dragons guys? Pete the Dragon, Puff the Magic Dragon, um . . . those Game of Thrones dragons . . . Smaug from *The Hobbit* . . . Mushu from *Mulan* . . . yeah, pretty much every dragon I can think of is a guy.

ANGELICA: I was almost wishing we had a female Dragon now, just to defy some of these mythological-beast gender stereotypes.

JENSY: But of all the dragons I know, *our* Dragon is by far my favorite. He's the cutest!!!

ANGELICA: Jensy seemed to love the school way too much to ever do anything that would hurt it, though. She had so much school spirit, I was almost surprised she hadn't tattooed SAN ANSELMO PREP somewhere on her body. I'd thought I loved homecoming, but I'd never met someone as excited for homecoming as Jensy Studenroth. Looking at her, and at Finn, so torn up about whether or not he'd be able to perform, it really started to hit me just how important this day was, and how important it was to so many different people. Not just to the football team and the cheerleaders, but to the marching band, and the AcaBat team, and to everyone who was working so hard on their Student Council speeches. And the people in *Much Ado*. How did I keep forgetting about the fall play?! What was going to happen to all of these people when they weren't going to be able to do all the things they wanted to do, because of the scheduling mix-up? Homecoming came only once a year. It's not like they'd get a do-over.

FINN: Angelica had turned the conversation pretty smoothly to the Dragon. Even if Jensy turned out not to have taken the head—and it seemed obvious she hadn't—I was glad I'd come to Angelica.

ANGELICA: I was pretty sure Jensy Studenroth wasn't our culprit in the case of the missing head.

151

JENSY: I can't wait to see the Dragon at homecoming!!! We haven't gotten to see him yet. Homecoming is the first game of the year he comes to, probably because he's busy, like, preparing in his Dragon ways after his long summer hibernation. He always does a cute little dance with the cheer squad, and it's the best. Seriously, it's the most adorable thing that ever happens at this school.

FINN: I couldn't even look at Jensy when she mentioned the annual homecoming Dragon–cheer squad dance. Of course I'd been looking forward to it, too! The Dragon Dougies at the front of the V-formation, and it's like all the cheer squad are his backup dancers. I wanted to have that rock star moment just like all the Dragons before me. What if it didn't happen this year?

JENSY: Tragically, I'm stuck way in the back of the V-formation, because I'm the tallest, so I'll barely even be close to the Dragon. Lucky Holly will probably be right next to him.

HOLLY CARPENTER, *cheerleader*: Yeah, lucky me. Because of my spot in the V-formation, I *would* be right next to the Dragon. Well, I would be right next to him if I came to the homecoming game. I still hadn't told anyone on cheer that the Student Council elections and the AcaBat Locals were at the same time. Mostly because I hadn't decided which event I was going to yet.

ANGELICA: Poor Holly. Whenever I brought up the homecoming game, she made a face just like Becca had that one time she'd accidentally swallowed a bug.

BECCA: I don't know why I thought I'd enjoy Rollerblading. Temporary insanity? Because Angelica had somehow convinced me it would be fun? She was wrong, by the way. The wind resistance basically created a superhighway for that bug to fly right up into my mouth. I promptly sold my Rollerblades on craigslist.

Note: It was fun. It's not the bug's fault that Becca's mouth zoomed right into where he was flying.

HOLLY: If I didn't come to the game, who was going to hold Momo's left foot? She couldn't fly without me! She wouldn't even *be* a flyer anymore, she'd just be . . . um . . . I don't know . . . a grounder? But I definitely had to give my Student Council speech. Otherwise, there was no way I could win. And I couldn't bear the thought of handing the presidency to Andrew Nithercott on a silver platter. But I also had to give my AcaBat speech! Otherwise, there was no way *we* could win. I don't mean to sound stuck-up or anything, we'd just never had anyone else practice giving the speech. And having someone wing it would have been a recipe for disaster. No matter what I did, someone was bound to be disappointed. And I just couldn't bear the thought of that.

THE ENEMY INVESTIGATES

ANGELICA: The very last thing I expected was that *I* would become the subject of somebody else's investigation. But much to my surprise, that is exactly what happened.

BEN WASHINGTON, *member of the San Rafael Academy Academic Battle team, junior editor of the* San Rafael Reporter: I had to make sure someone would set the record straight. And if that someone was me, well, fine. I could step up.

DAPHNE LEAKE-PALMER, *captain of the San Rafael Academy Academic Battle team*: Of course I told the team that Hutch's baby sister, of all people, was doing a story on us. That she had interviewed me. I thought it was hilarious.

BEN: But what questions had this person asked? How had Daphne answered?

DAPHNE: God, Ben is such a buzzkill. I didn't *remember* every question she asked. And I'm sure all my answers were *fine*. Why did it matter, anyway? It was just for some dumb little school paper.

BEN: It matters because the way you're portrayed in the media matters. Because even "dumb little school papers" live forever on the Internet. And, as a junior editor at the *San Rafael Reporter*, I objected to her use of the phrase "dumb little school paper." Print can still be powerful, no matter how small the audience. Maybe it's easy not to care when your father is a hedge fund manager at Palmer Capital, but, yeah, I care. You think admissions committees don't Google you? They do. One of our seniors last year had his admission to Yale rescinded because of a Facebook post.

DAPHNE: Ben needed to relax, not that he ever did. *Relax* was probably the only vocabulary word he didn't understand. He was always trying to assign the rest of us reading, all of these beyond dull texts by Laurence Perrine, everything Thomas Hardy had ever written, and, snooze, A *Dictionary of Composers*. I know plenty about composers. My family subscribes to both the orchestra and the ballet—I've been seeing full seasons of both since I was two. And I certainly don't need Ben telling me which newspapers I should be reading. It was completely inappropriate. Who is the captain of this team? *I* am.

BEN: Listen—I don't think there's anything wrong with doing a little extra reading. We need every competitive advantage we can get to take down San Anselmo Prep. They've been mopping the floor with us for *years*. And I would never *make* anyone read anything. I was just offering up suggestions of things I'd found helpful.

DAPHNE: Ben needs to wait until he's a senior to boss everyone around.

BEN: Oh, I know Daphne doesn't like me. Sometimes it feels like I'm the only person on our team who isn't in love with her or afraid of her. Or both.

DAPHNE: He just wouldn't let it go. No, I don't remember the name of Hutch's little sister. No, I don't remember what she said, I told him a thousand times. Blah blah blah. The same thing over and over again. I don't know how Ben does so well at the interview. He was practically putting me to sleep.

BEN: If someone at San Anselmo Prep was writing something about our AcaBat team, I wanted to know what it was. There was no way our rivals could possibly say anything good about us. And even worse, the reporter Daphne had talked to was *Hutch's little sister*?! This sounded like a disaster in the making. Everyone on the San Rafael Academy AcaBat team *hates* Hutch. We hate him with the burning fire of a thousand suns. With the kind of hate people usually reserved for war criminals and corrupt politicians. With the kind of hate I feel when I find raisins in carrot cake. Hutch had crushed us for four years, after all. Our hatred was pretty well justified. And I was sure the feeling was mutual—the San Anselmo Prep AcaBats hate us just as much as we hate them. I'd seen a girl on their team spit at Daphne last year. We may despise San Anselmo Prep, but at least we've never resorted to flinging bodily fluids at them.

CINTHIA ALVAREZ, *San Anselmo Prep AcaBat*: I didn't *spit* at Daphne Leake-Palmer! A little excess saliva just *happened* to leave my mouth while I was in her vicinity. It's not like any of the spit landed on her stupid Tory Burch wedges. Not that I'd been aiming for the wedges or anything.

BEN: If someone from San Anselmo Prep—who just so happened to be a *Hutcherson*—was writing something about us, it was bound to be a smear piece.

DAPHNE: Finally, I told Ben that if he was so worried about it, he could go find her himself, after we finished practicing for UltraQuiz.

BEN: I had a feeling Daphne was being sarcastic, but it wasn't a bad idea. Finding Hutch's little sister was the only way to set the record straight. It was easy enough to do some googling on my phone while Daphne drilled the other guys. I'm okay at UltraQuiz—it's not my forte. I'm on AcaBat for interview and essay writing, although I know I could kill the speech, if Daphne would let it out of her talons. Maybe next year, after she graduates, right?

DAPHNE: Ugh, I *know* Ben thinks he should be doing speech, just because that video he did for the Black Youth Project went viral for, like, two seconds. And yes, it was a very powerful piece of social justice, and great for Ben to make a stand and all that, and it was probably good press for the team, but I have a proven track record in Academic Battle, okay? Not YouTube.

BEN: Her name was Angelica. Luckily, typing in "James Hutcherson" turned up a lot of press clippings. Which proved my point exactly. This was what I'd been trying to convince Daphne of, with no luck. All of this stuff lives online forever. One of the pictures of Hutch with his family after he won the Broadcom MASTERS named Angelica. She was only a little kid then, though, so I wasn't sure I'd be able to find her now—maybe she didn't look the same anymore. Well, obviously, she didn't look the same anymore. Humans age. When I googled "Angelica Hutcherson," the first thing that came up was "The Little Ladybug Poem, by Angelica Marie Hutcherson, Age Eight." I wondered if it was the same Angelica.

> Note: I cannot believe my claim to fame is still "The Little Ladybug Poem." Mortifying! I need more accomplishments! If you google James, you get, like, twelve pages of contests he's won. And me? I have a poem about a bug. I peaked at eight. No wonder I have a complex.

DAPHNE: Ben was even suckier at UltraQuiz than usual. I had a feeling he was on his phone, which is obviously forbidden at AcaBat practice, but I couldn't catch him.

BEN: I have this theory that Daphne has terrible eyesight, but she refuses to get glasses because she can't admit there's anything about her that's less than perfect, including her vision. Which is fine by me, because the less she sees, the better. Anyway, I found Angelica's Facebook page. All I could see was her profile picture, but hopefully, that would be enough for me to find her. Unless something had changed really dramatically since that Broadcom MASTERS picture, I assumed Angelica was the girl with the box braids and not the one with the blue hair.

Note: The girl with the blue hair would be Becca, of course. Although I had a feeling that if Andrew Nithercott got reelected, her blue hair days might be numbered. I knew he was itching to outlaw hair dye.

DAPHNE: The minute practice ended, Ben ran out the door without even so much as the courtesy of a good-bye.

BEN: I had to make it to San Anselmo before Angelica left for the day. If she hadn't left already. Luckily, it's a pretty quick bike ride.

Note: !!! Not the only person here with a bike!

ANGELICA: As I walked out of school with Becca, it felt like Opposite Day. I was quiet and feeling dejected about my lack of progress on the hunt for the missing head, and Becca was chattering away about marching band. I knew she'd never admit it, but it seemed to me like she'd had a great time.

BECCA: Marching band practice was, obviously, torture, but the orchestrations were fairly impressive. They'd incorporated six different songs, and each had a seamless transition, and some included a mixing effect where you could hear the hooks from two songs at the same time. And, okay, fine, Natalie had been right about one thing: Being part of the horns at the beginning of "Crazy in Love" wasn't the worst.

Note: "Wasn't the worst" is Becca's designation for things at San Anselmo Prep she actually likes, as in "French Fry Friday wasn't the worst" or "That unit on Sylvia Plath wasn't the worst."

BEN: It was her. I knew it was her. She was even standing next to the girl with the blue hair, like her Facebook profile picture had come to life.

ANGELICA: For one crazy moment, I thought Daveed Diggs was in the quad, here to thank me and Becca for listening to *Hamilton* so, so many times.

BECCA: It was like Daveed Diggs had time-traveled back into his high school body, and had decided to wear a maroon sweater vest, which is a garment I am positive Daveed Diggs would never wear. Colonial vest, yes. Sweater vest, never.

ANGELICA: Young-Daveed-Diggs stood—he'd been sitting on the edge of the fountain—adjusted the strap of his messenger bag, and said, of all things, "Angelica?"

BECCA: I sang, "Eliza, and Peggy!" He looked confused.

ANGELICA: "I'm Angelica," I said, ignoring Becca, who was still singing "Work, work" in the background.

BECCA: Hey, for a show that doesn't have a tuba, *Hamilton* is pretty great. But would it be better with a tuba? Absolutely. Lin-Manuel Miranda ignored all my tweets about it for some reason, though. He was probably embarrassed about not putting a tuba in right from the get-go and didn't want to talk about it.

ANGELICA: "Ben," he said, and stuck out his hand. I shook it, and I have to admit, I was feeling distinctly and unfamiliarly fluttery. Like the way I felt when Captain Wentworth writes, "You pierce my soul. I am half agony, half hope," and had felt when reading, lots of times, but had never actually felt in real life. Ben obviously had not pierced my soul or anything, but I was also feeling kind of half agony, half hope, not that I even knew what I was hoping for.

BECCA: The guy was undeniably hot. I'm not even into guys, and he was still hot.

BEN: Angelica was staring at me. I'd forgotten I was still wearing my San Rafael Academy uniform. She must have been wondering what I could possibly be doing at San Anselmo Prep.

ANGELICA: Yeah, it was definitely the uniform I'd been staring at. It was the uniform.

BEN: I told her I was from the San Rafael Academy Academic Battle team, and I hoped we could talk for a few minutes.

CINTHIA ALVAREZ, *associate editor of the* Prepster, *member of the San Anselmo Prep AcaBats*: On my way back from the vending machine in the gym, I saw a maroon sweater vest in the quad. I froze. Someone from San Rafael Academy! And he was talking to Angelica! Could it have been someone from their AcaBat team?! I pressed my face up against the glass and squinted. Pretty sure it was Ben Washington: great at all things literature, fantastic interview. Had Daphne Leake-Palmer sent one of her minions to spy on us? Did she send Ben in particular to exploit our weaknesses in English, which is, admittedly, our weakest category?! Was he trying to infiltrate us through Angelica, the particular reporter who happened to be assigned to the AcaBat story?! It was all too convenient to be coincidence. There was no good reason for Ben Washington to be at San Anselmo Prep. Some kind of sabotage was afoot. I didn't trust it one bit. But I also didn't want to run out into the quad and let Ben know that I was onto him. I went back to the computer lab to figure out my next move.

SEBASTIAN "BASH" VON KOHORN, *age ten*: Cinthia banged the door open so hard she almost smooshed me. I was trying to hang up some new cat pictures. The old ones had disappeared, somehow. Colin said it was the maintenance team, but I suspected Cinthia.

CINTHIA: There was no time for cat pictures! The AcaBats were under attack! I shooed Bash out of the computer lab and shut the door.

COLIN VON KOHORN, *editor in chief*: Cinthia announced that Ben Washington had arrived on campus to steal all of her team's AcaBat secrets. I replied that the AcaBat team has no secrets.

CINTHIA: AcaBat has plenty of secrets! Like . . . um . . . well, I can't think of any right now. But that wasn't important. What was important was *why* was Ben talking to Angelica? Did he *know* her? I was pretty sure they had never met before . . . unless Angelica had been maintaining a secret friendship with the enemy this whole time?! I thought I knew Angelica pretty well, and I certainly didn't want to *accuse* her of anything, but this looked suspicious. Beyond suspicious. Maybe even downright nefarious. Man, what would Hutch think if he knew his own sister was fraternizing with a San Rafael Academy Knight?! I couldn't even imagine.

> *Note: Still not sure what kind of nefarious AcaBat sabotage Cinthia thought I was perpetrating. Conspiring to blunt everyone's number two pencils?*

COLIN: This San Rafael Academy person had been talking to Angelica? It looked like she really was pursuing all the angles of this AcaBat assignment after all. I texted her to keep up the good work. And told Cinthia to stop fussing about what was clearly a journalistic assignation, not a case of AcaBat sabotage. She was being even more distracting than usual.

ANGELICA: My phone buzzed. A text from Colin that read, "Proceed." No idea what that meant. So I just kept proceeding. Which was probably the intended effect of the text, now that I think about it.

BEN: I asked Angelica if she'd want to head over to Marin Coffee Roasters with me. I definitely didn't feel comfortable staying at San Anselmo Prep. I felt really out of place in my uniform, like this whole sea of people in navy was staring at me.

When we were in first grade, we'd had to fill in the following sentence: "I feel sad when . . ." I'd written, and I remember this, because my mom still has it hanging on the refrigerator, "I feel sad when the teacher gives me a mean mug." That quad was full of people mean mugging me. Luckily, I was a lot more emotionally equipped to handle a mean mug or two now that I was long past elementary school.

Note: On our fridge, aside from the China Villa menu, we have, you guessed it, a copy of "The Little Ladybug Poem." And a bunch of press clippings about the boy wonder.

BECCA: I had a feeling Angelica was going to follow this hot stranger to coffee. I asked him if he was a murderer, though, and he said no. Although a murderer probably wouldn't say yes.

BEN: Not a murderer. I even move spiders outside instead of squashing them. Basically, I'm the opposite of a murderer. Although that's sort of selfishly motivated, since spiders do eat a lot of other bugs.

ANGELICA: I was taking my own mode of transportation and meeting him at a public location. It was perfectly safe.

BEN: We left the blue-haired girl behind and pedaled off toward San Anselmo Ave.

BECCA: A best friend can't compete with a hottie on a bicycle. I texted Angelica to tell me everything once she was finished.

Mysterious Ben still hadn't told us what he'd been doing at San Anselmo Prep.

ANGELICA: Ben bought me a vanilla frappé. I felt like the employees of Marin Coffee Roasters were getting a really inaccurate impression of my social life. To the outside observer, it looked like I'd been on dates with two different guys in the span of one short week.

BEN: I just wanted to make sure that Angelica hadn't gotten the wrong impression about us. Daphne Leake-Palmer doesn't speak for all of San Rafael Academy, and she certainly doesn't speak for me. And I hoped I could get a better sense of what, exactly, Angelica was planning to write.

ANGELICA: Here I was, sitting across from a despised San Rafael Academy Knight, and he actually didn't seem that despicable. He seemed the opposite of despicable, in fact. And to be perfectly honest, I could kind of see where he was coming from. I wouldn't want Daphne Leake-Palmer speaking for me, either.

BEN: Of course we want to crush San Anselmo Prep. Just as bad as those guys want to crush us, I'm sure. We've been losing for so long, and they're probably desperate to hold on to their winning streak—the stakes could not be higher.

ANGELICA: Listening to Ben talk, *I* was almost starting to feel excited about the AcaBat Locals. The stakes *were* really high.

The defending champs versus our despised rivals, who also happened to be the underdogs, even if their captain was remarkably unpleasant. What was happening to me? I was *interested* in AcaBat? Maybe this actually was an exciting assignment! Should I have been *thanking* Colin Von Kohorn for giving it to me?!

BEN: I just wanted to make sure Angelica knew that we intended to crush her school in, you know, a thoroughly respectful and sportsmanlike fashion. Nothing underhanded, nothing sneaky, nothing nasty. None of that smoke-and-ashes stuff Daphne kept talking about.

ANGELICA: And *that* made me think she *had* written that great line in advance.

BEN: Daphne concludes almost every AcaBat meeting by bellowing, "There will be nothing left of San Anselmo Prep but smoke and ashes!" And then everyone cheers like they're about to storm the gates of Winterfell, and I try not to roll my eyes right out of their sockets.

ANGELICA: Well, I guess I'd learned that Daphne Leake-Palmer wasn't a master of crafting crushing lines on the spot, and I'd gotten a couple good sound bites for my article, but what had Ben gotten out of this meeting? This seemed like an awful lot of effort to go through to make sure I wouldn't print something negative in a newspaper that approximately nobody read.

BEN: What can I say? Maybe it wasn't just about the paper, or AcaBat, or the reputation of San Rafael Academy. Maybe I couldn't resist the chance to meet the girl who'd written "The Little Ladybug Poem."

ANGELICA: That damn ladybug poem. It would haunt me until the day I died.

BEN: I was pretty sure that Angelica wasn't going to trash us in her paper. She didn't seem to have the monomaniacal detestation of my school that I'd seen from all the San Anselmo Prep AcaBats in the past. She certainly hadn't come close to spitting on me.

ANGELICA: Of course I hate the Knights, as, like, an abstract construct, or a distant, adversarial entity. But I somehow couldn't hate Ben as he sat across from me, laughing at the things I said that probably weren't even that funny, and doing impressions of Daphne Leake-Palmer that made me choke on my vanilla frappé, and talking about books he'd read, which included, oddly, an astounding amount of Thomas Hardy, and asking me questions about books I'd read, and listening, listening to everything I was saying, like he really wanted to know what I thought. To know *me*.

BEN: We're all just people, right? People who want to compete in eleven different areas of academics? If that's not an extremely specific common ground, I don't know what is. Some people take this whole school rivalry thing just a little too seriously.

ANGELICA: School rivalry . . . of course! I realized, then, that Ben was my ticket in. I had to find a way to get into San Rafael Academy. And it would have been pretty difficult to get in there on my own. Not to mention that I would have no idea where to start looking.

BEN: It was time for me to head home for dinner, otherwise Mom would start sending out extremely aggressive text alerts. I asked Angelica if there was anything else I could do for her, or anything else she needed from me for her article.

ANGELICA: The odds that the Dragon's head was hidden behind the wrought-iron gates of San Rafael Academy were too high to be ignored. I needed to search that school, and I needed help.

BEN: "Actually, Ben," she said, "I need something from *you*." And when she reached across the table and grabbed my hand, sparks of excitement in her eyes . . . well, I had a feeling that whatever it was, I was going to do it.

INTERROGATION TWO:
THE SCHEDULE

ANGELICA: Ben promised he could get me into San Rafael Academy Wednesday night, after his AcaBat practice. Which, considering homecoming was on Friday, didn't give me a lot of wiggle room to find that head. It was a margin of error of only two days—ugh, even thinking about it made me sick.

BECCA: When Angelica told me the mysterious hot guy from San Rafael Academy had wanted to talk to her about the *Prepster* and Academic Battle, it was a bit of a letdown. Those were, quite possibly, the two most boring topics one could theoretically conceive of.

ANGELICA: Maybe the topics were sort of boring, but the conversation was anything but.

BECCA: Oh man. There were practically heart emojis shooting out of her phone. The mysterious Ben Washington had obviously made a big impact.

ANGELICA: I hadn't used any emojis. And Ben wasn't mysterious. He just seemed mysterious to Becca, because I couldn't explain what, exactly, we were going to be doing on Wednesday night.

BECCA: I tried to think of another time Angelica and I had kept secrets from each other. And honestly, I couldn't.

ANGELICA: Becca was right. Between the picture and the missing head, this was the most we'd ever *not* told each other. And I didn't like it. I just wanted to find the head and get the whole thing over and done with so I didn't feel like I was hiding something from my best friend. Being Finn Aquino's secret keeper was hard. I don't know how Timo and Tanner P. had lived with it for a whole year.

BECCA: And I wasn't mad at Angelica for not telling me what she was looking for—that would have been beyond hypocritical, seeing that I wouldn't tell her what the picture was of— but it seemed to me that she had decided to trust this Ben person awfully quickly. How could he help her find the missing whatever? Who even knew if he could be trusted?

ANGELICA: I *didn't* know if he could be trusted. But what other choice did I have? If I waltzed into San Rafael Academy on my own, I'd have no idea where to look. And I'm sure I'd look incredibly suspicious. All I'd said was I needed to get in the building. No mention of Dragons or heads or anything.

BEN WASHINGTON, *AcaBat competitor at San Rafael Academy*: Of course I'd asked Angelica why she needed to get into San Rafael Academy. But her response was "Classified." I was still going to get her in, even if she was a Dragon. Clearly, I read too many mysteries. I couldn't resist.

ANGELICA: But still. Ben was a Knight, after all. What if *he'd* taken the head? I mean, the Dragon doesn't go to the AcaBat Locals—*no one* goes to the AcaBat Locals—but maybe this was all part of an evil plot to demoralize the San Anselmo Prep AcaBat team.

CINTHIA ALVAREZ, *AcaBat member*: Would I feel demoralized if anything happened to the Dragon? You mean our school mascot? Um, no. The mascot only goes to sporting events. And I haven't gone to a single sporting event that wasn't mandatory. I see him, maybe, what, once or twice a year, at the pep rally? The Dragon has a pretty limited impact on my life.

ANGELICA: If none of our AcaBats cared about the Dragon, the grand head theft probably wasn't committed by anyone on the San Rafael Academy AcaBat team. The more likely culprit would be someone involved in football or cheer or even marching band—someone who would understand just how much the Dragon's presence would affect everyone at San Anselmo Prep on game day.

COLIN VON KOHORN, *editor in chief*: The Dragon was irrelevant. We had serious business to attend to—this scheduling disaster was my best chance at a front-page article that had nothing to do with French fries or our teacher's neckties. I asked Angelica to join me in the principal's office. I needed a reliable witness in case Patel tried to weasel his way out of the mess he'd gotten us all into.

ANGELICA: "A reliable witness." That was a real compliment, coming from Colin.

MS. HERNANDEZ, *administrative assistant to Principal Patel, registrar*: The two sophomores from the newspaper were back.

COLIN: I asked Ms. Hernandez to take us to the principal. Immediately.

ANGELICA: "WHERE IS HE?!" Colin barked, like he'd just kicked the door down, warrant in hand.

MS. HERNANDEZ: I told them that the principal was currently on the phone. Yet another parent concerned that the school wasn't certifiably peanut-free. I wasn't sure where this latest round of nut hysteria was coming from. I swear, there hasn't been a peanut on this campus since 2004.

COLIN: I'll believe in this alleged "phone call" when I can see the records. Clearly, Patel was dodging us. I'd expected no better from a man who was so reliant on the phrase "No comment."

ANGELICA: Poor Ms. Hernandez. She looked so busy—her desk was covered in colored Post-it notes and mountains of paper. The last thing she needed was Colin harassing her.

COLIN: We didn't have time for niceties. This whole mess had come straight from the top. Patel was clearly the culprit, and the people deserved answers. Was there something even more nefarious than a simple misunderstanding at play? If Patel didn't have some ulterior motive for creating chaos, then why didn't he just reschedule all of the homecoming events? Something was off about the whole situation.

ANGELICA: I'm not sure *what* Colin thought Principal Patel's motive for purposefully messing up homecoming would be. But I wondered, too, why they hadn't just rescheduled everything once they found out about the conflicts.

MS. HERNANDEZ: Well, we certainly couldn't move the Academic Battle Locals. Those are scheduled through National Headquarters, and we don't have any jurisdiction to change anything around. It's not a school-sponsored activity; it may take place at the school and feature our students, but all of the scheduling, and, well, everything about it is run by an outside organization.

ANGELICA: Homecoming, though, was the definition of a school-sponsored activity.

MS. HERNANDEZ: The homecoming game itself is a joint activity between us and San Rafael Academy, of course. We couldn't reschedule it without their consent, and when I'd called to see if they had any wiggle room, they refused. They said it was "the linchpin of their entire athletic calendar," and that moving it would be impossible.

COLIN: What about the Student Council elections? Certainly, the principal at least had control over his own student government!

MS. HERNANDEZ: Oh, well, the elections were no problem! It would happen right at the end of the day, and then everyone could scoot off to the game. Sure, the football players and the cheerleaders would leave a bit early, but that only affected a few students. And nothing can be scheduled perfectly, after all. There will always be a few overlaps.

COLIN: This was more than a few overlaps. This was a disaster. It would be like calling the punctured siding on the *Titanic* "a few holes."

ANGELICA: "And the fall play?" I prompted. It seemed like both Colin and Ms. Hernandez had forgotten about *Much Ado About Nothing*. Honestly, with everything that was going on, I kind of kept forgetting about it, too.

MS. HERNANDEZ: Oh. Yes. Well, our theater teacher specifically requested that weekend—she has a wedding to go to later in October—and when I asked her to move the play, she said she was tired of the school consistently prioritizing athletics, and she refused!

COLIN: Ms. Hernandez was responding to our questions, yes, but I still wasn't getting the answers I needed. There was only one man who could do that.

ANGELICA: Colin shouted, "The people demand answers!" the minute Principal Patel walked out of his office. Principal Patel looked like he wished he'd stayed in his office.

COLIN: How could an educator be so technologically incompetent as to allow such a grievous oversight to occur? And once the oversight had occurred, how could our *principal* be so ineffective at resolving it, so cavalier with the feelings of the students affected?

PRINCIPAL PATEL, *principal*: A small scheduling conflict hardly qualifies as a school emergency.

ANGELICA: I'd never seen Colin speechless before. His mouth opened and closed like a fish.

MS. HERNANDEZ: I gently reminded Colin and Angelica that the office closes fifteen minutes after the final bell, and well, it was about that time.

COLIN: I was going to bring down Principal Patel. No matter what it took. He was going to answer for his crimes against homecoming, and for his complete lack of perspective on the gravity of the situation.

ANGELICA: I ushered Colin out of the office before he said something he'd *really* regret. I practically had to pull him down the hall and back to the computer lab.

CINTHIA: Colin finally came back, thank God. DJ Li'l Monster clearly thought *I'd* thrown away his cat pictures, and our relationship was starting to deteriorate.

SEBASTIAN "BASH" VON KOHORN, *Colin's little brother, age ten*: I was working on a new portrait of Mrs. Fluff, since my last one had disappeared. I have three cats right now. Mrs. Fluff, King Richard, and Li'l Beastie. King Richard only has one eye, and Li'l Beastie's tongue sticks out all the time, so Mrs. Fluff is definitely my most normal cat. I finished my picture and taped it to the side of Colin's computer. He started talking about schedules, which sounded really boring. So I decided to go exploring.

CINTHIA: Finally, Bash got out of the office and stopped glaring at me. There were only so many Von Kohorn glares I could handle in one day. I brushed all the Cheeto dust off Colin's chair before he inevitably blamed me for it.

COLIN: This entire homecoming debacle was Principal Patel's fault. Just as I'd thought, this disaster had come straight from the top. And he didn't even seem to *care*!

ANGELICA: It seemed to me like it was nobody's *fault*, really, more like an oversight on a couple different people's parts. The way Colin was talking about it, it almost sounded like a conspiracy.

COLIN: I wasn't talking about *conspiracy*. I was talking about gross incompetence. And the outrage of apathy.

CINTHIA: When Colin powered up the computer and opened Word, I almost couldn't believe it. He hadn't sat down and written any articles yet this year.

COLIN: As editor in chief, my primary function is, of course, to edit. But every once in a while, a story comes along that is so big, so momentous, that even editors must go out into the field and do their own reporting. And this, I just knew, was my story.

INTERROGATION THREE:
THE HOOFER

HARRISON BAXTER, *senior, star of San Anselmo Prep's theater department, expert tapper*: If these questions are for the *Prepster*, I am not saying one more word.

CINTHIA ALVAREZ, *associate editor of the* Prepster: Colin has made himself a lot of enemies in the theater department.

COLIN VON KOHORN, *editor in chief of the* Prepster: Last year, I had no problem accepting the role of the *Prepster's* resident theater critic. I enjoy the arts. I was happy to take on the position. I just hadn't realized how *sensitive* everyone at this school was. They weren't looking for a theater critic. They were looking for someone to heap undeserved praise upon them.

BECCA: God, Colin's reviews were *incredible*. I'd forgotten how much I loved them last year. They were by far the best thing the *Prepster* has ever produced. I firmly believe Colin Von Kohorn was put on this earth to review bad theater. It was his calling. I still feel kind of bummed that they pulled him off that segment. His *Damn Yankees* review made me laugh so hard I *cried*.

CINTHIA: It was Colin's review of *Damn Yankees* that officially lost him the position, but it was his review of last year's spring musical, *Hello, Dolly!*, that had lost him a lot of friends. Well, friendly acquaintances, I guess. It's not like Harrison Baxter even knew who Colin was before the review was published.

HARRISON: I remember every word of that horrible review. I wish I could forget it. But it's burned into my retinas. I can still see it like it had just been printed: "You'll feel so down and out from seeing this production, not even putting on your Sunday clothes will help!"

CINTHIA: Harrison actually got off pretty light, all things considered. Colin *destroyed* the poor senior girl who was playing Dolly.

COLIN: You should never attempt to mount a production of *Hello, Dolly!* unless you have a real powerhouse set to play the titular role. Melanie Whatever-Her-Last-Name-Was was so forgettable she practically blended into the scenery. Her hats did more acting than she did.

HARRISON: Melanie was gutted. She cried so much her eyes are still puffy in her prom pictures. Look at the Facebook album if you don't believe me.

BECCA: Why do all these people give Colin Von Kohorn so much power? Who cares about his opinion? Yes, the reviews were hilarious, and I enjoyed reading them, but I didn't take them seriously. Why do any of these people take him seriously?! It's not like he's a *real* theater critic.

ANGELICA: I totally got it. It always hurts to read or hear people saying negative things about you, even if you know their opinion shouldn't *really* matter. Colin's theater reviews were basically just like all the rejection Post-its he'd written me, only in a much, much more public forum.

COLIN: I gave Harrison Baxter an extremely favorable review. Of course, it was nothing compared to the puff piece Cinthia did on his preparations to play Benedick in *Much Ado*, but I can't imagine he'd have any problems with me or what I'd written.

HARRISON: An extremely favorable review?! Seriously? That's what he said? *Extremely favorable?!* You tell me if this is favorable. "A notable tap solo from Harrison Baxter as Cornelius provides a welcome moment of respite from rarely riveting choreography. If only his acting were as competent as his footwork."

COLIN: I was *very* positive.

HARRISON: "If only his acting were as competent as his footwork." I have been *haunted* by that phrase! I played Billy in *Anything Goes* this summer, and I got so in my head about it, I could barely deliver a line. Sure, I was tapping just fine, maybe better than ever, triple-time steps flowing as easily as walking down the street, but any time I had to speak, I overthought all of it. It certainly wasn't my best work. It was a miracle I was cast as Benedick this fall. Hopefully, I'll be fine, since there's definitely no tapping in *Much Ado*, as long as I avoid Colin Von Kohorn at all costs. Good thing seniors rarely have to interact with sophomores.

ANGELICA: I assured Harrison that this was not for the *Prepster*, and after that, he was only too happy to answer my questions, and to keep bashing Colin.

HARRISON: Colin *should* praise my footwork. God knows I've been working on it for long enough.

COLIN: I *did* praise Harrison's footwork! What on earth was his issue?

ANGELICA: I knew Harrison was primarily a tapper, but I'd seen him do other kinds of dance in school assemblies, and even on the dance floor at homecoming, and the Valentine's dance, and the Spring Fling last year. He definitely had the skills necessary to be the Dragon. I'd still never actually seen Finn Aquino dance, so from what I'd seen, Harrison Baxter was by far the best dancer at our school.

HARRISON: The Dragon? You mean the mascot? I wouldn't say I have a lot of experiences with him. I think I took a picture with him, once, when I was a freshman. It's not like they send mascots to theatrical performances here. Not that I really *want* a mascot pumping up the crowd before curtain, but this school always gives preferential treatment to its athletes. I heard Ms. Hernandez asked Ms. Tussey to *change the weekend of the play*, just because opening night happens to be at the same time as some football game. Ridiculous. The fall play only has two performances! We can't just skip the Friday night show because of some athletic event. We've been rehearsing for this for months, too! Why are we less important than the football team?!

ANGELICA: Harrison had a good point about the play. I understood why the theater department didn't want to move it, even if that would have solved at least one problem. But I had to get back to the mascot head. I was quickly discovering that it was really difficult to ascertain whether someone had once been interested in being the Dragon without just asking them point-blank if they had once been interested in being the Dragon. Rookie detective problems, I supposed. I didn't know how to be subtle.

HARRISON: Did I ever want to *be* the Dragon? I'm sorry . . . just . . . give me a minute here. . . .

ANGELICA: His laughter seemed to indicate that, no, he had never wanted to be the Dragon.

HARRISON: God, no, I never wanted to be the Dragon. I suppose the Dragon gets to perform for a fairly large audience at homecoming intermission, but my God, it couldn't possibly be worth it. That green furry suit is horrible.

FINN AQUINO, *actually the Dragon*: The suit is *not* horrible. It's surprisingly comfortable, and you can see out of the eyes just fine. Maybe it gets a little ripe on hot days, but it's not nearly as bad as you would think it would be, considering how many

Dragons have worn it. Actually, thanks to Tripp Gomez-Parker, it mostly smells like Axe body spray.

HARRISON: Think about it: If you worked at Disneyland, would you rather be a furry or a face character? Do you want to be Prince Charming or Goofy? It's no contest. I'm not a furry. I'm face character material. And I'm going to go audition for Prince Eric as soon as I graduate.

ANGELICA: Harrison would make a great Prince Eric. And his disdain for the Dragon suit seemed genuine. As Colin had pointed out, much as I hated to admit it, he wasn't *that* good of an actor.

HARRISON: I'm going to perform, and I want people to be able to see my face. It would be a crime to hide this bone structure.

ANGELICA: Harrison definitely wasn't our head thief. And it didn't seem like there was anyone at San Anselmo Prep harboring resentful feelings toward the Dragon. Our culprit had to be at San Rafael Academy. And I could only hope that Ben could somehow lead me straight to that head.

HARRISON: As much as I love doing press, as long as it's not the *Prepster*, unfortunately, I didn't have time for any more questions. It was tech week! I had to get back to the auditorium for rehearsal.

ANGELICA: The auditorium. The play was in the auditorium.

HARRISON: Of course the play is in the auditorium. Where else would it be? It's not like this school would ever drop the money on a performing arts center, although God knows we *need* another lacrosse field. Please.

ANGELICA: I didn't have the heart to tell Harrison that not only was *Much Ado About Nothing* going up against homecoming, the best-attended after-school event of the entire year, but it was also, somehow, sharing a space with the AcaBat Locals. There was another layer to this homecoming scheduling nightmare we'd never even considered! The fall play and the AcaBat Locals weren't just happening at the same time—they were happening in the same place. Homecoming was getting closer and closer, and things were only getting *more* complicated. But I couldn't deal with the schedule right now. I had a head to hunt down.

INSIDE ENEMY TERRITORY

ANGELICA: I hung out in the computer lab for a bit after school on Wednesday, waiting for Ben's AcaBat practice to finish up before I biked over to San Rafael Academy.

COLIN VON KOHORN, *editor in chief of the* Prepster: Angelica was heading *back* to San Rafael Academy to do even more investigative reporting on Academic Battle. At first I'd thought it was unnecessary, but I'd come around to agreeing that interviewing the antagonist really did add another nice layer to the piece. I was impressed. Unfortunately, I couldn't join her this time, as I was mired in trying to make sense of this scheduling conflict, and seeing what kind of piece I could craft around it.

ANGELICA: Thank God Colin couldn't come with me. Because he would have soon discovered that although I was, in fact, on my way over to San Rafael Academy to see someone on their AcaBat team, it had nothing to do with AcaBat. This was all about finding that missing mascot head, and I wasn't leaving until I had it.

DAPHNE LEAKE-PALMER, *captain of the San Rafael Academy Academic Battle team*: Ben was acting *bizarre* at practice. He was being a total space cadet. Fidgety, distracted, and he kept looking out the window at absolutely nothing.

BEN WASHINGTON, *Academic Battle competitor at San Rafael Academy*: I couldn't stop looking for Angelica. I told her not to get there too early, because if people saw someone hanging around in that navy San Anselmo Prep uniform, they would definitely ask questions. But what if she got there early anyway? What if she couldn't get through the gates undetected? And worst of all, what if Daphne saw her? She would undoubtedly recognize Angelica, and then where would we be?

ANGELICA: There was an extremely large bush off to the side of San Rafael Academy, just where Ben had said it would be. I rolled up there and hopped off my bike at exactly the appointed time.

BEN: I tried to look nonchalant as I headed out of AcaBat practice. I ducked out the door in the science wing, and there was Angelica, hiding in the bush. She was hiding a little more thoroughly than was probably necessary.

ANGELICA: I realize now, of course, that I probably didn't have to climb *into* the bush. I think the pressure of finding the head was starting to get to me.

BEN: I handed Angelica the maroon sweater vest I'd brought her.

ANGELICA: The good thing is that the San Anselmo Prep and San Rafael Academy uniforms both feature a white button-down and a gray skirt—easy to make a changeover. The bad thing is that the maroon sweater vest Ben gave me was *his*.

BEN: It was sort of, uh, comically large.

ANGELICA: Okay, maybe it wasn't all bad. It smelled like clean laundry and something warm and wonderful, something I couldn't quite find the word for, which sort of drove me crazy because I hate when I can't find the right word to describe something. Well, it smelled the way Ben smelled, and I kind of wanted to steal it forever and then felt immediately embarrassed I was having such strong feelings for a sweater vest, nature's worst garment.

BEN: But hopefully, there wouldn't be too many people hanging around school anyway. AcaBats are usually some of the last people to leave the building. And I'd watched Daphne get into her car and drive away, and she had been our biggest concern. Angelica looked fine from a distance, and that was what really mattered.

ANGELICA: I left my bike in the bush, and followed Ben into a side door he'd propped open. I had made it into the belly of the beast.

BEN: I asked Angelica what, exactly, we were looking for. She said she couldn't tell me. Which was going to make this a whole lot more difficult than I'd anticipated.

ANGELICA: So, if I were a missing mascot head, where would I be? Probably not in some random hallway full of labs. I asked Ben to take me to the gym.

BEN: Angelica wanted to go on the weirdest tour of San Rafael Academy. I showed her the gym, the weight room, and then the jazz band room. She seemed really frustrated when I told her we didn't have a marching band, for some reason. In every room I showed her, she checked every corner, opened up any cabinets. She rifled through every single tub of athletic equipment in the PE department's storage closet, but it was clear she hadn't found what she was looking for. She kept sighing, and the wrinkle between her brows deepened. It would have been pretty cute, if she hadn't been so clearly distressed.

Note: Cute?! No. It was really dark in there. He must not have been able to see clearly.

ANGELICA: I checked the girls' locker room alone. No reason the head thief couldn't be a girl. Obviously, I couldn't open any of the lockers, but they were too narrow for the head to fit in, anyway.

BEN: The only place I balked at showing her was the guys' locker room.

ANGELICA: Of course I had to check the guys' locker room! That seemed like an obvious place to hide a head! After Ben checked three times to make sure there weren't any half-naked dudes lurking in there to offend my maidenly sensibilities, I went in. Again, no head. The only thing lurking in there was an unholy stench.

BEN: This was officially the latest I'd ever stayed at school before. The place was deserted. I kept waiting for a teacher or someone on maintenance to show up and kick us out, but we never saw anyone. Guess I didn't need to be so concerned about getting Angelica that sweater vest.

ANGELICA: I was starting to panic. I had been so sure the head would be there. Although, what was I expecting, a big neon sign that read STOLEN HEAD HERE!?! Well, to be fair, I bet if Brooks Mandeville stole the Knight's helmet, he would have mounted it in the cafeteria or something. San Rafael Academy had to have its very own Brooks Mandeville.

BEN: She started opening every closet we passed, mostly full of mops, vacuums, other cleaning supplies. She'd glance anxiously in every classroom, passing by when she didn't see whatever it was that she was looking for. The last place she asked me to take her was where we had AcaBat practice.

ANGELICA: There was still a chance Demon Sneak-Palmer had taken it, even if Cinthia seemed skeptical that any of the AcaBats cared about the Dragon.

BEN: Our adviser is an English teacher, so we just have AcaBat in a regular old classroom on the second floor. Angelica looked around the room hopefully, she looked under the desk, she looked in the closet where Ms. Schwartz stores extra books, and then she slammed the closet door, leaned against it, and slid down to the floor. She pulled my sweater vest over her knees, so it looked like she was sitting in a maroon tent.

ANGELICA: It wasn't anywhere. No head. Homecoming was in two days, and the Dragon remained completely and utterly headless. I had failed. I had failed Finn Aquino, and I had failed my whole school. It was over.

BEN: "You know, Angelica," I said, "it might help if you told me *what* you were looking for."

ANGELICA: Of course I couldn't tell him. He was a *Knight*. He might have been the one who'd stolen it, for all I knew.

BEN: I promised her I'd never stolen anything from San Anselmo Prep, not even a pen. That I had, in fact, never actually been inside its doors, since Locals were hosted at my school last year. The closest I'd ever gotten was when I'd talked to Angelica in the courtyard. And she could verify that I certainly had not taken anything then.

ANGELICA: I don't know why I said it. Oh, of course I know why—because I was panicked and exhausted.

BEN: She was looking for a *mascot head*?!

ANGELICA: I explained that the Dragon was essential to our homecoming celebration. And I had to find it. As soon as possible.

BEN: Unfortunately for Angelica, I was pretty sure the head wasn't here. It's really hard to keep a secret at a small school, and I hadn't heard anything about someone stealing the Dragon's head. Certainly, if Daphne had taken it, she would have mounted it to the wall like a trophy of war. And I'm sure the guys on the football team would have been even more ostentatious if they'd taken it. And even if someone had been trying to hide it, Angelica had turned the school upside down. I was reasonably sure the head wasn't here.

ANGELICA: And Knight or no, I believed him. And even though we hadn't found the head, I was grateful to Ben for helping me. Even though I really didn't understand *why* he had helped me.

BEN: I helped her because I thought she was cute, okay? Because I wanted to spend more time with her. Because I liked the questions she asked when she was interviewing me, because she wasn't afraid of Daphne, because there was something about the way she put her sentences together that made me need to know what she was going to say next, that made me want her to never stop talking. I helped her because I should have asked her out, but I was intimidated, and it seemed easier to wander around an empty school with her than actually put myself out there and do something about the fact that I liked her. Because I did. I liked her. A lot. And maybe we hadn't spent that much time together yet, but I intended to do something about that.

ANGELICA: I stared at Ben. He thought I was *cute*?! He wanted to *ask me out*?!

BEN: She was just staring at me. I had probably said too much. No, I had definitely said too much.

ANGELICA: How could tall, hot, smart Ben be intimidated by *me*, of all people? I could hear Becca in my head telling me that he *should* be intimidated, that I was short, sure, but just as hot and smart, but I was having a hard time believing imaginary Becca. Or believing that Ben *liked* me. This was the kind of thing that happened in made-for-TV movies on the Disney Channel. Were people going to pop out of lockers and start singing about how this was the start of something new?

BEN: I knew what I had to do. I had to stop talking.

ANGELICA: Much to my astonishment, Ben Washington, San Rafael Academy Knight, leaned over and kissed me.

BEN: I'd wanted to kiss her since I first stood up in the quad and asked, "Angelica?"

ANGELICA: Honestly? I'd wanted to kiss *him* since he first stood up in the quad and asked, "Angelica?"

BEN: It was worth the wait.

ANGELICA: Ben Washington liked me. And the more we kissed, the more I liked him, too. I mean, I'd liked him before. But kissing someone is a *great* way to get to know them. Highly recommended.

BEN: I could have sat on that ugly carpet kissing her forever.

ANGELICA: Somehow, I was less worried about the missing mascot head than I'd been in a long time. And all thoughts of working on my story had vanished. Man, it is really hard to maintain any semblance of journalistic integrity or focus on the investigation at hand when a cute boy is kissing you.

BEN: But I wanted to do this right. With a real date. Angelica deserved to go somewhere way nicer than the floor of Ms. Schwartz's room. So I asked if she was free Friday.

ANGELICA: Friday?! Was he insane?!

BEN: Right. Friday! AcaBat Locals! Homecoming! I couldn't believe I'd forgotten. But there was something about kissing Angelica that was making me forget a lot of things. Like my name. What state I was in. Who the president was.

ANGELICA: I wanted to go out with him, too. Just not, you know, on Friday.

BEN: Saturday, then. What about Saturday?

ANGELICA: Saturday. It was a date.

COLIN CRACKS THE CASE

ANGELICA: As I left San Rafael Academy, here is what I had: The phone number of an extremely cute boy. A date with said extremely cute boy. Lips that had kissed an extremely cute boy. Here's what I did not have: a missing mascot head. I guess this was the real definition of "half agony, half hope!"

BECCA: I got a text from Angelica that was fifteen fireworks emojis.

ANGELICA: That was the other dilemma: recount all the glorious details for my best friend, or deal with the unmitigated disaster that was my detective work?

BECCA: I had a feeling the fireworks were courtesy of mysterious Ben Washington.

ANGELICA: I'm only human. I'd had a totally firework-emoji-worthy kiss, yes, but now was not the time to discuss it.

BECCA: Now was *not the time*?! When was the time?! I had about a billion follow-up questions, but she wouldn't give me anything. Angelica promised she would explain soon, but that for now, she had "urgent homecoming business to deal with." Good God. There has never been anything urgent about homecoming at San Anselmo Prep. And there *certainly* wasn't anything more urgent than the juicy, juicy details Angelica was so cruelly withholding.

ANGELICA: I didn't want to tell anyone else about the missing head. I really, really didn't. I knew it compromised every bit of the detective-client confidentiality I shared with Finn. But I was stumped. And I was desperate. I needed help.

BECCA: Angelica had been looking for *the mascot head* this whole time?! That was not what I'd expected. I promised her I wouldn't tell anyone it was missing—not that I was ever particularly desperate to discuss the Dragon with anyone; the only thing I *wanted* to talk about was Ben Washington—but unfortunately, I had absolutely no idea where it could be. I certainly hadn't seen it anywhere. But if Angelica needed more help searching, all she had to do was tell me where to be, and I'd be there. Searching. And asking my billion follow-up questions about Ben Washington.

ANGELICA: I appreciated Becca's offer of help. But it didn't really help much with my current predicament. And I told her again that we could talk about Ben *after* we found the head. There are things in life called priorities, and unfortunately, finding the head was a bit more time-sensitive than discussing the world's most perfect kiss.

BECCA: If Angelica wanted to focus, then okay. Fine. I'd focus. There was one person I thought who might be able to help Angelica. Someone with an almost psychopathic attention to detail. Someone who should almost assuredly be used only as a last resort. But it sounded like Angelica was down to last resorts.

ANGELICA: When Becca suggested I ask Colin for help, I made her repeat herself three times. I thought I'd heard her wrong. But the more I thought about it, the more it did make a certain kind of grim sense. I had nowhere else to turn. And Colin *did* hear quite a lot of school business because of the *Prepster*. And Colin, for all of his many, many faults, is possessed of a logical mind. An almost pathologically logical mind. Maybe he could put the pieces together in a way I clearly couldn't.

BECCA: I made Angelica promise she would never let Colin know that I had recommended him for anything, even as junior detective on Angelica's missing mascot case. It went against everything I stood for.

COLIN VON KOHORN, *editor in chief*: I appreciated Angelica's compliments about my deductive prowess. But this case was solved by pure dumb luck. Or coincidence, I suppose.

ANGELICA: And so I biked back to San Anselmo Prep, shooting off a quick text to my dad that I was going to a friend's for dinner. He would undoubtedly send me fifty-seven follow-up questions guilting me about missing dinner, but I would deal with those later. For now, there were more important things than my dad being annoyed about me bailing. The last bell of the school day had rung long ago, but I had a feeling Colin might still be there. When I entered the computer lab, just as I'd thought, Colin was there, and he was alone. No Cinthia or Bash or Mr. Duncan in sight.

COLIN: Cinthia went out with Becca. Bash gets picked up early for karate on Wednesdays. And a bunch of the other English teachers stopped by to gossip with Mr. Duncan about something, so off he went. I was pretty sure he was out of the building ninety seconds after the final bell. Sometimes I seriously question Mr. Duncan's devotion to the *Prepster*.

ANGELICA: It seemed like Cinthia and Becca had been spending a lot of time together recently, but I didn't have time to think about what that meant right now. That needed to be filed under the Romantic-Intrigue-to-Be-Discussed-at-a-Later-Date folder along with Ben Washington. I needed to focus on the head.

COLIN: Angelica didn't tell me *who* the Dragon was, but she explained to me about the missing head.

ANGELICA: I told him about everyone I'd interviewed, and my fruitless search at San Rafael Academy, and how I'd hit nothing but dead ends. I was totally and completely stumped. The head was nowhere to be found.

COLIN: The Dragon's head . . . I knew I'd seen it before, but I couldn't quite remember what it looked like.

ANGELICA: It's green, it's fuzzy, and it looks like a dragon. There really wasn't that much to it.

COLIN: Green and fuzzy . . . when Angelica mentioned it, I realized I actually *had* seen something green and fuzzy recently. But could it possibly be the Dragon's head? That seemed so improbable as to be impossible. And yet, how many other big, green, fuzzy things could there be in this world?

ANGELICA: When Colin told me there was a chance the Dragon head might be at *his house*, I thought he had lost it. *Colin* was the self-confessed mascot head thief? Why?! Why could he possibly have wanted the head? I couldn't think of any use he'd have for it, and I couldn't imagine Colin being so upset *he* wasn't the Dragon that he'd stolen it in an act of sabotage. Colin was the least likely candidate for a school mascot on the San Anselmo Prep campus. Except for maybe Becca.

COLIN: Good God, of course I didn't want to be the Dragon! I wouldn't cavort about in a fur suit even if you paid me a healthy salary, and being the school mascot is a volunteer activity. I never said I'd stolen the Dragon head. What I'd said was that there was a chance that the head just might be at my house. Because there was definitely something green and fuzzy at my house—and maybe it was the Dragon head.

ANGELICA: There was no way I was letting Colin ride on my handlebars the whole way over to his house. I am not pedaling Colin Von Kohorn anywhere. It's the principle of the thing.

COLIN: And thusly, we were forced to rely on my least favorite mode of transportation: my mother.

MRS. VON KOHORN, *Colin's mother*: I had *just* dropped Bash at home after karate and now Colin was summoning me to head *back* to San Anselmo Prep to pick him up. Honestly. I think Colin thinks I spend the day sitting around, waiting for him to text me so I can pick him up somewhere.

SEBASTIAN "BASH" VON KOHORN, *Colin's brother, age ten*: I was *not* an unaccompanied minor. Dad was at home, too. Mom wants to make sure you put that in.

ANGELICA: Colin helped me get my bike into the back of the minivan, and I clambered into the backseat.

COLIN: Angelica was polite enough not to mention the cat hair.

ANGELICA: It was a *lot* of cat hair. But I could tell by Colin's pained expression when he tried to brush it off his khakis that he was well aware of it.

COLIN: I had hoped we could just listen to NPR in companionable silence, but no. My mother insisted on interrogating Angelica.

MRS. VON KOHORN: Colin *never* has friends over! I wanted to get to know the famous Angelica Hutcherson a little better. She was just delightful! And she would have been a real asset to my book club, let me tell you.

ANGELICA: I was *not* being delightful. The entire fate of homecoming was resting on my shoulders! I was so nervous that the head wouldn't be there, but apparently, I was doing an okay job of faking it.

COLIN: She seemed so upset, I had to do something. Something . . . comforting.

ANGELICA: When Colin stuck his hand in the backseat, I honestly had no idea what he wanted me to do with it. I reached out, and I shook his hand. I thought a handshake seemed like the only hand activity Colin Von Kohorn would engage in. But much to my surprise, he kept my hand in his and squeezed it.

COLIN: Making friends has never come easily for me. For most of my life, I've preferred to be on my own, doing things that I can have control over, that I know won't get messed up, because I'm the only person doing them. But watching Angelica attack this homecoming story with the vigor of Boudicca, and even, God help me, spending all that time in my office with Cinthia, was making me realize that there were some things, perhaps, that weren't best done alone. Maybe this *would* be the best edition of the *Prepster* ever. And if that were the case, it certainly wouldn't be just because of me. In fact, it would *barely* be because of me. It would mostly be because of Angelica, and a little bit because of Cinthia, too. Assuming she didn't screw up the formatting.

MRS. VON KOHORN: The minute we pulled into the driveway, Angelica and Colin leapt out of the car. I'd barely even put it in park! Angelica, at least, managed to say thank you.

COLIN: I raced up the stairs and down the hall, Angelica close behind me.

ANGELICA: We flew down the upstairs hall, until Colin stopped in front of a door that had big cutout letters reading DJ BASH and a bunch of different pictures of various Internet-famous cats.

COLIN: I pushed open the door. It swung open kind of anticlimactically. It would have been better with a dramatic bang. Or a sound track of suspenseful music.

BASH: Colin *never* knocks. It is *very* rude. Aren't little brothers entitled to their privacy, too? Just because I'm ten, it doesn't mean I don't have a rich inner life!

ANGELICA: Bash sat on the floor in his oversize headphones, surrounded by a pile of magazines. There was an orange cat draped over his neck.

COLIN: Bash blinked owlishly up at us. There was no time for niceties. We had to get that head—*if* it was the head.

ANGELICA: Colin completely ignored his little brother and strode toward the window. I followed him, totally unsure why he was glowering at a couple cats napping in the sunshine. But then I realized what, exactly, the cats were napping *in*.

COLIN: I guess I'd thought it was weird that Bash's new cat bed was bright green, but if I'm being honest, I hadn't paid much attention to it.

BASH: I'd shown my cat bed to Colin *ages* ago. Li'l Beastie was napping so nicely in it. He loved it. It was so cute and so I wanted Colin to see it, too. He came in and saw it, but all he said was "I don't have *time* for Li'l Beastie, Bash," and he was doing something on his phone, and I knew he wasn't really paying attention.

ANGELICA: I couldn't believe it. We had found the head!

COLIN: I think it was understandable that I hadn't recognized it as a mascot head, given that it was filled with cats.

ANGELICA: It was definitely the San Anselmo Prep Dragon mascot costume head. Bash had flipped it upside down and filled it with blankets. Currently, a big gray cat and a small black one were cuddling in it.

BASH: Li'l Beastie and King Richard love their new bed. They sleep in it all the time.

COLIN: Who ever expects to find a missing mascot head in their little brother's room?

BASH: Colin doesn't pay any attention to anything I do. I thought he'd think it was cool that I'd made such an awesome cat bed, but he just ignored it.

COLIN: I pay attention to Bash! I'd just been so busy lately, trying to get the *Prepster* off to a successful start, that it had needed a little bit more of my attention than usual.

BASH: Colin used to play with me all the time. But not anymore.

COLIN: As I looked down at Bash, cuddling Mrs. Fluff, something that felt unfamiliarly like guilt pricked at my conscience. I couldn't actually remember the last time I had played Takenoko with him, or drawn cat pictures with him, or listened when he played me some god-awful techno song. Maybe I *had* been ignoring him.

ANGELICA: Bash was awfully cute, with his freckles and over-size headphones. And when Colin crouched down to talk to him, I finally saw the other side of monomaniacal editor Colin Von Kohorn I knew existed. Colin was prickly and tough and difficult to get along with sometimes, but he treated his brother with a lot of kindness and patience. And that was the kind of person I wanted to be friends with.

COLIN: I told Bash that Angelica really, really needed his cat bed.

BASH: I had a feeling I'd have to give the cat bed back, eventually. I knew I'd taken something that wasn't mine, even if it was just sitting in that weird little room and no one was using it. Mom would probably be pretty mad if she knew I'd taken it. She's always telling me that I need to stop touching other people's stuff. And I definitely shouldn't *take* other people's stuff.

ANGELICA: I did wonder *how*, exactly, Bash had taken it.

BASH: A couple days ago, I was hanging out in the *Prepster* office, like I always do. I thought Colin might let me write an article or help with printing, or at least let me decorate his desk or something, but then he just sat there click-click-clicking on his computer, ignoring me, being boring. Wouldn't even look at the pictures I'd drawn. So I decided to go exploring.

ANGELICA: I remain surprised by how easily accessible San Anselmo Prep was after school hours. It's crazy that more things aren't stolen, honestly.

BASH: I went down to the weight room, because there's a lot of fun stuff to play with down there. There are mats and jump ropes and boxing gloves, and one of those big things boxers kick and punch. And a bar where I try to do chin-ups, like we do in PE sometimes. I'd found one of those little scooter things in a storage closet, and I sat down on it, scooting around the weight room. And then I noticed a door in the corner that I'd never noticed before.

COLIN: How was *Bash* the first person who had ever noticed that door? Maybe my generation is as self-involved as all those articles keep saying.

BASH: The door wasn't locked, so I pushed it open and went in.

ANGELICA: Finn hadn't bothered to lock the door to the ultra-super-top-secret Dragon's Lair?! *HE DIDN'T LOCK THE DOOR?!* I tried to quash the instinct to cheerfully murder him. Little wonder he had neglected to mention that tiny, insignificant detail when he'd come to me for help. This whole missing head thing was on him. I couldn't believe how easily this could have been avoided!

BASH: Inside, it was pretty boring. There was a big mirror and some squishy mats, like from gymnastics class. And then I noticed the Dragon costume.

ANGELICA: I couldn't believe that all of this stress had been caused by a curious ten-year-old.

BASH: I put the head on and danced around a little, but I didn't really like it, because it was too dark in there. I don't know how the Dragon sees anything! But I did really like how soft and fuzzy it was. And I thought my cats would like it, too. So I put it in a duffel bag I found in the weight room and brought it home. Huh. I guess I actually took two things. Wow. Mom would be *really* mad if she knew. This might be worse than the time I took the Kit Kats.

ANGELICA: I hugged Bash so hard he squeaked. We'd gotten the head back, and just in time for homecoming!

BASH: I got all the blankets out of my old, green, furry cat bed, and set up a nice blanket nest in the sunshine for Li'l Beastie and King Richard. They seemed just as happy on the floor, actually.

COLIN: I told Bash I would help him build a new cat bed as soon as possible—maybe sometime next week, after the home-coming edition went to the press. Maybe Mom could drive us to the fabric store and we could even get some fuzzy green fabric. And maybe Angelica would want to help us build it, too.

ANGELICA: I didn't know who the social poltergeist was who had possessed Colin Von Kohorn, but much to my surprise, I found I liked this new Colin. So I guess I had a lot of plans now. I had a date with Ben next weekend, *and* there was a cat bed in my future. But for now I had to get to school.

COLIN: I put the head back in the duffel bag Bash had stolen it in, and saluted him.

BASH: I saluted Colin, and waved bye to Angelica as she headed out with my cat bed. Mrs. Fluff climbed back up to sit on my shoulders. She likes it up there.

ANGELICA: We'd done it. I couldn't believe it. "Don't worry," I texted Finn. "I have the head." And then I texted him a dragon emoji, because, well, it seemed appropriate.

TIMOTHY "TIMO" WAKATSUKI, *sophomore*: Finn was lying on my couch, facedown. I'm surprised he even summoned up the energy to glance at his phone when it pinged. But he did, and then he shot up to his feet like he'd been poked with a cattle prod.

TANNER PETERSON, *the one in marching band, not the one on the football team*: "She did it," Finn whispered. "Angelica. She did it. She got the head back."

MOMO WAKATSUKI, *freshman*: And then all those dumb boys started jumping around and hugging each other and, like, crying and chest bumping. I slammed my coconut water down forcefully on the kitchen island, but nobody noticed me. There was no "Thank you, Momo!" No "Great idea, Momo!" No "Momo, we're so glad we called Angelica. Thanks for telling us to call Angelica!" And there was certainly no "Momo Wakatsuki, you are the girl who saved homecoming." Ugh. Whatever. The greatest heroes don't wear capes, you know what I mean? I shouldn't have expected praise from those yahoos.

FINN AQUINO, *restored Dragon*: I don't know how Angelica had done it, and I almost didn't care. I was just happy that the head was back. And I was definitely going to lock the Dragon's Lair every time I left from now on, even if I was just popping out for a quick pee break. Man. Who knew a pee break could have so many unintended consequences?

MRS. VON KOHORN, *Colin's mother*: And now Colin wanted to go *back* to school? Honestly. I will never understand anything about that boy's schedule.

ANGELICA: After thanking Mrs. Von Kohorn profusely for the many rides, I sat contentedly in the backseat, the Dragon's head resting in my lap. It felt, ironically, like cuddling a large green cat.

FINN: The head was on its way back to San Anselmo Prep, and it was safe. And now it was time for the Dragon to give the greatest homecoming halftime show performance this school had ever seen.

THE GREAT HOMECOMING RESCHEDULING

ANGELICA: Colin and I had found the head. And now, in order to truly save homecoming, we needed to fix the schedule.

COLIN VON KOHORN, *editor in chief*: Firstly, I wasn't sure it was possible to fix the schedule.

ANGELICA: Well, fixing it completely was definitely impossible, but we could certainly improve things.

COLIN: And secondly, I wasn't sure we *should* fix the schedule. It went against my journalistic instincts to get involved in this whole mess. For the sake of the story, I felt like it would be better to let it play out, and just report on what happened. That seemed like what a real reporter would do.

ANGELICA: Maybe it was what a real reporter would do. But it wasn't what a real friend would do. And if we didn't fix homecoming, it meant that AcaBat Locals would be totally screwed up for Cinthia. And as much as Colin complains about her "flamboyant formatting," and her soft touch with the theater reviews, and her processed snack habits, and the dirty cereal mugs she hides under her desk, I know he really cares about her. And that he would want to fix something that means so much to her. Because neither of them would probably admit it, but they're best friends.

COLIN: Best friends are for *children*, Angelica.

CINTHIA ALVAREZ, *associate editor of the* Prepster: Oh my God. Colin Von Kohorn *is* my best friend. How did this even happen?! I need to sit down.

COLIN: Angelica was right about one thing, though: I *did* want to help Cinthia. I'd seen how hard she'd been working with her AcaBat team, and how desperately she wanted to prove to everyone that the team was just as strong this year, no matter who had graduated. And if making sure the San Anselmo Prep AcaBat team could compete to the best of its abilities meant that I had to meddle in the story, well, then I'd meddle. I couldn't believe I was about to say this, but I guess there were some things that were more important than the *Prepster*.

ANGELICA: The first thing I had to do was get the fall play out of the auditorium, so that the AcaBats had the space to themselves. I couldn't believe I was prioritizing AcaBat. What had happened to me?! Had I been sucked into the cult of Academic Battle?!

COLIN: Angelica's solution to the space issue seemed like something our most dramatic extracurricular activity would embrace with open arms.

ANGELICA: My family had gone to see *Twelfth Night* at the Marin Shakespeare Company this summer, and it was outside. And we'd seen *Fences* at Cal Shakes, and that's August Wilson, not Shakespeare, but it was outside, too. And there's this little patio area in the back of the school that opens up onto a lawn that I thought would make a *perfect* stage.

COLIN: Angelica insisted I wait in my office while she talked to Harrison. These theater types. So sensitive.

HARRISON BAXTER, *Benedick in San Anselmo Prep's production of* Much Ado About Nothing: Angelica came to me with the most brilliant idea. Outdoor Shakespeare. Of course! Of course. How had we not instituted this sooner?! That was how *all* the big festivals did it. And are we not producing festival-caliber performances here? I knew mine would be.

MS. TUSSEY, *San Anselmo Prep theater teacher*: I loved the idea. I agreed immediately. Sometimes the most important thing you can say in life is "Yes, and!" So I said, "Yes, we will move the show outside, AND it will be the best fall play that's ever been produced at San Anselmo Prep!" Why *not* do the show under the stars, just as they did in the Bard's day?

HARRISON: And *then* I realized it would be easier to light the show if we waited until after the sun set. So, technically, no one would have to choose between the homecoming game and *Much Ado.*

ANGELICA: Phase one was complete—the fall play was no longer a conflict. And the Student Council elections weren't *that* problematic. Like Ms. Hernandez had pointed out, the football players, cheerleaders, and AcaBats would just cast their ballots first.

COLIN: It was an inelegant solution. I expected no better from the administration.

HOLLY CARPENTER, *candidate*: Luckily, my speech was scheduled to go first. Thank you, alphabetical order, for placing Carpenter in front of Nithercott! I felt like that gave me just a little bit more breathing room. Since elections were during the last period of the day, all of the AcaBats would be there for the speeches and would have time to cast their votes, which, let's be honest, I desperately needed. I wouldn't be able to stay while they tallied the votes, but I would be there for the two minutes that were allotted for me to give my speech. Which was obviously more important, although having to leave without knowing if I'd won or not sounded like torture. And then I would *hustle* up to the auditorium for the first event in AcaBat. Except, of course, I then realized I'd forgotten about cheerleading. Again.

ANGELICA: So I obviously didn't have as big of a problem as Holly had. But I realized that I was also supposed to be in two places at once. Of course I had to watch the AcaBat Locals, since that was what I was writing my article on, after all, but I certainly couldn't miss the halftime show at homecoming. This was Becca's big moment! I had to be there.

BECCA: I didn't care if Angelica came to halftime or not. I didn't care if my parents came or not. It's not like *I* wanted to be there. I had been *blackmailed* into playing. Honestly, I would have considered it a greater mark of respect if no one came.

ANGELICA: I knew she didn't mean it, though. I caught her practicing the footwork for "Formation," and humming "Love on Top," with a goofy little smile on her face, when she thought no one was listening or watching. She was excited. And I was going to be there. Just like I'd been there for every single Blitzkrieg Tuba Factory concert.

HOLLY: When Angelica told me she'd figured out a way to do both AcaBat and the homecoming game, I couldn't believe it. Was this seriously going to work? Had Angelica and Colin Von Kohorn, of all people, somehow made it possible for me to be in three places at once? Angelica said it would be tight, and I could only do the halftime show, but that was more than I'd ever imagined. The sideline cheers aren't that important, anyway. Halftime was what mattered. While we were on the sidelines, Momo would just be on her phone, and she probably wouldn't be the only one.

MOMO WAKATSUKI, *cheerleader*: I got my phone out one time, okay? It was just one time! Ugh, I'm going to tape a magazine to the back of the WIN sign I hold up for the "GO, FIGHT, WIN!" sideline chant so everyone will get off my butt about this.

ANGELICA: Typically, there is a brief intermission between the math and literature sections in AcaBat, which provides a much-needed pee-and-vending-machine break for the poor siblings who are forced to sit through the whole thing. If I could get the AcaBat intermission to line up with the halftime show, Holly and I could do both. It was a big ask. But luckily, I had a secret weapon.

JAMES "HUTCH" HUTCHERSON, *older brother, Academic Battle ceremonial judge*: Angelica wanted me to ask Mrs. Halzbach to schedule the AcaBat intermission at a specific time? That seemed like a huge overreach of my position as a ceremonial judge, and highly inappropriate. Judges can't mess with the schedule. The schedule is appointed by *National Headquarters*. Nobody messes with Nationals.

AVERY DENNIS, *older brother's girlfriend, superhero*: Okay, Hutch needed to get off his high horse. The schedule had already been messed with—by me! I felt terrible that I'd created so many problems for everyone at San Anselmo Prep by trying to get Hutch to homecoming. I should have just told him there were a bunch of Pokémon lures on the football field or something. Luckily, Angelica's idea of scheduling AcaBat intermission and halftime at the same time was completely brilliant. I would have been devastated if I'd missed the Dragon Dougie.

HUTCH: I love Avery, but I wasn't going to mess with the AcaBat schedule so she could watch a dragon dance.

AVERY: Honestly, Hutch needs to just *listen* sometimes. And he definitely needs to listen to Angelica more. When she explained what had happened with the schedule, with everything happening at the same time, *of course* I promised her that Hutch would do everything in his power to fix it. It was basically my fault, after all. Of course I had to help! And if helping meant I had to exploit this Halzbach woman's megalomaniacal obsession with Hutch, well then, I'd exploit.

HUTCH: Well, I've said it before, and I'll say it again: AD is the most stubborn human on earth. And, after thinking about it, I realized San Anselmo Prep couldn't win without Holly. I knew there was no way they'd had anyone else practice giving a speech. And that's not the kind of thing you can throw someone into cold. We needed Holly. As a judge, maybe I shouldn't have been so biased toward my alma mater, but hey, I'm only human. I wanted to make sure we had the A-team we needed to win. Besides, it's not like we'd be the only team benefiting. The San Rafael AcaBats could head out at halftime and support their football team, too! So when AD made me sit down and listen, really listen, to what Angelica was saying, I have to admit, I was kind of impressed. I couldn't believe Angelica had figured out this whole scheduling mess *and* taken it upon herself to fix it. I felt, well, proud of Angelica. Maybe I should listen to her more often.

Note: I'm sorry, did a pig just fly past my window?!

MRS. MARTINE HALZBACH, *regional director of Academic Battle*: I was absolutely delighted when James gave me a call! That boy is such a treasure.

ANGELICA: I had James call Mrs. Halzbach on speaker so I could listen in. The way she fawned over him was still the worst, but if I could take advantage of James's golden-boy status to fix this homecoming nightmare, I would.

MRS. HALZBACH: Of course I was more than happy to schedule the intermission at a time that was convenient for James! As regional director, I provide the timetable to Nationals, and they cleared it without issue. It was absolutely darling that James wanted both Academic Battle teams to be able to see the homecoming halftime show. I loved his whole idea about how the biggest athletically competitive day of the year is also now the most academically competitive day of the year. Why shouldn't the AcaBat teams get, er, "pumped up" by their school mascots and cheerleaders?

AVERY: I wrote that part, about the greatest day of intellectual combat of the year! Hutch toned it down a bit too much when he talked to Mrs. Halzbach, but he at least got the essence across.

ANGELICA: We had done it. There would be a break in Academic Battle just in time for the homecoming halftime show. The worst scheduling disaster in the history of San Anselmo Prep had been unraveled. Now Holly Carpenter, and anyone else who wanted to, could go to the Student Council elections, the Academic Battle Locals, the homecoming game, and the fall play. Oh, and the dance at night, too, if they were so inclined. It was a victory for humans with many interests everywhere.

CINTHIA: Watching Colin and Angelica work was incredible. They'd created this color-coded Excel spreadsheet, moving blocks around, freeing up spaces. I don't know why Principal Patel hadn't worked this hard to fix things when Colin and Angelica first told him it was a problem. It was really *his* problem, after all.

ANGELICA: Well, of course, it wouldn't have even been a problem—or as big of a problem—if Principal Patel just hadn't listened to Andrew Nithercott in the first place.

COLIN: I stopped dead in my tracks, leaving a word half-typed. What had Angelica just said?

ANGELICA: Oh my gosh. In the panic of trying to find the missing head, and then the total relief at finding it, and, um, I'm not going to lie, being kind of distracted by Ben, I had completely forgotten to tell Colin that Andrew Nithercott had purposefully scheduled the Student Council elections so that Holly wouldn't be there.

COLIN: I made her repeat it several times. Andrew Nithercott had willfully manipulated the democratic process? She couldn't possibly have proof.

ANGELICA: I did, though. I had Andrew saying it on the record. I had a voice recording.

COLIN: Right then, I needed to know exactly what Andrew Nithercott had said.

ANGELICA: I showed him everything. How Principal Patel had scheduled the elections when Andrew told him to, seemingly oblivious that he was blocking Holly from running. Andrew, however, was anything *but* oblivious.

COLIN: Forget the scheduling disaster. Or my little brother's Grand Theft Mascot Head. *This* was the story.

THE ELECTION

ANGELICA: I couldn't tell you a single thing that happened in school on Friday. I have no idea what we read in English or what we said in French or what we did in math. Well, I rarely remember what we did in math, so maybe that's not a great metric.

COLIN VON KOHORN, *editor in chief*: The schedule had been slightly condensed, so that there was an activity period at the end of the day for the Student Council elections. Each of these activity periods was staggered, so that only one grade at a time would be in the cafeteria. Somehow, the administration managed not to screw it up.

MS. HERNANDEZ, *registrar*: Now *these* are the types of things I schedule. Concurrent activity periods. Not major events.

BECCA: Student Council elections. What a charade. No one in student government can get anything done, anyway. Why even bother to enact this farce? I wondered if I should run next year on an anarchy platform and see if I could disband the whole thing. That would be an even greater legacy to leave behind than the memory of Blitzkrieg Tuba Factory.

HOLLY CARPENTER, *candidate*: Sophomore elections were being held second to last, after the juniors but before the freshmen. As I sat in study hall in homeroom, I looked over my notes for my speech, hoping that it was good enough to win. That *I* was good enough to win.

ANDREW NITHERCOTT, *candidate*: What a glorious day for democracy. Yes, an unknown bandit may have defaced my campaign posters, and yes, the aforementioned bandit had not been apprehended by either the administration or my investigative attempts at unmasking him, but in the end, his attempts to discredit me were futile. The posters were removed promptly, the name of Nithercott remained unsullied, and according to the informal poll I'd conducted, I knew my victory was assured. As I filed into the cafeteria, surrounded by my sloppily dressed classmates, I had never felt more confident. Change was on the horizon. Soon these untucked shirts and scuffed shoes would be a thing of the past, and San Anselmo Prep would return to its former greatness.

HOLLY: They had set up a podium along one side of the cafeteria wall, with a row of folding chairs behind for the candidates. The couple of people running for secretary and treasurer had already taken their seats.

JENNIFER "JENSY" STUDENROTH, *cheerleader*: Lunch had just happened, like, two hours ago, and the seats were *not* particularly clean. I had to pick a piece of lettuce out of a place *no one* should ever have a piece of lettuce.

HOLLY: I felt someone squeeze my hand. Tanner E. I looked up into his open, friendly face, and somehow I didn't feel as nervous as I had before. Together, we walked past the podium and took our seats.

TANNER ERICKSEN, *the kicker, not the one in marching band*: This was Holly's moment. She was here to win. She just needed to remember that.

ANGELICA: I was already sitting by the time Andrew Nithercott made his grand entrance. He walked toward the last open chair with the sort of swagger that suggested he thought Drake should be playing his campaign song. I told Colin that if he voted for Nithercott again this year, I'd kill him.

COLIN: I reminded Angelica that threats of violence have no place in the democratic process. Even if one of the candidates is an amoral malefactor.

HOLLY: The treasurer and secretary speeches went by in a blur.

TANNER E.: I didn't spend that much time on my speech. It seemed like a waste of time when you are running unopposed. I pretty much said, "Vote for me, because you have no other choice," and that was it. The applause was more enthusiastic than I'd expected.

HOLLY: And then it was my turn. Of course I was nervous. But as soon as I made it to the podium, and placed my hands on the worn wood, and looked out at my classmates, all the nerves went away. This was where I was supposed to be. I was ready.

TANNER E.: The eyes of the whole sophomore class were on Holly.

HOLLY: "Some of you know me as Holly Carpenter, cheerleader," I said.

JENSY: I gave Holly a thumbs-up. She so had this!

HOLLY: "Some of you know me from AcaBat. And some of you may know me from my tenure as your freshman class secretary. But the truth is, I'm not really any one of those things," I continued. "Who I am is Holly Carpenter, San Anselmo Prep student. Just like each and every one of you. Maybe you're not involved in as many activities as I am, or maybe you're involved in more, but none of those activities define who you are. At the end of the day, we all have one thing in common: this school. And that commonality is far bigger than any of our differences. There is no such thing as a perfect high school experience, but I promise, if you elect me as your Student Council president, I will work my hardest to make this the best sophomore year you could possibly have. I love this school. And if you don't love it, well, I'll do my best to find you something to love about it, too. Most of you know me. And if you don't know me, get to know me. I don't have an office, but my locker door is always open. Stop by. Introduce yourself. Tell me what can make our class, make this school, better. The president's most important role is to represent the students and to be their advocate. Let me be your advocate. I don't have any grand campaign promises of free pizza every afternoon, or an ability to get rid of the dress code. That's not realistic. What I do have is the promise that I am here to listen. I am here to fight for what you want. And I am here to be your class president."

TANNER E.: She. Was. Brilliant. I rose to my feet while the rest of the class exploded in applause.

HOLLY: It went well, I think. I mean, it felt like it went well. Weirdly, I started shaking after I sat down, like all the adrenaline was leaving my body in a big whoosh.

TANNER E.: She had done it. Now all we had to do was endure Andrew Nithercott, and hope that he didn't bamboozle anyone into voting him.

ANGELICA: Why was Andrew even giving his speech? As soon as I'd told Colin what Nithercott had done with the scheduling, I was sure he'd want to go confront Principal Patel with it, as part of his mission to "take down Patel." Maybe I should have gone to Principal Patel with it the minute I'd found out about it, but at first I wasn't sure it was that big of a deal, since Andrew said it so casually, and then I got way too caught up in everything that was going on. Which made me, I guess, not a very good reporter, or a very good detective, or a very good whistle-blower. Maybe I was only good at writing poems about bugs.

COLIN: Would Principal Patel disqualify Nithercott from running? There was no way of knowing what he would or wouldn't do. This was a situation that was outside the purview of the handbook. Nothing had, in fact, been added to it on the subject of student government since Principal Patel instituted a two-term limit for class presidents, and that was years ago. I did, of course, have every intention of alerting him to the extent of Nithercott's machinations, in the hopes that I might get him to implicate himself. But for now, it was time to let democracy run its course. If Holly did win, she deserved to feel like she beat him fair and square in an open race. Not because he'd been forced to resign before the election.

ANGELICA: Was this *empathy*, coming from Colin Von Kohorn?

COLIN: Angelica had a weird sort of misty look in her eyes. I told her to focus on the speeches.
  Note: I wasn't getting "misty." And even if I was, so what?! The Tin Man had found his heart! It had been there all along! It was a moment!

TANNER E.: Andrew Nithercott is so slimy, he practically left a trail behind him as he oozed up to the podium. I couldn't wait to get this over with. And then, hopefully, we'd never have to hear another Nithercott speech again. Or at least not this year, anyway.

ANDREW: I looked out over my assembled peers. The crowd was in the palm of my hand already. I could feel it. Holly's speech had been cute, I suppose, but it was hardly professional. Exactly the problem with her candidacy.

TANNER E.: I considered myself extremely fortunate that I got to look at the back of Nithercott's head. Definitely his best angle.

ANDREW: "Being a student at San Anselmo Prep used to mean something," I said. "It meant a firm handshake. A starched collar. A respectful young man who would look you in the eye and guarantee that his word was his bond, and that was a guarantee you could take to the bank."

BECCA: So in Andrew Nithercott's idealized version of San Anselmo Prep, women, what, just didn't exist?

COLIN: San Anselmo Prep used to be an all-boys school. It had only gone coed in the early 1960s. Perhaps Andrew Nithercott was calling for a return to single-sex education? Although I highly doubted that was the kind of thing the Student Council could make happen.

BECCA: What a sexist boob. I couldn't believe I had another ninety seconds of this trash to endure.

ANDREW: "That is the San Anselmo Prep I propose a return to," I continued. "What that hearkens back to is the values of an earlier era, where tradition, respect, and discipline were prized. These are the foundations upon which education was built. Sadly, in recent years, our foundation has shown its cracks. Sloppy adherence to the dress code. Frivolous after-school activities that drain our financial resources. Immodest uniforms in some of our athletic organizations."

JENSY: Immodest uniforms?! I was going to go up there and tackle him.

BECCA: I was sitting behind Jensy Studenroth. She looked like she was going to rush the podium, but then decided against it. Too bad. I would have *loved* to have seen a cheerleader take down Andrew Nithercott.

ANDREW: "We need discipline. Consistency. High expectations. Without these things, we may be good, but we will never be great. Good is the enemy of great. Join me, and let's make San Anselmo Prep great again."

BECCA: Nithercott's speech was finally over. And *that* was great.

ACABAT LOCALS, PART ONE

ANGELICA: The football team, the cheerleaders, the AcaBats, and the marching band got to cast their votes first so they could head off to their next activity and begin the marathon that was homecoming. Despite being in none of those groups, I slipped in next to Cinthia to cast my ballot. I couldn't miss a minute of AcaBat. I owed it to the *Prepster*'s readers to capture every single thing that happened—even if, as I suspected, nothing particularly interesting would happen.

CINTHIA ALVAREZ, *AcaBat*: Angelica walked up to the ballot box with the rest of the AcaBats, and it just felt right. Maybe spending so much time on this story had finally convinced her to join the team!

Note: We'll see about that.

HOLLY CARPENTER, *candidate*: It felt weird to vote for myself, but of course I did, since the only other option was Andrew Nithercott. And then we were off to the auditorium for Locals, and I had no idea when I would find out the election results.

COLIN VON KOHORN, *editor in chief*: The entire sophomore class voted with a minimum of chaos. Then the last bell rang, and I was off on a date with destiny. Well, an unscheduled appointment with Principal Patel.

DAPHNE LEAKE-PALMER, *captain of the San Rafael Academy AcaBats*: Here we were, back in the San Anselmo Prep auditorium once more. The whole place reeked of failure. And mediocrity. And improperly fried potatoes.

Note: The decreasing crispiness of French Fry Friday strikes again!

BEN WASHINGTON, *San Rafael Academy AcaBat*: I wondered if Angelica would be there. I kept scanning the small crowd for her as we sat on the stage, but I didn't see her anywhere. I was dangerously distracted, given that I needed all of my mental faculties for AcaBat. But Angelica was very distracting.

Note: !!!!! Now that the head had been found, I gave myself full permission to be distracted by Ben again. Because he was pretty distracting, too.

CINTHIA: The San Rafael Academy AcaBats were waiting in the auditorium already when we filed in, sitting in folding chairs on one side of the stage.

MASON BAUMGARTNER, *San Anselmo Prep AcaBat*: Daphne looked ravishing, as always. I knew she was my enemy, but I couldn't help the current that drew me inexorably toward her.

JAMES "HUTCH" HUTCHERSON, *older brother, ceremonial judge*: It was beyond surreal to be sitting on the auditorium floor at a table with the judges, instead of on the stage. If old Demon Sneak-Palmer was displeased to see me at the judges' table, she didn't let it show. Well, she did look like she'd smelled something particularly unpleasant, but that was kind of how she always looked.

AVERY DENNIS, *brother's girlfriend*: My first AcaBat competition. Someone had already told me I couldn't eat popcorn in here, so we weren't off to a great start, but I had hope that things would turn around.

ANGELICA: I don't think Ben could see me because I was sitting way in the back, trying to be unobtrusive, but I could see him. He looked so handsome in his maroon blazer and striped school tie. I could see him smile and laugh all the way from the back of the room, and I loved how confident he looked, how excited, like he knew he was about to do something he was really good at. It was a pretty stark contrast to all the nervous competitors I could see sweating clear from the other end of the auditorium. And of course I wanted San Anselmo Prep to win—I would *never* root against our school—but I really hoped Ben did well, too.

AVERY: I'll say this for AcaBats—those guys don't waste any time. Almost as soon as the San Anselmo Prep team took their seats, they started. I hadn't even gotten any of my candies unwrapped.

BEN: The first AcaBat event is UltraQuiz—my worst event. Luckily, for this one, you can work as a team. It's basically a live question-and-answer test, where you can confer with your teammates before buzzing in with your response. It covers seven different academic disciplines—teams need to be incredibly well rounded in order to succeed.

CINTHIA: Mason and Allison were particularly fantastic in UltraQuiz. We were off to an even better start than I'd hoped. Hutch who, am I right?

ALLISON WALSH, *San Anselmo Prep AcaBat*: We would have done *better* if Mason could stop looking at Daphne.

HUTCH: And this is where I started to get nervous—as UltraQuiz finished up, the Knights and the Dragons appeared to be almost exactly evenly matched. The Knights had done a little better in music and art, and we'd done a little better in math/science/econ, but no one had been able to take a commanding lead.

AVERY: Things took a dramatic turn for the worse after group Jeopardy, or whatever the first event was called. The second event was watching people write an essay?! What was I supposed to do with that?

BEN: "One aspect of the novel *Far from the Madding Crowd* is the Victorian cultural belief that women are dependent upon men. Explain how Bathsheba Everdene's conduct, both as a manager of her farm and in her relationships with others, conforms to and departs from this belief." *This* is why you need to be a well-read AcaBat. *This* was why I'd kept trying to get everyone to read the collected works of Thomas Hardy.

CINTHIA: A feminist essay prompt?! Thank you, AcaBat powers that be!

HUTCH: I'd known Cinthia was going to crush this essay. It was right in her wheelhouse. But I did *not* like the way Ben Washington was grinning while writing. It did not bode well.

BEN: AcaBat judges *love* feminist interpretations of dead white guys. And that's exactly why I roll hard with Thomas Hardy.

> *Note: I guess this explains why he talked so much about Thomas Hardy at Marin Coffee Roasters! Not that there's anything wrong with Thomas Hardy, I just have a certain threshold for distressed farm girls. There's only so much one can take.*

AVERY: I didn't think things could get worse than the essay. But they did. Or, I guess, they stayed the same. Now we were watching people silently take a multiple-choice test. I found some peanut M&M's in my purse, but that distraction didn't last long.

MRS. MARTINE HALZBACH, *regional director of Academic Battle*: There was a young woman in the front row who was extremely insistent on snacking. I probably should have had her removed, but I worried the removal would prove even more distracting to the competitors than simply confiscating her snacks.

> *Note: If she had known that young woman was the girlfriend of the perfect James Hutcherson, I think her brain might have exploded all over the auditorium floor. James Hutcherson*

would never snack in an AcaBat competition! How could he possibly associate with someone who did?!

ANGELICA: Multiple-choice proved to be as boring as I remembered. There is just nothing thrilling about watching a team of people silently take a series of seven multiple-choice tests. Even watching the cute way Ben bit his lip while he concentrated could only keep me engaged for so long. The only other fun thing was watching Avery try not to fall asleep in the front row. I could see her head bobbing as she struggled to stay awake. I was trying to come up with some way to make this interesting for the *Prepster's* readers when I felt a small poke in my side.

COLIN: I slid in the back and took a seat next to Angelica. Now that Cinthia and I had formally acknowledged that we were, in fact, friends, it seemed like going to watch her at Academic Battle Locals was the kind of thing a friend would do. And what a pleasant surprise it turned out to be! I had no idea Academic Battle involved multiple-choice tests! In a world filled with far too many shades of gray, I do enjoy the black-and-white clarity of an enumerated assessment. And I'd never been able to watch others take them before—the methodology was fascinating, if somewhat disturbing. From where I was sitting, it appeared that Cinthia's bubbling technique was inefficient, and Mason Baumgartner's was downright erratic. I looked forward to giving them some pointers after the competition.

ANGELICA: Way to bury the lede, Colin! Who had won the elections? What had Principal Patel said? Was anything going to happen to Andrew Nithercott?!

COLIN: Principal Patel seemed to be truly ignorant of the intent behind the malicious scheduling, although privately, I didn't feel that excused him from the entire debacle.

PRINCIPAL PATEL, *principal:* This was not San Anselmo Prep's Watergate. Colin Von Kohorn, despite his best efforts, is neither Woodward nor Bernstein, and I am no Nixon. You know what? Strike that. No comment.

COLIN: As for Andrew Nithercott, he has been banned from student government for life. If that's not an admission of guilt, I don't know what is. Just wait until the school board hears about this.

PRINCIPAL PATEL: There is nothing for the school board to hear about. I simply prohibited Andrew Nithercott from running for Student Council again as the most efficacious solution to the problem. I certainly have no intention of "resigning in a tempest of shame and a deluge of disgrace," as a certain student suggested. Who was it? No comment.

COLIN: But Nithercott's political ban turned out not to have mattered, anyway—Holly won by a landslide.

ANGELICA: Holly won! That was amazing. But there was no way we could tell her. She was currently sitting onstage, head bowed over her test.

COLIN: Angelica turned to a fresh sheet in her notebook, and hastily scribbled something in big block letters. I frowned at her. I hoped that wasn't distracting to the competitors! Allison Walsh had just executed a particularly sloppy page turn in her test. Maybe we had been whispering too loudly. I resolved to be quiet and give Academic Battle my complete focus. Angelica, however, had other ideas.

ANGELICA: I wasn't sure if she could see me way in the back, so I stood up on my chair, and held the notebook toward the stage.

HOLLY: I like to look up from time to time and keep an eye on the clock, so I know I'm pacing myself correctly. Hutch always said the clock can be your best friend or your worst enemy, and you should make it a friend. But when I looked toward the back of the auditorium, I didn't notice the clock. I saw Angelica standing on the chair, holding up her notebook. I squinted at what she'd written.

ANGELICA: All it said was: YOU WON.

HOLLY: And I couldn't think of two more beautiful words in the English language. But for now I had work to do. The presidency would have to wait. I flipped over to the next sheet of paper, and resumed testing.

CRAZY IN LOVE

BECCA: Well, it was happening. My overly militaristic jacket was buttoned, my horrific feather hat was fastened onto my reluctant head, and my tuba was in hand, ready to fulfill the obligation Natalie Wagner had blackmailed me into.

NATALIE WAGNER, *marching band clarinet*: Becca was waiting alone before it was time for us to head out onto the field, not talking to anyone, looking completely pissed off, like always. And then I realized that I didn't really want to blackmail her into playing. I wanted her to play for the satisfaction of a piece well played. So I took a big, huge, enormous risk. I put the whole marching band in jeopardy. I was worse than Martin!

BECCA: Natalie scampered over to me. I prepared myself for yet another "THIS IS THE GREATEST DAY OF OUR LIVES" pep talk.

CLEMENTINE RUTHERFORD, *flautist*: Natalie had shouted "THIS IS THE GREATEST DAY OF OUR LIVES" no fewer than fourteen separate times the Friday of homecoming. Was it the greatest day of our lives? I don't know. We hadn't even played anything yet. And the French fries at lunch were *not* crispy.

NATALIE: All week long, Becca had been, quite honestly, amazing. She had learned the piece perfectly, she had put in so much time at rehearsal, and she had proved herself to be incredibly dependable. She wasn't even acting particularly snarky when she was hanging out with us after school. I think I only counted, like, four eye rolls, the entire time she'd been playing with us. It was probably a new record for Becca Horn. And you know what? Maybe I had blackmailed her into being there. But she hadn't been acting like someone who'd been blackmailed.

BECCA: Natalie didn't give me a pep talk. She gave me the last thing I ever expected her to give me.

NATALIE: I was actually really sad to see it go. I'm sure Becca thinks I kept it just to blackmail her, but that's not it at all. I kept it because of how happy we both look. And how adorable we are. And even if Becca likes to pretend we weren't friends, I know we were. And I like having a picture to remind me of that.

BECCA: The picture. Natalie Wagner gave me the picture. I couldn't believe it. She must have had backups or a digital copy or something.

NATALIE: The picture I handed Becca was the one and only copy. My mom had taken it, and she wouldn't understand how to upload a picture to the cloud if her life depended on it. Almost the entire record of my early childhood had been obliterated when she dropped her phone in the sink. But luckily, this picture had been saved. I'd asked her to print out a copy because it was one of my favorites.

BECCA: I stared at the picture in disbelief, at young, dumb Becca, who looked so insanely happy.

NATALIE: I don't know why Becca is so embarrassed about the picture. We look so cute! But I guess she's embarrassed because it proves that Becca is, well, you know. Blond.

BECCA: I wasn't embarrassed that the picture revealed I was a natural blonde. We can't help the hair color we're born with. And I dyed it purple, then green, then blue, then black, then blue again, just as soon as my mom would let me. I'm embarrassed because of what dumb five-year-old Becca is wearing.

NATALIE: Becca loved that Cinderella dress. She would put it on the minute she got home, and I'd put on my Little Mermaid costume, and we would play princesses for hours and hours. I have to admit, it *is* pretty funny that Cinderella was her favorite princess. Can you even imagine Becca saying stuff like "Have courage and be kind"? Hard to picture it, right? Believe me, she used to say it all the time.

BECCA: I looked at little me, in her blue ball gown, proudly showing off her glass slippers, and *hugging* Natalie Wagner in her dumb fish dress. What. An. Idiot. How could Cinderella have been my favorite princess?! She is the worst! She doesn't *do* anything. She takes so much crap from her stepfamily, just cleaning and cleaning, and then a makeover and a man save the day? Ugh. You disgust me, little Becca.

NATALIE: Much to my surprise, Becca didn't rip the picture up. She carefully put it in her pants pocket.

BECCA: Yeah, I decided to keep it. It definitely wasn't something I wanted the whole school to see—but I thought I might show Angelica. And my mom. And maybe Cinthia, too. After all, even I could admit it was pretty funny. Sometimes Cinderella grows up to be a blue-haired lesbian, I guess.

> Note: If I hadn't seen it with my own eyes, I'm not sure I would have believed it. Becca Horn dressed as Cinderella. I wondered if I could get a copy, too.

NATALIE: And now it was time for the moment of truth. Would Becca still play, even though she had the picture?

BECCA: Natalie was just staring at me. Was she expecting me to hug her or something? That wasn't happening.

NATALIE: "What are you staring at, Wagner?" she snapped. "Don't we have a show to do?"

BECCA: And then, I should have seen this coming—she hugged *me*. I endured it.

NATALIE: I couldn't help it. The hug was involuntary! Becca was going to play—because she *wanted* to. Marching band had worked its magic, just like I'd hoped it would! And now all we had to do was deliver the greatest halftime show San Anselmo Prep had ever seen.

KATE ROWND, *percussion*: I heard the buzzer. It was go time. The Ramos twins and I set the beat, and we marched out onto the field. I know this sounds like something Natalie would say, but it honestly felt like we were marching out to meet our destiny.

CLEMENTINE: The roar of the crowd was deafening. It seemed like there were more people in the stands than there were last year.

ANGELICA: There probably *were* more people in the stands than there were last year. Because both schools' AcaBat teams were there, and I thought I spotted Harrison Baxter and some of the other theater kids there, too. And because Becca was here, for once, this might have been the first time in San Anselmo Prep history that the entire school was at homecoming.

JENNIFER "JENSY" STUDENROTH, *cheerleader*: We waited with our poms on our hips as the marching band filed onto the field, playing a percussive beat. But where was Holly?!

HOLLY CARPENTER, *cheerleader*: I made it! I'd cut it a little close, but I made it! I did a poorly executed cartwheel into my place in the V.

JENSY: I sent Holly a mental hug, because I obviously couldn't break my place in formation.

HOLLY: The Dragon, bless his furry heart, did a much better cartwheel that made mine look like it had been planned.

FINN AQUINO, *Dragon*: No exaggeration—homecoming was the best day of my life. When I jogged onto the field with the football team, for a minute, I was overwhelmed by how many people were in the stands. But then I did some coffee grinders, the crowd cheered, and just like that, it was on. That crowd was in the palm of my furry Dragon claw. I felt invincible.

MOMO WAKATSUKI, *cheerleader*: That dumb Dragon was so happy. I couldn't actually see Finn's face, obviously, because his precious head had been recovered, but I could just tell he was grinning from ear to ear. And I guess I was happy for him. Like, if a big, green, furry suit can make you that happy, well, then, you do you.

BECCA: The horns came in for the beginning of "Crazy in Love," and, well, Natalie was right. Being part of that was pretty incredible.

FINN: The standing backflip at the beginning of "Crazy in Love" went perfectly. I wished Tripp could have been there to see it. He would have been so proud.

TRIPP GOMEZ-PARKER, *former Dragon*: Of course I was there to see Li'l Dragon's big moment! I just didn't tell him because I didn't want him to get all, like, up in his head about Big Papa Dragon in the audience. That kind of pressure can really mess with you. Also, Avery would not leave me alone until I agreed to come to homecoming. Every morning, I woke up to a text that said, "WHY DIDN'T YOU RSVP TO MY E-VITE YET?!?!"

AVERY DENNIS, *alumni coordinator*: Ninety-five percent attendance. The highest alumni attendance of any class in the history of San Anselmo Prep homecoming. I coordinated those alumni like nobody's business. There were only three I couldn't get to commit to coming back, and, like, I *guess* "traveling the world in the name of science" is a valid excuse. Kind of.

JAMES "HUTCH" HUTCHERSON, *older brother*: Alex Manevitz isn't actually "on a quest for scientific truth." It just seemed easier to tell Avery that he was in a foreign country instead of refusing to "place one foot on that godforsaken soil ever again." Cressida actually *is* out of the country, though, and she wasn't flying back from Oxford for this. And then Tamsin Brewer fractured her pelvis at the last minute. Avery offered to drive her over from the hospital, but apparently, Tamsin's doctors strongly advised against it.

AVERY: Ninety-five percent. So close to perfection, and yet so far. Poor Tamsin Brewer and her fragile pelvis. Well, if anything, I just felt bad for those three. They were missing one heck of a show. This was even better than the "Bad Blood" halftime show had been last year! And I'd thought that was un-toppable.

HOLLY: Was it just my imagination, or were we actually dancing in sync? On the beat?! It seemed as though some sort of miracle had occurred, and for the first time in San Anselmo Prep history, everyone on the cheer squad actually looked like we knew what we were doing. I've gotta say, the Dragon was on point this year. Maybe that was what did it.

FINN: Holly said I was on point? That's awesome! I felt pretty on point. I was so high on adrenaline the whole thing feels like a blur of green fuzz and sweat.

NATALIE: As we played, I thought that might have been the happiest moment of my life. But then I realized that there was only one thing missing: someone to share it with. And there was only one person I wanted to share marching band and pizza and everything else with. I love Martin Shen. I do. I love him. And I don't care *what* he does with his wrists anymore. I just want to be with him.

MARTIN SHEN, *sidelined tuba player*: As marching band powered through their Beyoncé medley, each riff and hook better than the last, I had a moment of perfect clarity. I was Crazy in Love. Natalie was my Love on Top. I didn't want her to be a Single Lady anymore. I would wear that stupid wrist brace every day for the rest of my life if it meant that she would hold the hand attached to it. I mean, if she would hold my hand. Just in case that wasn't clear.

NATALIE: I played my heart out. Every note I blew was for Martin. I hoped he could hear me, or feel it, somehow, all the way out in the stands.

MARTIN: Watching marching band from the sidelines had been torture. I belonged out there on that field with them. I belonged with Natalie. So I ran to her.

TANNER ERICKSEN, *the kicker, not the one in marching band*: The stadium exploded when marching band finished their medley. It was the loudest noise I had ever heard, the roar of the crowd, and even though it wasn't for the football team, it still felt pretty amazing.

BECCA: It felt . . . incredible. I can't believe I'm saying this, but it did. I can admit it. Every note was perfect, and I felt like I really understood, for the first time, that there is power in being part of something that's bigger than myself. Because the music we had created was incredible. And as great as I am, one tuba couldn't have created that all by itself. We'd come together to make something so much better than anyone could have ever made alone. And I guess that was worth wearing the stupid feathery hat.

> Note: I'm so happy that Becca finally understands the joy of school activities! Maybe she'll even join French Club next year. The sky's the limit!

NATALIE: I wanted to cheer and jump around and scream and dance, because the number had gone so well! But that wouldn't have been professional. And then I saw him. Martin was racing down the stairs, he was running onto the field, and I knew, I just knew, that he was coming for me.

MARTIN: I ran to Natalie, as fast as I could, which is not, admittedly, very fast. She dropped her clarinet to the ground, and came running toward me, and that's when I knew it was love, because she would never drop her clarinet for anything less. Handling an instrument roughly can cause it to sustain long-term damage.

TANNER E.: I couldn't believe it. Martin Shen and Natalie Wagner were making out on the field *again*! Why didn't homecoming have these magical powers for me?

FINN: I forgot that I was supposed to be doing things. There was so much happening on that field! But obviously this was a moment the Dragon had to react to. I just started freestyling around Natalie and Martin. I had a feeling no one was looking at *me*, though.

JENSY: It happened again! Martin wasn't even playing the tuba this year, and I thought, okay, maybe this is my year, you go for it, Jensy, go ahead and make a move. And Natalie Wagner got to him first, *again*! Well, technically, he came to her, but still. Ugh. I guess it's officially over for me and Martin. Who am I to stand in the way of true love?

TANNER PETERSON, *the one in marching band*: Martin Shen started a tiny exodus from the stands. When I saw Timo running onto the field, I thought he was coming to congratulate me. Ha!

TIMO WAKATSUKI, *sophomore*: I was sitting close enough to the field that I could see Jensy Studenroth crying. I thought she might need a shoulder to cry on. I've always liked tall women.

TANNER P.: Timo thinks he has a chance with Jensy?! Good luck, buddy.

CLEMENTINE: Timo was running onto the field! Maybe he was coming for me?! Was this the moment to forgive him for his misadventures in dairy? Maybe we could start anew, now that he was fully aware of my dietary restrictions.

TIMO: I thought I was making my way to Jensy, but then I was intercepted by Clementine Rutherford, of all people! I knew hanging out in marching band long enough would pay off! Good thing I had seriously minted-up before the game.

AVERY: What. Was. Happening? I'd thought San Anselmo Prep had been dramatic when I'd gone there, but now everyone was just kissing, like, the entire marching band, right there on the field?! It was pandemonium.

ANDREW NITHERCOTT, *defeated sophomore class presidential candidate*: We were mere hours into the Carpenter presidency, and the school had already gone to hell in a handbasket, exactly as I'd expected. It was like the last days of Rome out there on the field.

TANNER E.: All I wanted to do was kiss Holly, but of course I couldn't, because it would look like I was just jumping on the bandwagon, and I'd wanted to kiss Holly forever, and if it ever happened, it couldn't be part of some, like, weird mass marching-band-make-out.

PRINCIPAL PATEL, *principal*: Unacceptable. This was completely unacceptable! Flagrant public displays of affection as far as the eye could see! It took the ref far too long to remove them all.

TANNER E.: That poor ref. This was definitely not what he'd signed up for. But eventually, he got all the marching band kids off the field, the cheerleaders went back to the sidelines, and it was time for the second half.

BROOKS MANDEVILLE, *quarterback*: Were we down thirty to nothing? Yes, yes, we were. But did that mean we were out of the game? No way. No way, man. This second half was our time. I could taste it. Victory was ours!

HOLLY: I sprinted down the field and back toward the auditorium. The football team would have to go on without me. The AcaBats needed me now.

ACABAT LOCALS, PART TWO

ANGELICA: The second half of AcaBat starts off with the last two multiple-choice tests, which gives you one last chance for a nap before it starts to get interesting.

COLIN VON KOHORN, *apparently obsessed with AcaBat now*: Angelica was missing *everything*! Mason Baumgartner must have finally hit a section he was confident in, because his bubbling had gone from erratic to *masterful*. He flew down the page with such speed, agility, and precision it felt like watching a virtuoso violinist play his Stradivarius. Not a note—or bubble—was out of tune. How could Angelica be sleeping through this?! There was *genius* happening on that stage!

> Note: I'm sure there was genius on that stage, but I don't think that's something you can detect from watching someone silently take a test. There definitely was an insane person in the audience, because he was sitting next to me and would not stop poking me.

HOLLY CARPENTER, *AcaBat*: Once the multiple-choice tests are done, interview and speech are the final two sections. I do both, for our team, which isn't totally typical, but we don't have anyone who loves to talk quite as much as I do. And interview is just like being in a pageant—you answer questions about yourself, and as long as you're polite and articulate, it's hard to screw it up. We have a lot of very, um, opinionated people on our team, though, who often, um, struggle with coming off as polite.

COLIN: Interview? The next section was interview?! I couldn't believe what I was hearing! What could be more thrilling than watching an interview, live, in real time?!

Note: I had never seen someone so excited about Academic Battle. When they announced the interview was next, he literally jumped out of his seat a little bit.

DAPHNE LEAKE-PALMER, *San Rafael Academy AcaBat captain*: Now that Hutch had graduated, it looked like they were having AcaBat Barbie do both speech *and* interview?! A truly unconventional move. Everyone else on the team must have been an inarticulate troll. I stifled a laugh when I saw her waltz back into the auditorium in her cheerleading uniform. Was this some kind of a joke?!

HOLLY: Obviously, competing at AcaBat in my cheer uniform wasn't my first choice. I felt more than a little embarrassed, but what else was I supposed to do? It was better to be in my cheer uniform and on time than in a more professional outfit but late. I just smiled and head my held high, like my mom had taught me, and pretended that this was exactly the outfit I wanted to be wearing. I'd conducted interviews wearing way more ridiculous outfits than this back when I did pageants. At least there were no rhinestones slowly working their way into my butt crack.

JAMES "HUTCH" HUTCHERSON, *older brother, ceremonial AcaBat judge*: Holly's interview was fantastic, as always. Super polite, super professional, everything the judges like to see.

HOLLY: The interview question they started me off with was "Do you feel it's important to be involved in extracurricular activities? Please explain." Hilarious, right? Luckily, I had a lot to say on that topic.

BEN WASHINGTON, *San Rafael Academy AcaBat*: I remembered Holly from last year, and her interview was as strong as I'd remembered. But I wasn't intimidated. I love interview. It's what I'm good at, and I know it's what I'm here for. I shook the judges' hands, and gave it my best shot.

ANGELICA: Watching Ben introduce himself to the judges— you have to start off with, like, thirty seconds of talking about yourself—I sort of felt like I was Facebook-stalking him, learning things I hadn't learned about him in real life yet, like that he has three older sisters, and he watches every 49ers game with his dad, and that he was on the school newspaper, although that last one I did know. And I wondered if maybe Ben and I would ever watch a 49ers game together, and I wondered what it would be like to watch football played by people who actually knew how to play football, and what it would be like to watch with Ben.

BEN: "What do you enjoy most about school?" It's a simple question. Sometimes the simple questions are the best, because you can take them in any direction you want. And, well, I *do* enjoy school.

ANGELICA: Words. That was what he said he enjoyed most about school—*words*. The different texts they read in English class, because even if he didn't love the book, he loved *talking* about the book, hearing other people's opinions, and expressing his own. He read as much as he possibly could, and then he felt like he understood so much more about the book and the world and himself after talking about it. And as much as he loved reading and talking, he might almost love writing more, not just in class, but for the newspaper, too. Because there was so much that was wrong with the world, and nothing would ever change if we didn't talk about it, write about it, read about it. Words might seem like small things, but they were the biggest instruments of change we had.

COLIN: Sure, they might have seemed like softball questions, but it is a testament to the skill of both interviewer and subject to have a softball question yield a riveting response—it's the art of making sure the right person gets the right question. And Ben Washington had certainly gotten the right question.

ANGELICA: I had never—*never*—heard someone speak about words like that. Who felt the same magic I felt while reading, who understood that a book had a whole second life beyond when you read it, when you wrestled with it and thought about it and talked about it and wrote about it, and that was how books stayed with you long after you'd finished them. How words changed you and made you who you are. Sometimes I felt like I was composed entirely of the words I'd read and written and spoken, and I knew that if I told Ben that, he'd know exactly what I'd meant. Because he loved words, too, and he understood everything they were, and everything they could be—and it was that *could be* that was the most beautiful thing about them. And I couldn't wait to talk to him about it.

HUTCH: As much as I hate to admit it, that Washington kid was good. Scary good. All of the judges were smiling and nodding, and from what I could see, it looked like he had gotten extremely high marks, all across the board. Could Washington be the X-factor that finally took us down?

Note: I don't know what James is going to do when he finds out I'm dating Ben. He might not even let a San Rafael Academy Knight through the front door. Maybe we'll have dinner on the lawn. At least that way no one will try to talk to us about particle physics.

COLIN: I hadn't thought anything could possibly improve on multiple choice, but interview had been *even better*. I couldn't wait to see what came next.

ANGELICA: The interviews were finished. Ben took his seat, and it felt sort of like he'd cast a spell over the auditorium that was now broken. I knew that was the kind of simile Colin would criticize as hopelessly inane, but, well, it was how I felt.

AVERY DENNIS, *brother's girlfriend*: People were talking! I was awake! I ate a pretzel and no one noticed! Things were looking up!

Note: In case you are keeping track, Avery packed no fewer than four separate snacks in her purse.

ANGELICA: I was surprised to find myself getting somewhat swept up in the rush of AcaBat, in a way I never really had before when watching James compete. The pressure in the room was *intense*.

DAPHNE: Finally, it was time for my big moment: the speeches.

HOLLY: In the impromptu speech section of AcaBat, you only have sixty seconds between when you see the prompt and when you start talking. After that, you only have between ninety seconds and two minutes to deliver your speech. That's it. We're looking at a maximum of three minutes, with almost no time to prepare, that can decide the fate of your entire team. You need to have nerves of steel.

COLIN: A speech with *no preparation*?! My God. These AcaBats were invincible.

MRS. CARPENTER, *Holly's mom*: Holly looked cool as a cucumber waiting for her prompt. Not a drop of sweat on her. And it wasn't just the pressed powder working its magic, either.

HOLLY: I did feel remarkably relaxed, waiting for the prompt. Maybe because I always think, "Hey, it could be worse. You could be wearing hair extensions and an uncomfortable sequined dress that's glued to your body."

HUTCH: I'd read the prompt before it was handed over to Holly and Demon Sneak-Palmer. "A triathlon consists of swimming, running, and biking. If you were to create your own triathlon, which three sports would you choose to make up this event?"

HOLLY: I almost laughed out loud. What had today been, if not a triathlon? Student Council, cheerleading, and Academic Battle. Maybe they weren't really sports, except for cheer. And you're supposed to shy away from personal anecdotes for speech, and save that for interview, but I couldn't help myself. And last year, I'd gotten some pretty solid advice from one of the greats.

HUTCH: Trust your first instinct. Go with your gut. Sixty seconds isn't long enough to second-guess yourself.

DAPHNE: I was all too happy to go first. I knew instantly what I would discuss. This country has enough sporting events. What we need is a cultural triathlon. First, one would create an artistic work from a pre-agreed-upon medium, such as oil paints or watercolors. Secondly, one would play an instrument of one's own choosing. Thirdly, one would recite one of Shakespeare's sonnets. Contestants would be graded on proficiency and selection of theme and materials.

BEN: I winced as Daphne gave her speech. I didn't think she knew how elitist she sounded, but man, it was rough.

COLIN: Not a poor idea from the opposing team, but severely lacking in its execution.

HUTCH: A total snooze from Demon Sneak-Palmer, as per usual. San Rafael Academy was really shooting themselves in the foot by not letting Ben Washington do the speech. He'd nailed the interview. I'm sure his speech would have been phenomenal.

TANNER ERICKSEN, *the kicker, not the one in marching band*: I'd made it! I had run all the way from the field, still in my grass-stained uniform. I never know how it gets those grass stains, considering that I never do anything, but that's a mystery for another day. Sure, we had been destroyed, but I wasn't even that bummed out about it. I was just happy I'd made it.

BROOKS MANDEVILLE, *quarterback*: Fifty-two to nothing. They had destroyed us. *Fifty-two to nothing.* I'm sorry, I just . . . I can't talk about it right now.

JENNIFER "JENSY" STUDENROTH, *cheerleader*: Poor Brooks! He looked so sad when he was walking off the field. After the game, I found him sitting under the bleachers, crying. I sat down next to him and gave him a little hug. I really wanted to make it to AcaBat to support Holly, but have you ever tried to move a weeping quarterback? It's tricky.

TANNER E.: I slipped into the back doors of the auditorium as a dark-haired girl I didn't recognize left the stage among a smattering of polite applause. And there was Holly, walking center stage, the light shining on her blond hair, standing tall and confident in her cheer uniform. She was radiant.

255

HOLLY: Honestly, I can't even remember what I said. I think I just told them about my day. About all three of the things I'd done, and why they were all so important to me, and the people who had made it possible for me to do all those things, and how they were what had really made it so special. And then I'm pretty sure I related that back to being a triathlon, metaphorically. Somehow.

HUTCH: It was certainly an unconventional move, especially coming from Holly, who tended to deliver pitch-perfect variations on your textbook AcaBat speeches. But sometimes risks pay off, like with what I did with my "Math is a universal language" speech. Because I'd . . . You know what? You're probably sick of me talking about that, huh, Angelica? And what I did last year doesn't really matter. What really matters is that Holly spoke right from her heart, and for two minutes, she let us into her world. And that, to me, is what speech is supposed to be about. A two-minute window into someone else's world, someone else's viewpoint. Don't get me wrong, I love UltraQuiz, and all those multiple-choice tests, but in some ways, I think speech shows what's best about AcaBat. Seeing how people think, because that's what shows you who they are. Je pense, donc je suis. I just hoped the judges felt the same way I did. Demon Sneak-Palmer's speech had been pretty wretched, but it did follow your typical AcaBat speech a little more closely.

ANGELICA: I could not believe James had cut himself off from talking about "Math is a universal language." Previously, it had been his favorite topic of conversation. But listening to James talk about speech, I felt like I didn't just understand AcaBat, finally, but I understood James a little bit better, too. This was what he really loved, maybe even more than his experiments and science fair projects, and certainly more than winning all his contests and competitions—he loved thinking, and he loved learning about the way other people think. And you know what? *I* love learning about the way other people think, too. It's why I love reading so much. And I finally saw that maybe James and I weren't so different after all. "Je pense, donc je suis"—I think, therefore I am. It pretty much summed up who James is. And it pretty much summed up who I am, too. And that was something I was proud to have in common with my brother. So maybe being "Hutch's little sister" wasn't such a bad thing after all. He was smart, but that didn't mean I was stupid. It just meant that we were smart in different ways. And watching all the different categories in AcaBat, I realized the whole point of AcaBat was to celebrate all the different ways there were to be smart, and that, actually, was pretty cool.

DAPHNE: Had AcaBat Barbie gone completely insane? Maybe the sorry excuse for a cartwheel she'd done while shaking her pom-poms had rattled her brain. I don't know what I'd just witnessed. But it certainly wasn't an Academic Battle–caliber speech.

TANNER E.: Holly was perfect. Listening to her talk about homecoming had been even better than living it, and it had just happened. I hoped she could see me from where I was. I unfolded my poster and held it high above my head.

HOLLY: Something caught my eye in the back of the room. What was going on with all these people holding up posters today? I swear, that has never happened at any AcaBat event I've ever been to before. It's really not a posters-and-face-paint kind of thing. And when I saw what it was, this time, I actually did laugh out loud. Luckily, I was offstage by that point.

TANNER E.: She saw me. I know she did, because she looked right at me and laughed, and even though I was too far away to actually hear anything, I knew exactly what it sounded like, because I'd heard her laugh a hundred times before, and I wanted to hear it a hundred times more.

HOLLY: I guess I knew who had defaced all of Andrew Nithercott's campaign posters. Because Tanner E. was holding one over his head, and he'd drawn a magnificent mustache on Andrew, and above his head, in a little speech bubble, he'd written HOLLY, WILL YOU GO TO THE DANCE WITH ME?

TANNER E.: She looked right at me and mouthed, "YES."

THE DANCE

BEN WASHINGTON, *San Rafael Academy AcaBat*: The rest of the team could not get out of San Anselmo Prep fast enough.

DAPHNE LEAKE-PALMER, *captain of the San Rafael Academy AcaBats*: It was appalling. Outrageous. Disgraceful. The judges had obviously been prejudiced against us. Including Hutch on the judging panel was almost certainly illegal. I was going to launch a formal complaint with AcaBat Nationals, and I was confident that they would rescind San Anselmo Prep's "victory."

JAMES "HUTCH" HUTCHERSON, *older brother, ceremonial judge*: As I tried to explain to Demon Sneak-Palmer, I was a ceremonial judge only, and my scores weren't tabulated. I had literally nothing to do with the scores. But I don't think she could hear me because of how loudly she was yelling.

MASON BAUMGARTNER, *San Anselmo Prep AcaBat*: Somehow Daphne looked a lot less attractive when she was being carried out of the room screaming. I didn't know a human face could get that red.

BEN: Yeah, we'd lost. But I still felt good about it. Going into the speech, we were almost exactly tied. And it was kind of vindicating, to have lost because of Daphne's speech. Next year, when she's graduated, I'm going to do the speech. And San Anselmo Prep is going *down*.

CINTHIA ALVAREZ, *San Anselmo Prep AcaBat*: Five AcaBat Locals victories *in a row*. Now *that* was a beautiful sentence. We had done it. Even without Hutch and Cressida Schrobenhauser-Clonan, we had done it. Undefeated for five years! Never underestimate the San Anselmo Prep AcaBats!

COLIN VON KOHORN, *editor in chief*: It was hard to come down after the heady rush of Academic Battle, but there was still work to be done.

ANGELICA: I'd gone straight to the computer lab after Locals finished to try to get some of my ideas down. I didn't want to forget a moment! Colin was in there, too, typing away, and Cinthia sat next to him, recounting her glorious victory, silver heels propped up on the table. I had no idea why she'd changed to come hang out in the computer lab.

CINTHIA: I was dressed up because of the *dance*. From the way the two of them stared blankly at me, Colin and Angelica had clearly forgotten about it.

ANGELICA: The dance. I *had* totally and completely forgotten about it. And it had apparently started ten minutes ago. And I obviously hadn't brought a dress with me. So I guess that meant I was spending the homecoming dance in the computer lab with Colin Von Kohorn. As the Dance Committee had promised on the posters, it would truly be An Enchanted Evening.

CINTHIA: I was just killing time in the computer lab until my date showed up. And when she did, she looked gorgeous.

BECCA: I'd joined marching band, and now I was going to a school dance. It sounds so wrong when I say it out loud, but playing at homecoming was . . . well, it wasn't the worst. And when Natalie said they'd love to have a second tuba in marching band, permanently, well, I said yes. And when Cinthia asked if I wanted to go to the dance with her, well, I said yes. Because I wanted to dance with her. And if I *had* to dance with her *at* San Anselmo Prep, well, then, that's where I'd dance.

ANGELICA: Of course, I finally stop trying to convince Becca to go to a school dance, and *now* she goes. Literally, the one time I forgot a dance was happening. I love her, but she has got to be the most contrary person I've ever met.

BECCA: *I* was going to a dance *Angelica* wasn't going to?! Nothing made sense anymore.

ANGELICA: Look at all these activities Becca was participating in! When the Valentine's Day dance rolled around, when, hopefully, there wouldn't be quite so many things going on, we were all going to have the best time. Maybe I'd bring Ben. And maybe we could even drag Colin out of the computer lab.

COLIN: A school dance? Valentine's Day?! Inarguably America's worst annual holiday. I told Angelica not to push her luck.

BEN: Finally, I found the computer lab. I'd had to ask three different people where the school newspaper office was before someone could point me in the right direction.

COLIN: I assumed the gentleman caller at the door was not there for me. I cleared my throat.

ANGELICA: I looked up from my computer, blinking fuzzily at having my concentration broken. Ben Washington was standing in the door, tie loosened, blazer draped over his arm, still incredibly handsome.

BEN: I'd heard the music coming out of the gym. Looked like San Anselmo Prep was having their homecoming dance tonight.

ANGELICA: I think Colin and I were just staring at Ben as he talked about the homecoming dance. He moved closer to my computer, and I felt suddenly self-conscious of the uniform I'd been sweating in for the past eleven hours.

BEN: What I was trying to say, in an incredibly awkward, roundabout way, was that I'd love to go to the dance with Angelica. Maybe just for a little bit. If she'd take me.

ANGELICA: But . . . but I was still wearing my uniform. Everyone else there would be all dressed up.

BEN: Hey, I was still wearing my uniform, too. And I didn't care what we were wearing. I just wanted to dance with her.

ANGELICA: I grabbed on to Ben's outstretched hand and stood, feeling a bit like Cinderella being helped out of her carriage instead of Angelica being helped out of her uncomfortable computer lab chair. Ben and I started walking toward the door, but I felt bad leaving Colin alone in there. Was he sure he didn't want to come?

COLIN: I was sure. In fact, the solitude would be refreshing. God knows I'd hardly gotten a minute to myself since I'd agreed to take on Angelica Marie Hutcherson, reporter-at-large. I shooed them out of my office and shut the door.

ANGELICA: "Probably just one dance," I said, heart speeding up as I realized that Ben was in no hurry to let go of my hand, the music louder as we got closer and closer to the gym. "I still have a lot of work to do."

BEN: "How about we start with one dance," I suggested, "and then we'll see where it goes?"

ANGELICA: "We'll see where it goes," I agreed, because we'd barely written a paragraph of what might turn out to be the story of Ben and Angelica, but there was the possibility that it might be more. And I loved possibility—that was the thing I loved best about writing, after all. We walked into the dance, and this time, there was no agony. Just hope.

ALL THE NEWS THAT'S FIT TO PRINT

ANGELICA: The Monday after homecoming weekend felt decidedly anticlimactic. I couldn't believe it was all over.

CINTHIA ALVAREZ, *associate editor of the* Prepster: What a weekend. Sweetest AcaBat victory *ever*, best homecoming dance *ever*, and then Becca and I had an awesome time at the play on Saturday night, too. This was the kind of Monday that had launched a thousand *Garfield* comic strips. Such a bummer.

ANGELICA: One dance turned into two, and then before I knew it, I was in Ben's arms for the last slow dance of the night, and the teachers turned on the lights and the gym was just a gym again. On Saturday, we rode our bikes all over San Anselmo, and I introduced Ben to the wonder that is Fairfax Scoop. And then on Sunday, I went over to Becca's house, and we sat in her backyard and ate our way through a package of Oreos, and talked about absolutely *everything*, and that was maybe the best part of the whole weekend.

CINTHIA: I was a little tired, but I wasn't sure if Colin had actually slept. Or gone home. He was in the computer lab when I stopped by before the homeroom bell rung, clutching a gallon-size mug of coffee and blinking red-rimmed eyes.

MR. DUNCAN, *academic adviser to the* Prepster: Okay, fine. You got me. I let Colin drink coffee in the computer lab. But if you'd seen him that Monday morning, you would have let him drink coffee, too. That kid looked like Gollum.

MRS. VON KOHORN, *Colin's mother*: Colin *tried* to stay at school the whole weekend, but I was able to extract him on Friday evening after the dance, with the assistance of Mr. Ross.

COLIN VON KOHORN, *editor in chief of the* Prepster: Forget the game or the Academic Battle or the elections or any of it. This was the big moment—when the homecoming edition of the *Prepster* went to print.

ANGELICA: Of course. When I looked at caffeine-jittery Colin, I realized that homecoming wasn't actually over. This, the printing of the *Prepster*, was Colin's homecoming. It was his big game and his fall play and his AcaBat Locals and his Student Council election all rolled into one. And in some ways, it was bigger than all of those things, because it *was* all of those things and more. All wrapped up in one place.

COLIN: I'd texted Angelica and Cinthia and asked them to meet me in my office before the first bell.

CINTHIA: A text from Colin?! A text from Colin that wasn't disparaging my formatting?! This was unprecedented. Obviously, I came.

ANGELICA: Colin had actually responded to the text I'd sent him over the weekend, too. It seemed newly social Colin Von Kohorn was here to stay.

COLIN: Angelica had asked for more than two hundred and fifty words. I told her to take all the space she needed.

ANGELICA: My article was four hundred and ninety-seven words, which Colin said was fine. But I told him I had something else for him to read, too. All the interviews I'd compiled about homecoming were too good to just drag into the trash folder. I hadn't even known I'd been doing it, but I'd written a complete and authoritative oral history of the craziest homecoming weekend San Anselmo Prep had ever seen. And I felt like we should do *something* with it. The story of homecoming was so much bigger than two hundred and fifty words. Or even four hundred and ninety-seven.

COLIN: I told Angelica I'd read whatever she gave me. And then I offered her a full-time position on staff.

ANGELICA: I told Colin I'd think about it. After all, I had to help Becca get *Riot Prep!* up and running. And if Cinthia still thought there was a place for me in AcaBat, well, I'd decided that I wanted to be up onstage with them, writing the best essay I possibly could for our team. And if I'd learned anything from these past couple weeks, it was that I didn't want to pull a Holly Carpenter and overcommit myself.

COLIN: Angelica was *Prepster* staff already, whether she liked it or not. I had Cinthia clean out the mugs she'd been storing under an unused chair in the office so Angelica could have her own desk.

CINTHIA: I'd printed out a piece of paper that said ANGELICA MARIE HUTCHERSON, COLUMNIST and taped it to the back of the chair. She was stuck with us. This wasn't a job offer. It was a mandate.

COLIN: Going forward, Angelica could have her own column, to write whatever she wanted, including, yes, fiction sometimes. If she absolutely had to. If keeping Angelica meant that the *Prepster* would have a fiction column, well then, the *Prepster* would have a fiction column. Because Cinthia and I needed Angelica, and we'd do whatever it took to keep her. But that was a discussion for another day. Right now, the *Prepster* was ready to print. And it was a masterpiece.

CINTHIA: Angelica and I looked over the layout, giving the articles one last proofread, and I've gotta say, it was fantastic. This was Colin's Sistine Chapel.

ANGELICA: I looked over my column, and I was pretty happy with it, and I'd already seen Cinthia's articles, and loved them, and then I read Colin's story. And I have to admit, I was kind of shocked. It was a pretty boundary-pushing move for the *Prepster*. Was he sure he wanted to print this? I worried Principal Patel might force him to resign.

COLIN: I was positive I wanted to publish the article the way I'd written it. Yes, I knew it was a risky move. Yes, I knew it might result in my removal as editor in chief, which, I'm not going to lie, was an almost unbearable thought. But the only thing that would have been more unbearable would have been burying the story. This was the exact reason I'd wanted to work on the school paper. Because I wanted to take risks and publish stories that our students had a right to know about. That they deserved to know about. I'd wanted to uncover the truth, and to tell that truth. And that was exactly what I'd done.

CINTHIA: I couldn't believe it. Colin Von Kohorn, a self-described boundary pusher? I'd never have thought it. And I've never been more proud of him.

MR. DUNCAN: Of course I read the homecoming edition. Can't have a repeat of the tie article, right? Should I have stopped Colin's story? Maybe. But I was proud of the kid. A take-down of political corruption? It looked like Colin Von Kohorn had turned the *Prepster* into a real newspaper after all.

COLIN: The *Prepster* has always been a real newspaper.

CINTHIA: I think what the *Prepster* had always needed was a real editor. And now, in Colin, it had one.

ANGELICA: Cinthia, Colin, and I stood in the darkened computer lab before the first bell rang, listening to the whirring sounds as the giant copy machine printed out hundreds of copies of the *Prepster*. Standing there together, Cinthia reached out and grabbed my hand, and I reached out for Colin's, and yes, I'm sure it sounds super weird and cheesy that we were standing there holding hands, but it felt right in the moment. It was a *big* moment. And who knew what would happen next? We waited, and we listened.

THE PREPSTER

MARCHING BAND SLAYS BEY WHILE
DRAGONS GET FLAMBÉED
by Cinthia Alvarez

As the marching band does the unthinkable and tops last year's performance, the San Anselmo Prep Dragons lose the homecoming game for a record-breaking sixteenth year in a row.

In a stunning loss, the San Rafael Academy Knights defeated the San Anselmo Prep Dragons 52–0. This marked the sixteenth consecutive loss for San Anselmo Prep at the homecoming game.

The Dragons weren't the only thing destroyed on that field—as always, the San Anselmo Prep Marching Band absolutely crushed some sick beats. Queen Bey herself would have been wowed by the inventive medley that included six of her greatest hits. Clarinet Natalie Wagner called it "the single greatest thing that has literally ever happened, to anyone, not just here at San Anselmo Prep, but in the whole world," while newly instated tuba Becca Horn said it "wasn't the worst."

The Dragon Dougie was, as always, a highlight of the event, with the Dragon bringing a special panache this year, including more flips and gymnastic tricks than we've seen in previous years.

"That dumb Dragon really brought it," freshman Momo Wakatsuki said. "He almost made me forget how boring football

270

is." Cheerleader Wakatsuki expressed an emphatic hope that basketball season would be here soon.

DIRTY POLITICS: NITHERCOTT BARRED FROM STUDENT GOVERNMENT DUE TO INSIDER DEAL WITH PATEL
by Colin Von Kohorn

Andrew Nithercott's career in student government comes to an end as the ethics of San Anselmo Prep's principal are tested.

Student Council: The phrase conjures up a wholesome image of young American government, one supposedly free from the corruption that taints the democratic process on our national stage. At San Anselmo Prep, however, one of the candidates in this year's sophomore class presidential race decided to emulate his elders.

"It must be nice to have the principal on your side," senior class president Brooks Mandeville said. "Andrew Nithercott and Patel are basically BFFs, and *that's* what makes [Nithercott] so scary. He's got Patel in his pocket."

This shocking allegation was proven unfortunately true when it came time to schedule this year's student government elections. Andrew Nithercott, sophomore, had become remarkably unpopular with the student body, thanks to an endless series of ludicrous proposals he attempted to push through during his tenure as freshman class president. "All of his proposals were nutso," Mandeville stated. "Mandatory shoeshines? How would you enforce that? Who shines their shoes anymore?" Nithercott, however, was desperate to hold on to his position of power, and resolved to do so—by any means necessary.

The greatest challenge to Nithercott's reign of terror was presented by sophomore Holly Carpenter, cheerleader and Academic Battle whiz kid. "Holly should have been president last year," Tanner Ericksen, sophomore class vice president, said before the elections. "And she should definitely be president this year." The tide of popular opinion seemed to have turned inexorably toward Carpenter.

Nithercott, however, had an underhanded trick up his sleeve. Noticing that the student government elections had not yet been scheduled for this fall, he privately petitioned Patel to schedule them on the first Friday in October, knowing full well that Carpenter would be otherwise occupied, cheering at the homecoming game and delivering the speech portion of the Academic Battle Locals. As Nithercott himself pointed out, "You can't lose to a candidate who doesn't show up."

Principal Patel, however, does not appear to be the villain of this piece. His only crime is unfamiliarity with Google Calendar's interface, and, perhaps, a more cavalier attitude toward San Anselmo Prep's schedule than one might wish for in a principal. His own administrative assistant admitted, "I'm not completely sure he really understands Google Calendar . . . bless his heart."

Andrew Nithercott willfully and deliberately scheduled the elections to block the democratic process, hoping to hinder Holly Carpenter's chances at the voting booth. Patel, to his credit, when apprised of the situation, slapped Nithercott with a lifetime ban on student government activities. It may not, however, have mattered. Nithercott's misdeeds came to light after the votes were tallied, and Carpenter won in a landslide. "This is a great day for democracy," incumbent sophomore class vice president Tanner Ericksen said. He then proceeded to kiss newly elected President Carpenter, who, by all appearances, was very happy with that turn of events. She was heard to exclaim, "FINALLY!" by several bystanders.

At press time, neither Andrew Nithercott nor Principal Patel could be reached for comment.

A MUCH ADO WORTH GUSHING ABOUT
by Cinthia Alvarez

A fantastic evening of theater under the stars features a nearly pitch-perfect production of Shakespeare's classic romantic comedy.

Although this reviewer missed opening night due to a scheduling conflict, it seems impossible to imagine that Harrison Baxter's first outing as Benedick, the Bard's quick-witted hero, could have been any more magical than his second. The decision to move the production outside cast an enchanted spell over the entire evening, and the brightest stars weren't the ones twinkling above us in the night sky, but the ones in the making onstage in front of us. Harrison Baxter has finally shed his reputation as solely a dance talent, and established himself as an actor to be taken seriously. His wordplay is wicked, and I dare you not to swoon as he falls, against his will, for Imogen Llewellyn's brilliant Beatrice. Bring someone special with you. By the time the actors take their final bows, you may find you've fallen in love, too.

Five Stars—Highly Recommended

I THINK, THEREFORE I COMPETE
by Angelica Marie Hutcherson

*In which the author finally understands the appeal of Academic
Battle, and discovers something about herself in the process.*

I have made no secret of my disdain for Academic Battle. As
the younger sister of San Anselmo Prep's most celebrated AcaBat,
Academic Battle had been, at best, a boring afternoon to endure,
and, at worst, a reminder of all the ways I could never quite
measure up to my brilliant older sibling. In the mundane envi-
rons of our school's auditorium, however, I recently underwent a
transformative experience. AcaBat is more than the sum of its
multiple-choice tests, essay, interviews, and speeches. It's a chance
for students who excel academically to experience the same thrill
of competition usually reserved for athletes, but it's more than
that, too. As the previously mentioned older sibling said, the real
joy of AcaBat is "seeing how people think, because that's what
shows you who they are." And there was a lot to see in the San
Anselmo Prep auditorium on Friday afternoon.

San Anselmo Prep has won AcaBat Locals for the last four
years, in addition to our historic victory at Nationals last year.
Unsurprisingly, this has left our rivals, the San Rafael Academy
Knights, captained by Daphne Leake-Palmer, desperate for ven-
geance. Leake-Palmer assured me that she intended to reduce
San Anselmo Prep to "smoke and ashes." Luckily for all of us,
the building is still standing, even after a particularly dramatic
Locals competition.

Up until the final event in AcaBat, both teams found themselves evenly matched. It was Holly Carpenter's speech, however, that clinched the victory for San Anselmo Prep. Prompted

to speak about the invention of a new triathlon, Carpenter shared a personal anecdote, an unconventional move. That very day, Carpenter had competed in the triathlon known as San Anselmo Prep's homecoming, running for Student Council, cheering at the homecoming game, and, of course, competing with the other AcaBats. James Hutcherson, ceremonial judge, noted, "Holly spoke right from her heart, and for two minutes, she let us into her world. And that, to me, is what speech is supposed to be about." Apparently, the other judges agreed, because San Anselmo Prep emerged victorious for the fifth year in a row. The AcaBats next head on to Regionals, where this reporter is proud to announce she will be joining the team.

I always thought that I couldn't join AcaBats, that it would do nothing but invite unflattering comparisons to my brother. But what I learned on Friday is that Academic Battle is much more nuanced than a straightforward competition. Rather than simply pit contestants against one another, AcaBat celebrates our differences. It celebrates what makes each of us unique because it celebrates how we think about the world—a process that is always unique. To put it, perhaps, too simplistically, there are many different ways to be smart. And all of those ways are valued amongst the AcaBats.

"I definitely recommend checking out an AcaBat match if you have the opportunity," spectator Avery Dennis said. "But for the love of all that is holy, eat your snacks *before* you arrive."

ACKNOWLEDGMENTS

I am so grateful for the opportunity to dive back into the wacky world of San Anselmo Prep, and so thankful for everyone who came on this journey with me!

Thank you to Matt Ringler for bringing me back to San Anselmo and for loving all of these characters as much as I do, especially Principal Patel. Thank you for always knowing the right direction to take all forty-seven different plotlines in, and for making sure all the characters get where they're going in the funniest, most authentic way possible. You can never have too many marching-band-make-outs.

Everyone at Scholastic, thank you for your continued love for me and these books, and for making them so stinking beautiful I might just replace all the art in my apartment with framed copies of these covers.

Molly Ker Hawn, you remain the Supreme Grand Empress of agents. Thank you for making things happen, for talking through anything that needs to be talked through, and for bothering those who need to be bothered. I can't imagine a better person to have on my side.

Thank you to everyone at the Book Cellar in Lincoln Square. You guys are my literary home away from home, and I will come eat cake with you anytime.

Mom, Dad, and Ali, thank you for being my support system

and sales team. Max, you are the best husband any writer could ever ask for—like Professor Bhaer, but much, much cooler. You know Friedrich Bhaer never made his own kimchi. Love you.

ABOUT THE AUTHOR

Author photo by Braden Nesin

Stephanie Kate Strohm is the author of *Pilgrims Don't Wear Pink*, *Confederates Don't Wear Couture*, *The Taming of the Drew*, and *It's Not Me, It's You*. She graduated from Middlebury College with a dual degree in theater and history and has acted her way around the United States, performing in more than twenty-five states. She currently lives in Chicago with her husband and a dog named Lorelei Lee.

It's Not Me It's **You**

Stephanie Kate Strohm

DON'T MISS